The Eagle's Heart

Hamlin Garland

Alpha Editions

This edition published in 2021

ISBN : 9789354547188

Design and Setting By
Alpha Editions
www.alphaedis.com
Email - info@alphaedis.com

THE EAGLE'S HEART
PART I
CHAPTER I

HIS YOUTH

Harold was about ten years of age when his father, the Rev. Mr. Excell, took the pastorate of the First Church in Rock River. Many of the people in his first congregation remarked upon "the handsome lad." The clear brown of his face, his big yellow-brown eyes, his slender hands, and the grace of his movements gave him distinction quite aside from that arising from his connection with the minister.

Rev. John Excell was a personable man himself. He was tall and broad shouldered, with abundant brown hair and beard, and a winning smile. His eyes were dark and introspective, but they could glow like sunlit topaz, or grow dim with tears, as his congregation had opportunity to observe during this first sermon—but they were essentially sad eyes.

Mrs. Excell, a colorless little woman who retained only the dim outline of her girlhood's beauty, sat gracelessly in her pew, but her stepdaughter, Maud, by her side, was carrying to early maturity a dainty grace united with something strong and fine drawn from her father. She had his proud lift of the head.

"What a fine family!" whispered the women from pew to pew under cover of the creaking fans.

In the midst of the first sermon, a boy seated in front of Harold gave a shrill whoop of agony and glared back at the minister's son with distorted face, and only the prompt action on the part of both mothers prevented a clamorous encounter over the pew. Harold had stuck the head of a pin in the toe of his boot and jabbed his neighbor in the calf of the leg. It was an old trick, but it served well.

The minister did not interrupt his reading, but a deep flush of hot blood arose to his face, and the lids of his eyes dropped to shut out the searching gaze of his parishioners, as well as to close in a red glare of anger. From that moment Harold was known as "that preacher's boy," the intention being to convey by significant inflections and a meaning smile that he filled the usual description of a minister's graceless son.

Harold soon became renowned in his own world. He had no hard-fought battles, though he had scores of quarrels, for he scared his opponents by the suddenness and the intensity of his rage, which was fairly demoniacal in fury.

"You touch me and I'll *kill you*," he said in a low voice to the fat boy whose leg he had jabbed, and his bloodless face and blazing eyes caused the boy to leap frenziedly away. He carried a big knife, his playmates discovered, and no one, not even youths grown to man's stature, cared to attempt violence with him. One lad, struck with a stone from his cunning right hand, was carried home in a carriage. Another, being thrown by one convulsive effort, fell upon his arm, breaking it at the elbow. In less than a week every boy in Rock River knew something of Harry Excell's furious temper, and had learned that it was safer to be friend than enemy to him.

He had his partisans, too, for his was a singularly attractive nature when not enraged. He was a hearty, buoyant playmate, and a good scholar five days out of six, but he demanded a certain consideration at all times. An accidental harm he bore easily, but an intentional injury—that was flame to powder.

The teachers in the public school each had him in turn, as he ran rapidly up the grades. They all admired him unreservedly, but most of them were afraid of him, so that he received no more decisive check than at home. He was subject to no will but his own.

The principal was a kind and scholarly old man, who could make a boy cry with remorse and shame by his Christlike gentleness, and Harold also wept in his presence, but that did not prevent him from fairly knocking out the brains of the next boy who annoyed him. In his furious, fickle way he often defended his chums or smaller boys, so that it was not easy to condemn him entirely.

There were rumors from the first Monday after Harold's pin-sticking exploit that the minister had "lively sessions" with his boy. The old sexton privately declared that he heard muffled curses and shrieks and the sound of blows rising from the cellar of the parsonage—but this story was hushed on his lips. The boy admittedly needed thrashing, but the deacons of the church would rather not have it known that the minister used the rod himself.

The rumors of the preacher's stern measures softened the judgment of some of the townspeople, who shifted some of the blame of the son to the shoulders of the sire. Harry called his father "the minister," and seemed to have no regard for him beyond a certain respect for his physical strength. When boys came by and raised the swimming sign he replied, "Wait till I ask 'the minister.'" This was considered "queer" in him.

He ignored his stepmother completely, but tormented his sister Maud in a thousand impish ways. He disarranged her neatly combed hair. He threw mud on her dress and put carriage grease on her white stockings on picnic day. He called her "chiny-thing," in allusion to her pretty round cheeks and clear complexion, and yet he loved her and would instantly fight for her, and no one else dared tease her or utter a word to annoy her. She was fourteen years of age when Mr. Excell came to town, and at sixteen considered herself a young lady. As suitors began to gather about her, they each had a vigorous trial to undergo with Harold; it was indeed equivalent to running the gantlet. Maud was always in terror of him on the evenings when she had callers.

One day he threw a handful of small garter snakes into the parlor where his sister sat with young Mr. Norton. Maud sprang to a chair screaming wildly, while her suitor caught the snakes and threw them from the window just as the minister's tall form darkened the doorway.

"What is the matter?" he asked.

Maud, eager to shield Harry, said: "Oh, nothing much, papa—only one of Harry's jokes."

"Tell me," said the minister to the young man, who, with a painful smile on his face, stammeringly replied:

"Harry thought he'd scare me, that's all. It didn't amount to much."

"I insist on knowing the truth, Mr. Norton," the minister sternly insisted.

As Norton described the boy's action, Mr. Excell's face paled and his lips set close. His eyes became terrible to meet, and the beaded sweat of his furious anger stood thick on his face. "Thank you," he said with ominous calmness, and turning without another word, went to his study.

His wife, stealing up, found the door locked and her husband walking the floor like a roused tiger. White and shaking with a sort of awe, Mrs. Excell ran down to the kitchen where Harold crouched and said:

"Harold, dear, you'd better go out to Mr. Burns' right away."

Harold understood perfectly what she meant and fled. For hours neither Mrs. Excell nor Maud spoke above a whisper. When the minister came down to tea he made no comment on Harry's absence. He had worn out his white-hot rage, but was not yet in full control of himself.

He remained silent, and kept his eyes on his plate during the meal.

The last time he had punished Harold the scene narrowly escaped a tragic ending. When the struggle ended Harold lay on the floor, choked into insensibility.

When he had become calm and Harold was sleeping naturally in his own bed, the father knelt at his wife's knee and prayed God for grace to bear his burden, and said:

"Mary, keep us apart when we are angry. He is like me: he has my fiendish temper. No matter what I say or do, keep us apart till I am calm. By God's grace I will never touch his flesh again in anger."

Nevertheless he dared not trust himself to refer to the battles which shamed them all. The boy was deeply repentant, but uttered no word of it. And so they grew ever more silent and vengeful in their intercourse.

Harold early developed remarkable skill with horses, and once rode in the races at the County Fair, to the scandal of the First Church. He not only won the race, but was at once offered a great deal of money to go with the victor to other races. To his plea the father, with deep-laid diplomacy, replied:

"Very well; study hard this year and next year you may go." But the boy was just at the age to take on weight rapidly, and by the end of the year was too heavy, and the owner of the horse refused to repeat his offer. Harold did not fail to remark how he had been cheated, but said nothing more of his wish to be a jockey.

He was also fond of firearms, and during his boyhood his father tried in every way to keep weapons from him, and a box in his study contained a contraband collection of his son's weapons. There was a certain pathos in this little arsenal, for it gave evidence of considerable labor on the boy's part, and expressed much of buoyant hope and restless energy.

There were a half-dozen Fourth of July pistols, as many cannons for crackers, and three attempts at real guns intended to explode powder and throw a bullet. Some of them were "toggled up" with twine, and one or two had handles rudely carved out of wood. Two of them were genuine revolvers which he had managed to earn by working in the harvest field on the Burns' farm.

From his fifteenth year he was never without a shotgun and revolver. The shotgun was allowed, but the revolver was still contraband and kept carefully concealed. On Fourth of July he always helped to fire the anvil and fireworks, for he was deft and sure and quite at home with explosives. He had acquired great skill with both gun and pistol as early as his thirteenth year, and his feats of marksmanship came now and then to the ears of his father.

The father and son were in open warfare. Harold submitted to every command outwardly, but inwardly vowed to break all restraint which he considered useless or unjust.

His great ambition was to acquire a "mustang pony," for all the adventurous spirits of the dime novels he had known carried revolvers and rode mustangs. He did not read much, but when he did it was always some tale of fighting. He was too restless and active to continue at a book of his own accord for any length of time, but he listened delightedly to any one who consented to read for him. When his sister Maud wished to do him a great favor and to enjoy his company (for she loved him dearly) she read Daredevil Dan, or some similar story, while he lay out on his stomach in the grass under the trees, with restless feet swinging like pendulums. At such times his face was beautiful with longing, and his eyes became dark and dreamy. "I'm going there, Beauty," he would say as Maud rolled out the word *Colorado* or *Brazos*. "I'm going there. I won't stay here and rot. I'll go, you'll see, and I'll have a big herd of cattle, too."

His gentlest moments were those spent with his sister in the fields or under the trees. As he grew older he became curiously tender and watchful of her. It pleased him to go ahead of her through the woods, to pilot the way, and to help her over ditches or fences. He loved to lead her into dense thickets and to look around and say: "There, isn't this wild, though? You couldn't find your way out if it wasn't for me, could you?" And she, to carry out the spirit of the story, always shuddered and said, "Don't leave me to perish here."

Once, as he lay with his head in the grass, he suddenly said: "Can't you hear the Colorado roar?"

The wind was sweeping over the trees, and Maud, eager to keep him in this gentle mood, cried: "I hear it; it is a wonderful river, isn't it?"

He did not speak again for a moment.

"Oh, I want to be where there is nobody west of me," he said, a look of singular beauty on his face. "Don't you?"

"N—no, I don't," answered Maud. "But, then, I'm a girl, you know; we're afraid of wild things, most of us."

"Dot Burland isn't."

"Oh, she only pretends; she wants you to think she's brave."

"That's a lie." He said it so savagely that Maud hastened to apologize.

CHAPTER II

HIS LOVE AFFAIRS

Naturally a lad of this temper had his loves. He made no secret of them, and all the young people in the town knew his sweethearts and the precise time when his passion changed its course. If a girl pleased him he courted her with the utmost directness, but he was by no interpretation a love-sick youth. His likings were more in the nature of proprietary comradeship, and were expressed without caresses or ordinary words of endearment.

His courtship amounted to service. He waited about to meet and help his love, he hastened to defend her and to guide her; and if the favored one knew her rôle she humored his fancies, permitting him to aid her in finding her way across a weedy pasture lot or over a tiny little brook which he was pleased to call a torrent. A smile of derision was fatal. He would not submit to ridicule or joking. At the first jocular word his hands clinched and his eyes flamed with anger. His was not a face of laughter; for the most part it was serious in expression, and his eyes were rapt with dreams of great deeds.

He had one mate to whom he talked freely, and him he chose often to be his companion in the woods or on the prairies. This was John Burns, son of a farmer who lived near the town. Harry spent nearly every Saturday and Sunday during the summer months on the Burns farm. He helped Jack during haying and harvest, and when their tasks were done the two boys wandered away to the bank of the river and there, under some great basswood tree on delicious sward, they lay and talked of wild animals and Indians and the West. At this time the great chieftains of the Sioux, Sitting Bull and Gall, were becoming famous to the world, and the first reports of the findings of gold in the Black Hills were being made. A commission appointed by President Grant had made a treaty with the Sioux wherein Sitting Bull was told, "If you go to this new reservation and leave Dakota to the settlers, you shall be unmolested so long as grass grows and water runs."

But the very guard sent in to protect this commission reported "gold in the grass roots," and the insatiate greed of the white man broke all bounds—the treaty was ignored, and Sitting Bull, the last chieftain of the Sioux, calling his people together, withdrew deeper into the wilderness of Wyoming. The soldiers were sent on the trail, and the press teemed for months with news of battles and speeches and campaigns.

All these exciting events Harry and his friend Jack read and discussed hotly. Jack was eager to own a mine. "I'd like to pick up a nugget," he said, but Harold was not interested. "I don't care to mine; I'd like to be with General Custer. I'd like to be one of the scouts. I'd like to have a coat like that." He pointed at one of the pictures wherein two or three men in fringed buckskin shirts and wide hats were galloping across a rocky plain.

Many times as the two boys met to talk over these alluring matters the little town and the dusty lanes became exceedingly tame and commonplace.

Harold's eyes glowed with passion as he talked to his sweetheart of these wild scenes, and she listened because he was so alluring as he lay at her feet, pouring out a vivid recital of his plans.

"I'm not going to stay here much longer," he said; "it's too dull. I can't stand much more school. If it wasn't for you I'd run away right now."

Dot only smiled back at him and laid her hand on his hair. She was his latest sweetheart. He loved her for her vivid color, her abundant and beautiful hair, and also because she was a sympathetic listener. She, on her part, enjoyed the sound of his eager voice and the glow of his deep brown eyes. They were both pupils in the little seminary in the town, and he saw her every day walking to and from the recitation halls. He often carried her books for her, and in many other little ways insisted on serving her.

Almost without definable reason the "Wild West" came to be a land of wonder, lit as by some magical light. Its cañons, *arroyos*, and mesquite, its bronchos, cowboys, Indians, and scouts filled the boy's mind with thoughts of daring, not much unlike the fancies of a boy in the days of knight errantry.

Of the Indians he held mixed opinions. At times he thought of them as a noble race, at others—when he dreamed of fame—he wished to kill a great many of them and be very famous. Most of the books he read were based upon the slaughter of the "redskins," and yet at heart he wished to be one of them and to taste the wild joy of their poetic life, filled with hunting and warfare. Sitting Bull, Chief Gall, Rain-in-the-Face, Spotted Tail, Star-in-the-Brow, and Black Buffalo became wonder-working names in his mind. Every line in the newspapers which related to the life of the cowboys or Indians he read and remembered, for his plan was to become a part of it as soon as he had money enough to start.

There were those who would have contributed five dollars each to send him, for he was considered a dangerous influence among the village boys. If a window were broken by hoodlums at night it was counted against the minister's son. If a melon patch were raided and the fruit scattered and broken, Harold was considered the ringleader. Of the judgments of their elders the rough lads were well aware, and they took pains that no word of theirs should shift blame from Harold's shoulders to their own. By hints and sly remarks they fixed unalterably in the minds of their fathers and mothers the conception that Harold was a desperately bad and reckless boy. In his strength, skill, and courage they really believed, and being afraid of him, they told stories of his exploits, even among themselves, which bordered on the marvelous.

In reality he was not a leader of these raids. His temperament was not of that kind. He did not care to assume direction of an expedition because it carried too much trouble and some responsibility. His mind was wayward and liable to shift to some other thing at any moment; besides, mischief for its own sake did not appeal to him. The real leaders were the two sons of the village shoemaker. They were under-sized, weazened, shrewd, sly little scamps, and appeared not to have the resolution of chickadees, but had a singular genius for getting others into trouble. They knew how to handle spirits like Harold. They dared him to do evil deeds, taunted him (as openly as they felt it safe to do) with cowardice, and so spurred him to attempt some trifling depredation merely as a piece of adventure. Almost invariably when they touched him on this nerve Harold responded with a rush, and when discovery came was nearly always among the culprits taken and branded, for his pride would not permit him to sneak and run. So it fell out that time after time he was found among the grape stealers or the melon raiders, and escaped prosecution only because the men of the town laid it to "boyish deviltry" and not to any deliberate intent to commit a crime.

After his daughter married Mr. Excell made another effort to win the love of his son and failed. Harold cared nothing for his father's scholarship or oratorical powers, and never went to church after he was sixteen, but he sometimes boasted of his father among the boys.

"If father wasn't a minister, he'd be one of the strongest men in this town," he said once to Jack. "Look at his shoulders. His arms are hard, too. Of course he can't show his muscle, but I tell you he can box and swing dumb-bells."

If the father had known it, in the direction of athletics lay the road to the son's heart, but the members of the First Church were not sufficiently advanced to approve of a muscular minister, and so Mr. Excell kept silent on such subjects, and swung his dumb-bells in private. As a matter of fact, he had been a good hunter in his youth in Michigan, and might have won his son's love by tales of the wood, but he did not.

For the most part, Harold ignored his father's occasional moments of tenderness, and spent the larger part of his time with his sister or at the Burns' farm.

Mr. and Mrs. Burns saw all that was manly and good in the boy, and they stoutly defended him on all occasions.

"The boy is put upon," Mrs. Burns always argued. "A quieter, more peaceabler boy I never knew, except my own Jack. They're good, helpful boys, both of 'em, and I don't care what anybody says."

Jack, being slower of thought and limb, worshiped his chum, whose alertness and resource humbled him, though he was much the better scholar in all routine work. He read more than Harold, but Harold seized upon the facts and transmitted them instantly into something vivid and dramatic. He assumed all leadership in the hunting, and upon Jack fell all the drudgery. He always did the reading, also, while Harold listened and dreamed with eyes that seemed to look across miles of peaks. His was the eagle's heart; wild reaches allured him. Minute beauties of garden or flower were not for him. The groves along the river had long since lost their charm because he knew their limits—they no longer appealed to his imagination.

A hundred times he said: "Come, let's go West and kill buffalo. To-morrow we will see the snow on Pike's Peak." The wild country was so near, its pressure day by day molded his mind. He had no care or thought of cities or the East. He dreamed of the plains and horses and herds of buffalo and troops of Indians filing down the distant slopes. Every poem of the range, every word which carried flavor of the wild country, every picture of a hunter remained in his mind.

The feel of a gun in his hands gave him the keenest delight, and to stalk geese in a pond or crows in the cornfield enabled him to imagine the joy of hunting the bear and the buffalo. He had the hunter's patience, and was capable of creeping on his knees in the mud for hours in the attempt to kill a duck. He could imitate almost all the birds and animals he knew. His whistle would call the mother grouse to him. He could stop the whooping of cranes in their steady flight, and his honking deceived the wary geese. When complimented for his skill in hunting he scornfully said:

"Oh, that's nothing. Anyone can kill small game; but buffaloes and grizzlies—they are the boys."

During the winter of his sixteenth year a brother of Mr. Burns returned from Kansas, which was then a strange and far-off land, and from him Harold drew vast streams of talk. The boy was insatiate when the plains were under discussion. From this veritable cattleman he secured many new words. With great joy he listened while Mr. Burns spoke of *cinches*, ropes, corrals, *buttes*, *arroyos* and other Spanish-Mexican words which the boys had observed in their dime novels, but which they had never before heard anyone use in common speech. Mr. Burns alluded to an *aparejo* or an *arroyo* as casually as Jack would say "singletree" or "furrow," and his stories brought the distant plains country very near.

Harold sought opportunity to say: "Mr. Burns, take me back with you; I wish you would."

The cattleman looked at him. "Can you ride a horse?"

Jack spoke up: "You bet he can, Uncle. He rode in the races."

Burns smiled as a king might upon a young knight seeking an errant.

"Well, if your folks don't object, when you get done with school, and Jack's mother says *he* can come, you make a break for Abilene; we'll see what I can do with you on the 'long trail.'"

Harold took this offer very seriously, much more so than Mr. Burns intended he should do, although he was pleased with the boy.

Harold well knew that his father and mother would not consent, and very naturally said nothing to them about his plan, but thereafter he laid by every cent of money he could earn, until his thrift became a source of comment. To Jack he talked for hours of the journey they were to make. Jack, unimaginative and engrossed with his studies at the seminary, took the whole matter very calmly. It seemed a long way off at best, and his studies were pleasant and needed his whole mind. Harold was thrown back upon the company of his sweetheart, who was the only one else to whom he could talk freely.

Dot, indolent, smiling creature of cozy corners that she was, listened without emotion, while Harold, with eyes ablaze, with visions of the great, splendid plains, said: "I'm going West sure. I'm tired of school; I'm going to Kansas, and I'm going to be a great cattle king in a few years, Dot, and then I'll come back and get you, and we'll go live on the banks of a big river, and we'll have plenty of horses, and go riding and hunting antelope every day. How will you like that?"

Her unresponsiveness hurt him, and he said: "You don't seem to care whether I go or not."

She turned and looked at him vacantly, still smiling, and he saw that she had not heard a single word of his passionate speech. He sprang up, hot with anger and pain.

"If you don't care to listen to me you needn't," he said, speaking through his clinched teeth.

She smiled, showing her little white teeth prettily. "Now, don't get mad, Harry; I was thinking of something else. Please tell me again."

"I won't. I'm done with you." A big lump arose in his throat and he turned away to hide tears of mortified pride. He could not have put it into words, but he perceived the painful truth. Dot had considered him a boy all along, and had only half listened to his stories and plans in the past, deceiving him for some purpose of her own. She was a smiling, careless hypocrite.

"You've lied to me," he said, turning and speaking with the bluntness of a boy without subtlety of speech. "I never'll speak to you again; good-by."

Dot kept swinging her foot. "Good-by," she said in her sweet, soft-breathing voice.

He walked away slowly, but his heart was hot with rage and wounded pride, and every time he thought of the tone in which she said "Good-by," his flesh quivered. He was seventeen, and considered himself a man; she was eighteen, and thought him only a boy. She had never listened to him, that he now understood. Maud had been right. Dot had only pretended, and now for some reason she ceased to pretend.

There was just one comfort in all this: it made it easier for him to go to the sunset country, and his wounded heart healed a little at the thought of riding a horse behind a roaring herd of buffaloes.

CHAPTER III

THE YOUNG EAGLE STRIKES

A farming village like Rock River is one of the quietest, most humdrum communities in the world till some sudden upheaval of primitive passion reveals the tiger, the ram, and the wolf which decent and orderly procedure has hidden. Cases of murder arise from the dead level of everyday village routine like volcanic mountain peaks in the midst of a flowering plain.

The citizens of Rock River were amazed and horrified one Monday morning to learn that Dot Burland had eloped with the clerk in the principal bank in the town, a married man and the leader of the choir in the First Church. Some of the people when they heard of it, said: "I do not believe it," and when they were convinced, the tears came to their eyes. "She was such a pretty girl, and think of Mrs. Willard—and then Sam—who would have supposed Sam Willard could do such a thing."

To most of the citizens it was drama; it broke the tedious monotony of everyday life; it was more productive of interesting conversation than a case of embezzlement or the burning of the county courthouse. There were those who smiled while they said: "Too bad, too bad! Any p'ticlers?"

Some of the women recalled their dislike of the lazy, pink-and-white creature whom they had often seen loitering on the streets or lying day after day in a hammock reading "domestic novels." The young girls drew together and conveyed the news in whispers. It seemed to overturn the whole social world so far as they knew it, and some of them hastened to disclaim any friendship with "the dreadful thing."

Of course the related persons came into the talk. "Poor Mrs. Willard and Harry Excell!" Yes, there was Harry; for a moment, for the first time, he was regarded with pity. "What will he do? He must take it very hard."

At about eleven o'clock, just as the discussion had reached this secondary stage, where new particulars were necessary, a youth, pale and breathless, with his right hand convulsively clasping his bloody shoulder, rushed into the central drug store and fell to the floor with inarticulate cries of fear and pain. Out of his mouth at last came an astonishing charge of murderous assault on the part of Harold Excell. His wounds were dressed and the authorities notified to arrest his assailant.

When the officers found Harold he was pacing up and down the narrow alley where the encounter had taken place. He was white as the dead, and his eyes were ablaze under his knitted brows.

"Well, what do you want of me?" he demanded, as the officer rushed up and laid hands upon him.

"You've killed Clint Slocum," replied the constable, drawing a pair of handcuffs from his pocket.

"Oh, drop those things!" replied Harold; "I'm not going to run; you never knew me to run."

Half ashamed, the constable replaced the irons in his pocket and seized his prisoner by the arm. Harold walked along quietly, but his face was terrible to see, especially in one so young. In every street excited men, women, and children were running to see him pass. He had suddenly become alien and far separated from them all. He perceived them as if through a lurid smoke cloud.

On most of these faces lay a smile, a ghastly, excited, pleased grin, which enraged him more than any curse would have done. He had suddenly become their dramatic entertainment. The constable gripped him tighter and the sheriff, running up, seized his other arm.

Harold shook himself free. "Let me alone! I'm going along all right."

The officers only held him the closer, and his rage broke bounds. He struggled till his captors swayed about on the walk, and the little boys screamed with laughter to see the slender youth shake the big men.

In the midst of this struggle a tall man, without hat or coat and wearing slippers, came running down the walk with great strides. His voice rang deep and clear:

"Let the boy alone!"

It was the minister. With one sweep of his right hand he tore the hands of the sheriff from the boy's arms; the gesture was bearlike in power. "What's the meaning of all this, Mr. Sawyer?" he said, addressing the sheriff.

"Your boy has killed a man."

"You lie!"

"It's true—anyhow, he has stabbed Clint Slocum. He ain't dead, but he's hurt bad."

"Is that true, Harold?"

Harold did not lift his sullen glance. "He struck me with a whip."

There was a silence, during which the minister choked with emotion and his lips moved as if in silent prayer. Then he turned. "Free the boy's arm. I'll guarantee he will not try to escape. No son of mine will run to escape punishment—leave him to me."

The constable, being a member of the minister's congregation and a profound admirer of his pastor, fell back. The sheriff took a place by his side, and the father and son walked on toward the jail. After a few moments the minister began to speak in a low voice:

"My son, you have reached a momentous point in your life's history. Much depends on the words you use. I will not tell you to conceal the truth, but you need not incriminate yourself—that is the law"—his voice was almost inaudible, but Harold heard it. "If Slocum dies—oh, my God! My God!"

His voice failed him utterly, but he walked erect and martial, the sun blazing on his white forehead, his hands clinched at his sides. There were many of his parishioners in the streets, and several of the women broke into bitter weeping as he passed, and many of the men imprecated the boy who was bringing white lines of sorrow into his father's hair. "This is the logical end of his lawless bringing up," said one.

The father went on: "Tell me, my boy—tell me the truth—did you strike to kill? Was murder in your heart?"

Harold did not reply. The minister laid a broad, gentle hand on his son's shoulder. "Tell me, Harold."

"No; I struck to hurt him. He was striking me; I struck back," the boy sullenly answered.

The father sighed with relief. "I believe you, Harold. He is older and stronger, too: that will count in your favor."

They reached the jail yard gate, and there, in the face of a crowd of curious people, the minister bowed his proud head and put his arm about his son and kissed his hair. Then, with tears upon his face, he addressed the sheriff:

"Mr. Sheriff, I resign my boy to your care. Remember, he is but a lad, and he is my only son. Deal gently with him.—Harold, submit to the law and all will end well. I will bring mother and Maud to see you at once."

As the gate closed on his son the minister drew a deep breath, and a cry of bitter agony broke from his clinched lips: "O God, O God! My son is lost!"

The story of the encounter, even as it dribbled forth from Slocum, developed extenuating circumstances. Slocum was man grown, a big, muscular fellow, rather given to bullying. A heavy carriage whip was found lying in the alley, and this also supported Harold's story to his father. As told by Slocum, the struggle took place just where the alley from behind the parsonage came out upon the cross street.

"I was leading a horse," said Slocum, "and I met Harry, and we got to talking, and something I said made him mad, and he jerked out his knife and jumped at me. The horse got scared and yanked me around, and just then Harry got his knife into me. I saw he was in for my life and I threw down the whip and run, the blood a-spurting out o' me, hot as b'ilin' water. I was scared, I admit that. I thought he'd opened a big artery in me, and I guess he did."

When this story, amplified and made dramatic, reached the ears of the minister, he said: "That is Clinton's side of the case. My son must have been provoked beyond his control. Wait till we hear his story."

But the shadow of the prison was on Harold's face, and he sullenly refused to make any statement, even to his sister, who had more influence over him than Mrs. Excell.

A singular and sinister change came over him as the days passed. He became silent and secretive and suspicious, and the sheriff spoke to Mr. Excell about it. "I don't understand that boy of yours.

He seems to be in training for a contest of some kind. He's quiet enough in daytime, or when I'm around, but when he thinks he's alone, he races up and down like a lynx, and jumps and turns handsprings, and all sorts of things. The only person he asks to see is young Burns. I can't fathom him."

The father lowered his eyes. He knew well that Harry did not ask for him.

"If it wasn't for these suspicious actions, doctor, I'd let him have the full run of the jail yard, but I dassent let him have any liberties. Why, he can go up the side of the cells like a squirrel! He'd go over our wall like a cat—no doubt of it."

The minister spoke with some effort. "I think you misread my son. He is not one to flee from punishment. He has some other idea in his mind."

To Jack Burns alone, plain, plodding, and slow, Harold showed a smiling face. He met him with a boyish word—"Hello, Jack! how goes it?"—and was eager to talk. He reached out and touched him with his hands wistfully. "I'm glad you've come. You're the only friend I've got now, Jack." This was one of the morbid fancies jail life had developed; he thought everybody had turned against him. "Now, I want to tell you something—we're chums, and you mustn't give me away. These fools think I'm going to try to escape, but I ain't. You see, they can't hang me for stabbing that coward, but they'll shut me up for a year or two, and I've got to keep healthy, don't you see? When I get out o' this I strike for the West, don't you see? And I've got to be able to do a day's work. Look at this arm." He stripped his strong white arm for inspection.

In the midst of the excitement attending Harold's arrest, Dot's elopement was temporarily diminished in value, but some shrewd gossip connected the two events and said: "I believe Clint gibed Harry Excell about Dot—I just believe that's what the fight was about."

This being repeated, not as an opinion but as the inside facts in the case, sentiment turned swiftly in Harold's favor. Clinton was shrewd enough to say very little about the quarrel. "I was just givin' him a little guff, and he up and lit into me with a big claspknife." Such was his story constantly repeated.

Fortunately for Harold, the case came to trial early in the autumn session. It was the most dramatic event of the year, and it was seriously suggested that it would be a good thing to hold the trial in the opera house in order that all the townspeople should be able to enjoy it. A cynical young editor made a counter suggestion: "I move we charge one dollar per ticket and apply the funds to buying a fire engine." Naturally, the judge of the district went the calm way of the law, regardless of the town's ferment of interest in the case.

The county attorney appeared for the prosecution, and old Judge Brown and young Bradley Talcott defended Harold.

Bradley knew Harold very well and the boy had a high regard for him. Lawyer Brown believed the boy to be a restless and dangerous spirit, but he said to Bradley:

"I've no doubt the boy was provoked by Clint, who is a worthless bully, but we must face the fact that young Excell bears a bad name. He has been in trouble a great many times, and the prosecution will make much of that. Our business is to show the extent of the provocation, and secondly, to disprove, so far as we can, the popular conception of the youth. I can get nothing out of him which will aid in his defense. He refuses to talk. Unless we can wring the truth out of Slocum on the stand it will go hard with the boy. I wish you'd see what you can do."

Bradley went down to see Harold, and the two spent a couple of hours together. Bradley talked to him in plain and simple words, without any assumption. His voice was kind and sincere, and Harold nearly wept under its music, but he added very little to Bradley's knowledge of the situation.

"He struck me with the whip, and then I—I can't remember much about it, my mind was a kind of a red blur," Harold said at last desperately.

"Why did he strike you with the whip?"

"I told him he was a black-hearted liar."

"What made you say that to him?" persevered Bradley.

"Because that's what he was."

"Did he say something to you which you resented?"

"Yes—he did."

"What was it?"

Right there Harold closed his lips and Bradley took another tack.

"Harry, I want you to tell me something. Did you have anything to do with killing Brownlow's dog?"

"No," replied Harold disdainfully.

"Did you have any hand in the raid on Brownlow's orchard a week later?"

"No; I was at home."

"Did your folks see you during the evening?"

"No; I was with Jack up in the attic, reading."

"You've taken a hand in *some* of these things—raids—haven't you?"

"Yes, but I never tried to destroy things. It was all in fun."

"I understand. Well, now, Harold, you've got a worse name than belongs to you, and I wish you'd just tell me the whole truth about this fight, and we will do what we can to help you."

Harold's face grew sullen. "I don't care what they do with me. They're all down on me anyway," he slowly said, and Bradley arose and went out with a feeling of discouragement.

CHAPTER IV

THE TRIAL

The day of his trial came as a welcome change to Harold. He had no fear of punishment and he hated delay. Every day before his sentence began was a loss of time—kept him just that much longer from the alluring lands to the West. His father called often to see him, but the boy remained inexorably silent in all these meetings, and the minister went away white with pain. Even to his sister Harold was abrupt and harsh, but Jack's devotion produced in him the most exalted emotion, and he turned upon his loyal chum the whole force of his affectionate nature. He did not look up to Jack; he loved him more as a man loves his younger brother, and yet even to him he would not utter the words young Slocum had flung at him. Lawyer Talcott had asked young Burns to get at this if possible, for purpose of defense, but it was not possible.

The court met on the first Tuesday in September. The day was windless and warm, and as Harold walked across the yard with the sheriff he looked around at the maple leaves, just touched with crimson and gold and russet, and his heart ached with desire to be free. The scent of the open air made his nostrils quiver like those of a deer.

Jack met them on the path—eager to share his hero's trouble.

"Please, sheriff, let me walk with Harry."

"Fall in behind," the sheriff gruffly replied; and so out of all the town people Jack alone associated himself with the prisoner. Up the stairs whereon he had romped when a lad, Harold climbed spiritlessly, a boy no longer.

The halls were lined with faces, everyone as familiar as the scarred and scratched wall of the court room, and yet all were now alien—no one recognized him by a frank and friendly nod, and he moved past his old companions with sullen and rigid face. His father met him at the door and walked beside him down the aisle to a seat.

The benches were crowded, and every foot of standing space was soon filled. The members of the First Church were present in mass to see the minister enter, pale and haggard with the disgrace of his son.

The judge, an untidy old man of great ability and probity, was in his seat, looking out absently over the spectators. "The next case" to him was *only* a case. He had grown gray in dealing with infractions of the law, and though kindly disposed he had grown indifferent—use had dulled his sympathies. His beard, yellow with tobacco stain, was still venerable, and his voice, deep and melodious, was impressive and commanding.

He was disposed to cut short all useless forms, and soon brought the case to vital questions. Naturally, the prosecution made a great deal of Harold's bad character, drawing from ready witnesses the story of his misdeeds. To do this was easy, for the current set that way, and those who had only *thought* Harold a bad boy now *knew* that he was concerned in all the mischief of the village.

In rebuttal, Mr. Talcott drew out contradictory statements from these witnesses, and proved several alibis at points where Harold had been accused. He produced Jack Burns and several others to prove that Harold liked fun, but that he was not inclined to lead in any of the mischief of the town—in fact, that he had not the quality of leadership.

He pushed young Burns hard to get him to say that he knew the words of insult which Slocum had used. "I think he used some girl's name," he finally admitted.

"I object," shouted the prosecution, as if touched on a hidden spring.

"Go on," said the judge to Talcott. He had become interested in the case at last.

When the lawyer for the prosecution cross-examined young Burns he became terrible. He leaned across the table and shook his lean, big-jointed finger in Jack's face. "We don't want what you *think*, sir; we want what you know. Do you *know* that Slocum brought a girl's name into this?"

"No, sir, I don't," replied Jack, red and perspiring.

"That's all!" cried the attorney, leaning back in his chair with dramatic complacency.

Others of Harold's companions were brow-beaten into declaring that he led them into all kinds of raids, and when Talcott tried to stem this tide by objection, the prosecution rose to say that the testimony was competent; that it was designed to show the dangerous character of the prisoner. "He is no gentle and guileless youth, y'r Honor, but a reckless young devil, given to violence. No one will go further than I in admiration of the Reverend Mr. Excell, but the fact of the son's lawless life can not be gainsaid."

Slocum repeated his story on the stand and was unshaken by Bradley's cross-examination. Suddenly the defense said: "Stand, please."

Slocum arose—a powerful, full-grown man.

Bradley nodded at Harold. "Stand also."

"I object," shrieked the prosecution.

"State the objection," said the judge.

"Keep your position," said Bradley sternly. "I want the jury to compare you."

As the prisoner and the witness faced each other the court room blossomed with smiles. Harold looked very pale and delicate beside the coarse, muscular hostler, who turned red and looked foolish.

Ultimately the judge sustained the objection, but the work was done. A dramatic contrast had been drawn, and the jury perceived the pusillanimity of Slocum's story. This was the position of the defense. Harold was a boy, the hostler had insulted him, had indeed struck him with a whip. Mad with rage, and realizing the greater strength of his assailant, the prisoner had drawn a knife.

In rebuttal, the prosecution made much of Harold's fierce words. He meant to kill. He was a dangerous boy. "Speaking with due reverence for his parents," the lawyer said, "the boy has been a scourge. Again and again he has threatened his playmates with death. These facts must stand. The State is willing to admit the disparity of strength, so artfully set forth by the defense, but it must not be forgotten that the boy was known to carry deadly weapons, and that he was subject to blind rages. It was not, therefore, so much a question of punishing the boy as of checking his assaults upon society. To properly punish him here would have a most salutary effect upon his action in future. The jury must consider the case without sentiment."

Old Brown arose after the State had finished. Everyone knew his power before a jury, and the room was painfully silent as he walked with stately tread to a spittoon and cleared his mouth of a big wad of tobacco. He was the old-fashioned lawyer, formal, deliberate; and though everybody enjoyed Bradley Talcott's powerful speech, they looked for drama from Brown. The judge waited patiently while the famous old lawyer played his introductory part. At last, after silently pacing to and fro for a full minute, he turned, and began in a hard, dry, nasal voice.

"Your Honor, I'm not so sure of the reforming effect of a penitentiary. I question the salutary quality of herding this delicate and high-spirited youth with the hardened criminals of the State." His strident, monotonous tone, and the cynical inflections of his voice made the spectators shiver with emotion as under the power of a great actor. He paced before the judge twice before speaking again. "Your Honor, there is more in this case than has yet appeared. Everyone in this room knows that the elopement of Dorothy Burland is at the bottom of this affair, everyone but yourself, judge. This lad was the accepted sweetheart of that wayward miss. This man Slocum is one of the rough, loud-spoken men of the village, schooled in vice and fisticuffery. You can well imagine, gentlemen of the jury," he turned to them abruptly, "you can well imagine the kind of a greeting this town loafer would give this high-spirited boy on that morning after the night when his *inamorata* disappeared with a married man. The boy has in him somewhat of the knight of the old time, your Honor; he has never opened his lips in dispraise of his faithless love. He has refused to repeat the insulting words of his assailant. He stands to-day at a turning point of his life, gentlemen of the jury, and it depends on you whether he goes downward or upward. He has had his faith in women shaken: don't let him lose faith in law and earthly justice." His first gesture was on the word "downward," and it was superb.

Again he paused, and when he looked up again a twinkle was in his eyes and his voice was softer. "As for all this chicken roasting and melon lifting, you well know the spirit that is in that; we all had a hand in such business once, every man Jack of us. The boy is no more culpable now than you were then. Moreover, Excell has had too much of the mischief of the town laid on his shoulders—more than he deserves. 'Give a dog a bad name and every dead sheep is laid at the door of his kennel.'

"However, I don't intend to review the case, y'r Honor. My colleague has made the main and vital points entirely clear; I intend merely to add a word here and there. I want you to take another look at that pale, handsome, poetic youth and then at that burly bully, and consider the folly, the idiocy, and the cowardice of the charge brought against our client." He waited while the contrast which his dramatic utterance made enormously effective was being felt; then, in a deep, melodious voice, touched with sadness, he addressed the judge:

"And to you, your Honor, I want to say we are old men. You on the bench and I here in the forum have faced each other many times. I have defended many criminals, as it was my duty to do, and you have punished many who deserved their sentences. I have seen innocent men unable to prove their freedom from guilt, and I have known men who are grossly criminal, because of lack of evidence—these things are beyond our cure. We are old, your Honor: we must soon give place to younger men. We can not afford to leave bench and bar with the stain of injustice on our garments. We can not afford to start this boy on the road to hell at seventeen years of age."

He stopped as abruptly as he had begun, and the room was silent for a long time after he had taken his seat. To Harold it seemed as though he and all the people of the room were dead—that only his brain was alive. Then Mrs. Excell burst into sobbing. The judge looked away into space, his dim eyes seeing nothing that was near, his face an impassive mask of colorless flesh. The old lawyer's words had stirred his blood, sluggish and cold with age, but his brain absorbed the larger part of his roused vitality, and when he spoke his voice had an unwontedly flat and dry sound.

"The question for you to decide," he said, instructing the jury, "is whether the boy struck the blow in self-defense, or whether he assaulted with intent to do great bodily injury. The fact that he was provoked by a man older and stronger than himself naturally militates in his favor, but the next question is upon the boy's previous character. Did he carry deadly weapons? Is he at heart dangerous to his fellows? His youth should be in mind, but it should also be remembered that he is a lad of high intellectual power, older than most men of his age. I will not dwell upon the case; you have heard the testimony; the verdict is in your keeping."

During all this period of severe mental strain Mr. Excell sat beside Lawyer Brown, motionless as a statue, save when now and again he leaned forward to whisper a suggestion. He did not look at his son, and Harold seldom looked at him. Jack Burns sat as near the prisoner as the sheriff would permit, and his homely, good face, and the face of the judge were to Harold the only spots of light in the otherwise dark room. Outside the voices of children could be heard and the sound of the rising wind in the rustling trees. Once a breeze sent a shower of yellow and crimson leaves fluttering in at the open window, and the boy's heart swelled high in his throat, and he bowed his head and sobbed. Those leaves represented the splendor of the open spaces to him. They were like messages from the crimson sunsets of the golden West, and his heart thrilled at the sight of them.

It was long after twelve o'clock, and an adjournment for dinner was ordered. Harold was about to be led away when his father came to him and said:

"Harold, would you like to have your mother and me go to dinner with you?"

With that same unrelenting, stubborn frown on his face the boy replied: "No—let me alone."

A hot flush swept over the preacher's face. "Very well," he said, and turned away, his lips twitching.

The jury was not long out. They were ready to report at three o'clock. Every seat was filled as before. The lawyers came in, picking their teeth or smoking. The ladies were in Sunday dress, the young men were accompanied by their girls, as if the trial were a dramatic entertainment. Those who failed of regaining their seats were much annoyed; others, more thrifty, had hired boys to keep their places for them during the noon hour, and others, still more determined, having brought lunches, had remained in their seats throughout the intermission, and were serene and satisfied.

Harold was brought back to his seat looking less haggard. He was not afraid of sentence; on the contrary he longed to have the suspense end.

"I don't care what they do with me if they don't use up too much of my life," he said to Jack. "I'll pound rock or live in a dungeon if it will only shorten my sentence. I hate to think of losing time. Oh, if I had only gone last year!"

The Reverend Excell came in, looming high above the crowd, his face still white and set. He paid no heed to his parishioners, but made his way to the side of Lawyer Brown. The judge mounted his bench and the court room came to order instantly.

"Is the jury ready to report on the case of the State *vs.* Excell?" he asked in a low voice. He was informed that they were agreed. After the jury had taken their seats he said blandly, mechanically: "Gentlemen, we are ready for your verdict."

Harold knew the foreman very well. He was a carpenter and joiner in whose shop he had often played—a big, bluff, good-hearted man whom any public speaking appalled, and who stammered badly as he read from a little slip of paper: "Guilty of assault with intent to commit great bodily injury, but recommended to the mercy of the judge." Then, with one hand in his breeches pocket, he added: "Be easy on him, judge; I believe I'd 'a' done the same."

The spectators tittered at his abrupt change of tone, and some of the young people applauded. He sat down very hot and red.

The judge did not smile or frown; his expressionless face seemed more like a mask than ever. When he began to speak it was as though he were reading something writ in huge letters on a distant wall.

"The Court is quite sensible of the extenuating circumstances attending this sad case, but there are far-reaching considerations which the Court can not forget. Here is a youth of good family, who elects to take up a life filled with mischief from the start. Discipline has been lacking. Here, at last, he so far oversteps the law that he appears before a jury. It seems to the Court necessary, for this young man's own good, that he feel the harsh hand of the law. According to the evidence adduced here to-day, he has been for years beyond the control of his parents, and must now know the inflexible purpose of law. I have in mind all that can be said in his favor: his youth, the disparity of age and physical power between himself and his accuser, the provocation, and the possession of the whip by the accuser—but all these are more than counterbalanced by the record of mischief and violence which stands against the prisoner."

There was a solemn pause, and the judge sternly said: "Prisoner, stand up." Harold arose. "For an assault committed upon the person of one Clinton Slocum, I now sentence you, Harold Excell, to one year in the penitentiary, and may you there learn to respect the life and property of your fellow-citizens."

"Judge! I beg——" The tall form of Mr. Excell arose, seeking to speak.

The judge motioned him to silence.

Brown interposed: "I hope the court will not refuse to hear the father of the prisoner. It would be scant justice if——"

Mr. Excell's voice arose, harsh, stern, and quick. He spoke like the big man he was, firm and decided. Harold looked up at him in surprise.

"I claim the right to be heard; will the Court refuse me the privilege of a word?" His voice was a challenge. "I am known in this community. For seven years as a minister of the Gospel I have lived among these citizens. My son is about to be condemned to State's prison, and before he goes I want to make a statement here before him and before the judge and before the world. I understand this boy better than any of you, better than the mother who bore him, for I have given him the disposition which he bears. I have had from my youth the same murderous rages: I have them yet. I love my son, your Honor, and I would take him in my arms if I could, but he has too much of my own spirit. He literally can not meet me as an affectionate son, for I sacrificed his good-will by harsh measures while he was yet a babe. I make this confession in order that the Court may understand my relation to my son. He was born with my own temper mingled with the poetic nature of his mother. While he was yet a lad I beat him till he was discolored by bruises. Twice I would have killed him only for the intervention of my wife. I have tried to live down my infirmity, your Honor, and I have at last secured control of myself, and I believe this boy will do the same, but do not send him to be an associate with criminals. My God! do not treat him as I would not do, even in my worst moments. Give him a chance to reform outside State's prison. Don't fix on him that stain. I will not say send me—that would be foolish trickery—but I beg you to make some other disposition of this boy of mine. If he goes to the penitentiary I shall strip from my shoulders the dress of the clergyman and go with him, to be near to aid and comfort him during the term of his sentence. Let the father in you speak for me, judge. Be merciful, as we all hope for mercy on the great day, for Jesus' sake."

The judge looked out over the audience of weeping women and his face warmed into life. He turned to the minister, who still stood before him with hand outstretched, and when he spoke his voice was softened and his eyes kindly.

"The Court has listened to the words of the father with peculiar interest. The Court *is* a father, and has been at a loss to understand the relations existing between father and son in this case. The Court thinks he understands them better now. As counsel for the defense has said, I am an old man, soon to leave my seat upon the bench, and I do not intend to let foolish pride or dry legal formalities stand between me and the doing of justice. The jury has decided that the boy is guilty, but has recommended him to the mercy of the Court. The plea of the father has enlightened the Court on one or two most vital points. Nothing is further from the mind of the Court than the desire to do injury to a handsome and talented boy. Believing that the father and son are about to become more closely united, the Court here transmutes the sentence to one hundred dollars fine and six months in the county jail. This will make it possible for the son and father to meet often, and the father can continue his duties to the church. This the Court decides upon as the final disposition of the accused. The case is closed. Call the next case."

CHAPTER V

THE EAGLE'S EYES GROW DIM

The county jail in Cedar County was a plain, brick structure set in the midst of the Court House Square. Connected with it was the official residence of the sheriff, and brick walks ran diagonally from corner to corner for the convenience of citizens. Over these walks magnificent maples flung gorgeous banners in autumn, and it was a favorite promenade for the young people of the town at all seasons, even in winter.

At times when the jail was filled with disorderly inmates these innocent lovers could hear the wild yells and see the insulting gestures of the men at the windows, but ordinarily the grounds were quiet and peaceful. The robins nested in the maples, the squirrels scampered from tree to tree, and little children tumbled about on the grass, unmindful of the sullen captives within the walls.

For seven years Harold himself had played about this yard, hearing the wild voices of the prisoners and seeing men come and go in irons. Over these walks he had loitered with Dot—now he was one of those who clawed at the window bars like monkeys in a cage in order to look out at the sunshine of the world. The jail pallor was already on his face and a savage look was in his eyes. He refused to see anyone but Jack, who came often and whose coming saved him from despair.

In one respect the county jail was worse, than the State's prison; it had nothing for its captives to do. They ate, amused themselves as best they could through the long day, and slept. Most of them brooded, like Harold, on the sunshine lost to them, and paced their cells like wild animals. It had, however, the advantage of giving to each man a separate bed at night, though during the day they occupied a common corridor. Some of them sang indecent songs and cursed their fellows for their stupidity, and fights were not uncommon.

The jailer was inclined to allow Harold more liberty after his trial, but the boy said: "I'm not asking any favors from you. I'm working out a sentence."

He continued his systematic exercise, eating regularly and with care in order that he should keep his health. He spent several hours each day leaping up the stairway which led from the lower cells to the upper, and his limbs were like bundles of steel rods. He could spring from the floor, catch the hand rail of the runway above, and swing himself with a single effort to the upper cells. Every possible combination of strength and agility which the slender variety of means allowed he used, and not one of all the prisoners cared to try muscular conclusions with him. Occasionally a new prisoner would experiment, but those who held over knew better than to "bother the kid." When a rash and doubting man tried it, he repented it in cotton cloth and arnica.

The only way in which Harold could be enticed into the residence part of the jail was by sending Jack to call upon him.

At such times the jailer gave him plenty of time, and Harold poured forth his latest plans in a swift torrent. He talked of nothing but the West. "My sentence will be out in April," he said; "just the right time to go. You must make all arrangements for me, old man. You take my money and get these things for me. I want a six-shooter, the best you can find, the kind they use out on the plains, and a belt and ammunition. I want a valise—a good strong one; and I want you to put all my clothes in it—I mean my underclothes—I won't need cuffs and collars and such knickknacks out there. I shall never enter father's door again. Then I want you to be on the lookout for a chance to drive cattle for somebody going West. We'll find chances enough, and we'll strike for Abilene and your uncle's place. I haven't money enough to carry me out there on the train. Oh! won't it be good fun when we have a good horse apiece and go riding across the plains herding the longhorns! That's life, that is! If I'd only gone last year, out where the buffalo and the antelope are!"

At such times the eagle's heart in the youth could scarcely endure the pale, cold light of the prison. For an hour after one of these talks with Jack he tore around his cell like a crazed wolf, till his weary muscles absorbed the ache in his heart.

During the winter the Young Men's Christian Association of the town organized what they called a Prison Rescue Band, which held services in the jail each Sunday afternoon. They were a great bore to Harold, who knew the members of the band and disliked most of them. He considered them "a little off their nut"—that is to say, fanatic. He kept his cell closely, and the devoted ones seldom caught a glimpse of him, though he was the chief object of their care. They sang Pull for the Shore, Trust it all with Jesus, and other well-worn Moody and Sankey hymns, and the leader prayed resoundingly, and then, one by one, the others made little talks to the prison walls. There was seldom a face to be seen. Muttered curses occasionally rumbled from the cells where the prisoners were trying to sleep.

But the leader was a shrewd young man, and not many Sundays after his initial attempt the prisoners were amazed to hear female voices joining in the songs. Heads appeared at every door to see the girls, who stood timidly behind the men and sang (in quavering voices) the songs that persuaded to grace.

Some of these girlish messengers of mercy Harold knew, but others were strange to him. The seminary was in session again and new pupils had entered. For the most part they were colorless and plain, and the prisoners ceased to show themselves during the singing. Harold lay on his iron bed dreaming of the wild lands whose mountains he could see shining through his prison walls. Jack had purchased for him some photographs of the Rocky Mountains, and when he desired to forget his surroundings he had but to look on the seamless dome of Sierra Blanca or the San Francisco peaks, or at the image of the limpid waters of Trapper's Lake, and like the conjurer's magic crystal sphere, it cured him of all his mental maladies, set him free and a-horse.

But one Sabbath afternoon he heard a new voice, a girl's voice, so sweet and tender and true he could not forbear to look out upon the singer. She was small and looked very pale under the white light of the high windows. She was singing alone, a wonderful thing in itself, and in her eyes was neither fear nor maidenly shrinking; she was indeed thrillingly absorbed and self-forgetful. There was something singular and arresting in the poise of her head. Her eyes seemed to look through and beyond the prison walls, far into some finer, purer land than any earthly feet had trod, and her song had a touch of genuine poetry in it:

"If I were a voice, a persuasive voice,
That could travel the whole earth through,

I would fly on the wings of the morning light
And speak to men with a gentle might
And tell them to be true—
If I were a voice."

The heart of the boy expanded. Music and poetry and love were waked in him by the voice of this singing girl. To others she was merely simple and sweet; to him she was a messenger. The vibrant, wistful cadence of her voice when she uttered the words "And tell them to be true," dropped down into the boy's sullen and lonely heart. He did not look at her, but all the week he wondered about her. He thought of her almost constantly, and the words she sang lay in his ears, soothing and healing like some subtle Oriental balm. "On the wings of the morning light" was one haunting phrase—the other was, "And tell them to be true."

The other prisoners had been touched. Only one or two ventured coarse remarks about her, and they were speedily silenced by their neighbors. Harold was eager to seek Jack in order to learn the girl's name, but Jack was at home, sick of a cold, and did not visit him during the week.

On the following Sunday she did not come, and the singing seemed suddenly a bitter mockery to Harold, who sought to solace himself with his pictures. The second week wore away and Jack came, but by that time the image of the girl had taken such aloofness of position in Harold's mind that he dared not ask about her, even of his loyal chum.

At last she came again, and when she had finished singing Not half has ever been told, some prisoner started hand clapping, and a volley of applause made the cells resound. The girl started in dismay, and then, as she understood the meaning of this noise, a beautiful flush swept over her face and she shrank swiftly into shadow.

But a man from an upper cell bawled: "Sing The Voice, miss! sing The Voice!"

The leader of the band said: "Sing for them, Miss Yardwell."

Again she sang If I were a Voice, and out of the cells the prisoners crept, one by one, and at last Harold. She did not see him till she had finished the last verse, and then he stood so close to her he could have touched her, and his solemn dark eyes burned so strangely into her face that she shrank away from him in awe and terror. She knew him—no one else but the minister's son could be so handsome and so refined of feature.

"You're that voice, miss," one of the men called out.

"That's right," replied the others in chorus.

The girl was abashed, but the belief that she was leading these sinners to a merciful Saviour exalted her and she sang again. Harold crept as near as he could—so near he could see her large gray eyes, into which the light fell as into a mountain lake. Every man there perceived the girl's divine purity of purpose. She was stainless as a summer cloud—a passionless, serene child, with the religious impulse strong within her. She could not have been more than seventeen years of age, and yet so dignified and composed was her attitude she seemed a mature woman. She was not large, but she was by no means slight, and though colorless, her pallor was not that of ill health.

Her body resembled that of a sturdy child, straight in the back, wide in the waist, and meager of bosom.

Her voice and her eyes subdued the beast in the men. An indefinable personal quality ran through her utterance, a sadness, a sympathy, and an intuitive comprehension of the sin of the world unusual in one so young. She had been carefully reared: that was evident in every gesture and utterance. Her dress was a studiously plain gray gown, not without a little girlish ornament at the neck and bosom. Every detail of her lovely personality entered Harold's mind and remained there. He had hardly reached the analytic stage in matters of this kind, but he knew very well that this girl was like her song; she could die but never deceive. He wondered what her first name could be; no girl like that would be called "Dot" or "Cad." It ought to be Lily or Marguerite. He was glad to hear one of the girls call her Mary.

He gazed at her almost without ceasing, but as the other convicts did the same he was not observably devoted, and whenever she raised her big, clear eyes toward him both shrank, he from a sense of unworthiness, she from the instinctive fear of men which a young girl of her type has deep-planted within her. She studied him shyly when she dared, and after the first song sang only for him. She prayed for him when the Band knelt on the stone floor, and at night in her room she plead for him before God.

The boy was smitten with a sudden sense of his crime, not in the way of a repentant sinner, but as one who loves a sweet and gentle woman. All that his father's preaching and precept could not do, all that the judge, jury, and prison could not do, this slip of a girl did with a glance of her big gray eyes and the tremor of her voice in song. All his misdeeds arose up suddenly as a wall between him and the girl singer. His hard heart melted. The ugly lines went out of his face and it grew boyish once more, but sadder than ever.

His was not a nature to rest inactive. He poured out a hundred questions to Jack who could not answer half a dozen of them. "Who is she? Where does she live? Do you know her? Is she a good scholar? Does she go to church? I hope she don't talk religion. Does she go to parties? Does she dance?"

Jack replied as well as he was able. "She's a queer kind of a girl. She don't dance or go to parties at all. She's an awful fine scholar. She sings in the choir. Most of the boys are afraid to speak to her, she's so distant. She just says 'Yes,' or 'No,' when you ask her anything. She's religious—goes to prayer meeting and Sunday school. About a dozen boys go to prayer meeting just because she goes and sings. Her folks live in Waverly, but she boards with her aunt, Mrs. Brown. Now, that's all I can tell you about her. She's in some of my classes, but I dassent talk to her."

"Jack, she's the best and grandest girl I ever saw. I'm going to write to her."

Jack wistfully replied: "I wish you was out o' here, old man."

Harold became suddenly optimistic. "Never you mind, Jack. It won't be long till I am. I'm going to write to her to-day. You get a pencil and paper for me quick."

Jack's admiration of Harold was too great to admit of any question of his design. He would have said no one else was worthy to tie Mary's shoe, for he, too, worshiped her—but afar off. He was one of those whom women recognize only as gentle and useful beings, plain and unobtrusive.

He brought the pad and pencil and sat by while the letter was written. Harold's was not a nature of finedrawn distinctions; he wrote as he fought, swift and determined, and the letter was soon finished, read, and approved by Jack.

"Now, don't you let anybody see you give that to her," Harold said in parting.

"Trust me," Jack stanchly replied, and both felt that here was business of greatest importance. Jack proceeded at once to walk on the street which led past Mary's boarding place, and hung about the corner, in the hope of meeting Mary on her return from school. He knew very exactly her hours of recitation and at last she came, her arms filled with books, moving with such stately step she seemed a woman, tall and sedate. She perceived Jack waiting, but was not alarmed, for she comprehended something of his goodness and timidity.

He took off his cap with awkward formality. "Miss Yardwell, may I speak with you a moment?"

"Certainly, Mr. Burns," she replied, quite as formally as he.

He fell into step with her and walked on.

"You know—my chum—" he began, breathing hard, "my chum, Harry Excell, is in jail. You see, he had a fight with a great big chap, Clint Slocum, and Clint struck Harry with a whip. Of course Harry couldn't stand that and he cut Clint with his knife; of course he had to do it, for you see Clint was big as two of him and he'd just badgered the life out of Harry for a month, and so they jugged Harry, and he's there—in jail—and I suppose you've seen him; he's a fine-looking chap, dark hair, well built. He's a dandy ball player and skates bully; I wish you could see him shoot. We're going out West together when he gets out o' jail. Well, he saw you and he liked you, and he wrote you a letter and wanted me to hand it to you when no one was looking. Here it is: hide it, quick."

She took the letter, mechanically moved to do so by his imperative voice and action, and slipped it into her algebra. When she turned to speak Jack was gone, and she walked on, flushed with excitement, her breath shortened and quickened. She had a fair share of woman's love of romance and of letters, and she hurried a little in order that she might the sooner read the message of the dark-eyed, pale boy in the jail.

It was well she did not meet Mrs. Brown as she entered, for the limpid gray of her eyes was clouded with emotion. She climbed the stairs to her room and quickly opened the note. It began abruptly:

"DEAR FRIEND: It is mighty good of you to come and sing to us poor cusses in jail. I hope you'll come every Sunday. I like you. You are the best girl I ever saw. Don't go to my father's church, he ain't good enough to preach to you. I like you and I don't want you to think I'm a hard case. I used up Clint Slocum because I had to. He had hectored me about enough. He said some mean things about me and some one else, and I soaked him once with my fist. He struck me with the whip and downed me, then a kind of a cloud came into my mind and I guess I soaked him with my knife, too. Anyhow they jugged me for it. I don't care, I'd do it again. I'd cut his head off if he said anything about you. Well, now I'm in here and I'm sorry because I don't want you to think I'm a tough. I've done a whole lot of things I had not ought to have done, but I never meant to do anyone any harm.

"Now, I'm going West when I get out. I'm going into the cattle business on the great plains, and I'm going to be a rich man, and then I'm going to come back. I hope you won't get married before that time for I'll have something to say to you. If you run across any pictures of the mountains or the plains I wisht you'd send them on to me. Next to you I like the life in the plains better than anything.

"I hope you'll come every Sunday till I get out. Yours respec'fly,

"HAROLD EXCELL.

"Jack will give this to you. Jack is my chum; I'd trust him with my life. He's all wool."

The girl sat a long time with the letter in her hand. She was but a child, after all, and the lad's words alarmed and burdened her, for the meaning of the letter was plain. It was a message of love and admiration, and though it contained no subtleties, it came from one who was in jail, and she had been taught to regard people in jail as lost souls, aliens with whom it was dangerous to hold any intercourse, save in prayer and Scripture. The handsome boy with the sad face had appealed to her very deeply, and she bore him in her thoughts a great deal; but now he came in a new guise—as a lover, bold, outspoken, and persuasive.

"What shall I do? Shall I tell Aunt Lida?" she asked herself, and ended by kneeling down and praying to Jesus to give the young man a new heart.

In this fashion the courtship went on. No one knew of it but Jack, for Mary could not bring herself to confide in anyone, not even her mother, it all seemed too strange and beautiful. It was God's grace working through her, and her devoutness was not without its human mixture of girlish pride and exaltation. She worshiped him in her natural moments, and in her moments of religious fervor she prayed for him with impersonal anguish as for a lost soul. She did not consider him a criminal, but she thought him Godless and rebellious toward his Saviour.

She wrote him quaint, formal little notes, which began abruptly, "My Friend." They contained much matter which was hortatory, but at times she became girlish and very charming. Gradually she dropped the tone which she had caught from revivalists and wrote of her studies and of the doings of each member of the class, and all other subjects which a young girl finds valuable material of conversation. She was just becoming acquainted with Victor Hugo and his resounding, antithetic phrases, and his humanitarian outcries filled her mind with commotion. Her heart swelled high with resolution to do something to help the world in general and Harold in particular.

She was not one in whom passion ruled; the intellectual dominated the passional in her, and, besides, she was only a child. She was by no means as mature as Harold, although about the same age. Naturally reverent, she had been raised in a family where religious observances never remitted; where grace was always spoken. In this home her looks were seldom alluded to in any way, and vanity was not in her. She had her lovelinesses; her hair was long and fair, her eyes were beautiful, and her skin was of exquisite purity, like her eyes. Her charm lay in her modesty and quaint dignity, her grave and gentle gaze, and in her glorious voice.

The Reverend Excell was pleased to hear that his son was bearing confinement very well, and made another effort to see him.

Simply because Mary wished it, Harold consented to see his father, and they held a long conversation, at least the father talked and the boy listened. In effect, the minister said:

"My son, I have forfeited your good will—that I know—but I think you do me an injustice. I know you think I am a liar and a hypocrite because you have seen me in rages and because I have profaned God in your presence. My boy, let me tell you, in every man there are two natures. When one is uppermost, actions impossible to the other nature become easy. You will know this, you should know it now, for in you there is the same murderous madman that is in me. You must fight him down. I love you, my son," he said, and his voice was deep and tremulous, "and it hurts me to have you stand aloof from me. I have tried to do my duty. I have almost succeeded in putting my worst self under my feet, and I think if you were to come to understand me you would not be so hard toward me. It is not a little thing to me that you, my only son, turn your face away from me. On the day of your trial I thought we came nearer to an understanding than in many years."

Harold felt the justice of his father's plea and his heart swelled with emotion, but something arose up between his heart and his lips and he remained silent.

Mr. Excell bent his great, handsome head and plead as a lover pleads, but the pale lad, with bitter and sullen mien, listened in silence. At last the father ended; there was a pause.

"I want you to come home when your term ends," he said. "Will you promise that?"

Harold said, "No, I can't do that. I'm going out West."

"I shall not prevent you, my son, but I want you to come and take your place at the table just once. There is a special reason for this. Will you come for a single day?"

Harold forced himself to answer, "Yes."

Mr. Excell raised his head.

"Let us shake hands over your promise, my boy."

Harold arose and they shook hands. The father's eyes were wet with tears. "I can't afford to forfeit your good opinion," Mr. Excell went on, "especially now when you are leaving me, perhaps forever. I think you are right in going. There is no chance for you here; perhaps out there in the great West you may get a start. Of my shortcomings as a father you know, and I suppose you can never love me as a son should, but I think you will see some day that I am not a hypocrite, and that I failed as a father more through neglect and passion than through any deliberate injustice."

The boy struggled for words to express himself; at last he burst forth: "I don't blame you at all, only let me go where I can do something worth while: you bother me so."

The minister dropped his son's hand and a look of the deepest sadness came over his face. He had failed—Harold was farther away from him than ever. He turned and went out without another word.

That he had hurt his father Harold knew, but in exactly what other way he could have acted he could not tell. The overanxiety on the father's part irritated the boy. Had he been less morbid, less self-accusing, he would have won. Harold passionately loved strength and decision, especially in a big man like his father, who looked like a soldier and a man of action, and who ought not to cry like a woman. If only he would act all the time as he did when he threw the sheriff across the walk that day on the street. "I wish he'd stop preaching and go to work at something," he said to Jack. The psychology of the father's attitude toward him was incomprehensible. He could get along very well without a father; why could not his father get along without him? He hated all this fuss, anyway. It only made him feel sorry and perplexed, and he wished sincerely that his father would let him alone.

Jack brought a letter from Mary which troubled him.

> "I am going home in March, a week before the term ends. Mother isn't very well, and just as soon as I can I must go. If I do, you must not forget me."

Of course he wrote in reply, saying:

> "Don't you go till I see you. You must come in and see me. Can't you come in when Jack does, he knows all about us, COME SURE. I can't go without a good-by kiss. Don't you go back on me now. Come."

"I'm afraid to come," she replied, "people would find out everything and talk. Besides you mustn't kiss me. We are not regularly engaged, and so it would not be right."

"We'll be engaged in about two minutes if you'll meet me with Jack," he replied. "You're the best girl in the world and I'm going to marry you when I get rich enough to come back and build you a house to be in, I'm going out where the cattle are thick as grasshoppers, and I'm going to be a cattle king and then you can be a cattle queen and ride around with me on our ranch, that's what they call a farm out there. Now, you're my girl and you must wait for me to come back. Don't you get impatient, sometimes a chap has a hard time just to get a start, after that it's easy. Jack will go with me, he will be my friend and share everything.

"Now you come and call me sweetheart and I'll call you angel, for that's what you are. Get to be a great singer, and go about the country singing to make men like me good, you can do it, only don't let them fall in love with you, they do that too just the way I did, but don't let 'em do it for you are mine. You're my sweetheart. From your sweetheart,

"HARRY EXCELL, Cattle King."

CHAPTER VI

THE CAGE OPENS

Before Harold's day of freedom came Mary was called home by a telegram from her father. She longed to see Harold before she left, but she was too much hurried to seek out Jack, the loyal go-between, and dared not send a letter by any other hands. She went away without sending him a word of good-by.

So it happened that the last week of Harold's captivity was spent in loneliness and bitter sorrow, and even when Jack came he brought very little information concerning Mary's flight, and Harold was bitter and accusing.

"Why didn't she write to me? Why didn't she come to see me?"

Jack pleaded for her as well as he was able. "She hadn't time, maybe."

Harold refused to accept this explanation. "If she had cared for me, she'd have sent me word—she could take time for that."

No letter came in the days which followed, and at last he put her out of his heart and turned his face to the sunset land which now called to the sad heart within him with imperious voice. Out there he could forget all his hurts.

On the morning when the jailer opened the door for him to leave the iron corridor in which he had spent so many months, his father met him, and the white face of the boy made the father's heart contract. Harold's cheeks were plump and boyish, but there was a look in his face which made him seem a youth of twenty.

The family stood in the jailer's parlor to receive him, and he submitted to their caresses with cold dignity. His manner plainly expressed this feeling: "You are all strangers to me." But he turned to Jack and gripped his hand hard. "Now for the plains!"

Side by side the father and son passed out into the sunshine. The boy drew an audible breath, as if in sudden, keen pain. Around him lay the bare, brown earth of March. The sun was warm and a subtle odor of lately uncovered sward was in the air. The wind, soft, warm, and steady, blew from the west. Here and there a patch of grass, faintly green, showed where sullen snow banks had lately lain. And the sky! Filled with clouds almost as fleecy and as white as June, the sky covered him, and when he raised his eyes to it he saw a triangular flock of geese sweeping to the northwest, serene and apparently effortless.

He could not speak—did not wish to hear any speech but that of Nature, and the father seemed to comprehend his son's mood, for he, too, walked in silence.

The people of the village knew that Harold was to return to freedom that day, and with one excuse or another they came to the doors to see him pass. Some of them were genuinely sympathetic, and bowed and smiled, intending to say, "Let by-gones be by-gones," but to their greetings Harold remained blankly unresponsive. Jack would gladly have walked with Harold, but out of consideration for the father fell into step behind.

The girls—some of them—had the grace to weep when they saw Harold's sad face. Others tittered and said: "Ain't he awful pale." For the most part, the citizens considered his punishment sufficient, and were disposed to give him another chance. To them, Harold, by his manner, intended to reply: "I don't want any favors. I won't accept any chance from you. I despise you and I don't want to see you again."

He looked upon the earth and the sky rather than upon the faces of his fellows. His natural love of Nature had been intensified by his captivity, while a bitter contempt and suspicion of all men and women had grown up in his mind. He entered his father's house with reluctance and loathing.

The day was one of preparation. Jack had carried out, so far as he well could, the captive's wishes. His gun, his clothing, and his valise were ready for him, and Mrs. Excell had washed and ironed all his linen with scrupulous care. His sister Maud had made a little "housewife" for him, and filled it with buttons and needles and thread, a gift he did not value, even from her.

"I'm going out West to herd cattle, not to cobble trousers," he said contemptuously.

Jack had a report to make. "Harry, I've found a chance for you," he said when they were alone. "There was a man moving to Colorado here on Saturday. He said he could use you, but of course I had to tell him you couldn't go for a few days. He's just about to Roseville now. I'll tell you what you do. You get on the train and go to Roseville—I'll let you have the money—and you strike him when he comes through. His name is Pratt. He's a tall old chap, talks queer. Of course he may have a hand now, but anyway you must get out o' here. He wouldn't take you if he knew you'd been in jail."

"Aren't you going?" asked Harold sharply.

Jack looked uneasy. "Not now, Harry. You see, I want to graduate, I'm so near through. It wouldn't do to quit now. I'll stay till fall. I'll get to Uncle John's place about the time you do."

Harold said no more, but his face darkened with disappointment.

The call to dinner brought them all together once more, and the minister's grace became a short prayer for the safety of his son, broken again and again by the weakness of his own voice and by the sobs of Maud and Mrs. Excell. Harold sat with rigid face, fixed in a frown. The meal proceeded in sad silence, for each member of the family felt that Harold was leaving them never to return.

Jack's plan was determined upon, and after dinner he went to hitch up his horse to take Harry out to the farm. The family sat in painful suspense for a few moments after Jack went out, and then Mr. Excell said:

"My son, we have never been friends, and the time is past when I can expect to win your love and confidence, but I hope you will not go away with any bitterness in your heart toward me." He waited a moment for his son to speak, but Harold continued silent, which again confused and pained the father, but he went on: "In proof of what I say I want to offer you some money to buy a horse and saddle when you need them."

"I don't need any money," said Harold, a little touched by the affection in his father's voice. "I can earn all the money I need."

"Perhaps so, but a little money might be useful at the start. You will need a horse if you herd cattle."

"I'll get my own horse—you'll need all you can earn," said Harold in reply.

Mr. Excell's tone changed. "What makes you say that, Harold? What do you mean?"

"Oh, I didn't mean anything in particular."

"Have you heard of the faction which is growing up in the church against me?"

Harold hesitated. "Yes—but I wasn't thinking of that particularly." He betrayed a little interest. "What's the matter with 'em?"

"There has been an element in the church hostile to me from the first, and during your trial and sentence these persons have used every effort to spread a feeling against me. How wide it is I can not tell, but I know it is strong. It may end my work here, for I will not cringe to them. They will find me iron."

Harold's heart warmed suddenly. Without knowing it the father had again struck the right note to win his son. "That's right," the boy said, "don't let 'em tramp on you."

A lump arose in the minister's throat. There was something very sweet in Harold's sympathy. His eyes smiled, even while they were dim with tears. He held out his hand and Harold took it.

"Well, now, my son, it's time for you to start. Don't you worry about me. I am a fighter when I am aroused."

Harold smiled back into his face, and so it was that the two men parted, for the father, in a flash of insight, understood that no more than this could be gained; but his heart was lighter than it had been for many months as he saw his son ride away from his door.

"Write often, Harold," he called after them.

"All right. You let me know how the fight comes out. If they whip you, come out West," was Harold's reply; then he turned in his seat. "Drive ahead, Jack; there's no one now but your folks for whom I care."

As they drove out along the muddy lanes the hearts of the two boys became very tender. Harold, filled with exaltation by every familiar thing—by the flights of ground sparrows, by the patches of green grass, by the smell of the wind, by the infrequent boom of the prairie chickens—talked incessantly.

"What makes me maddest," he broke out, "is to think they've cheated me out of seeing one fall and one winter. I didn't see the geese fly south, and now here they are all going north again. Some time I mean to find out where they go to." He took off his hat. "This wind will mighty soon take the white out o' me, won't it?" He was very gay. He slapped his chum on the shoulder and shouted with excitement. "We must keep going, old man, till we strike the buffalo. They are the sign of wild country that *is* wild. I want to get where there ain't any fences."

Jack smiled sadly in reply. Harold knew he listened and so talked on. "I must work up a big case of sunburn before I strike Mr. Pratt for a job. Did he have extra horses?"

"'Bout a dozen. His girl was driving the cattle, but he said——"

"Girl? What kind of a girl?"

"Oh, a kind of a tomboy, freckled—chews gum and says 'darn it!' That kind of a girl."

Harold's face darkened. "I don't like the idea of that girl. She might have heard something, and then it would go hard with me."

"Don't you worry. The Pratts ain't the kind of people that read newspapers; they didn't stop here but a day, anyhow."

The sight of Mr. Burns and his wife at the gate moved Harold deeply. Mrs. Burns came hurrying out: "You blessed boy! Get right down and let me hug you," and as he leaped down she put her arms around him as if he were her own son, and Harold's eyes smarted with tears.

"I declare," said Mr. Burns, "you look like a fightin' cock; must feed you well down there?"

No note of doubt, hesitation, concealment, or shame was in their greetings and the boy knew it. They all sat around the kitchen, and chatted and laughed as if no ill thing had ever happened to him. Burns uttered the only doubtful word when he said: "I don't know about this running away from things here. I'd be inclined to stay here and fight it out."

"But it isn't running away, Dad," said Jack. "Harry has always wanted to go West and now is the first time he has really had the chance."

"That's so," admitted the father. "Still, I'm sorry to see him look like he was running away."

Mrs. Burns was determined to feed Harry into complete torpor. She put up enough food in a basket to last him to San Francisco at the shortest. Even when the boys had entered the buggy she ordered them to wait while she brought out some sweet melon pickles in a jar to add to the collection.

"Well, now, good-by," said Harold, reaching down his hand to Mrs. Burns, who seized it in both hers.

"You poor thing, don't let the Indians scalp ye."

"No danger o' that," he called back.

"Be good to yourself," shouted Burns, and the buggy rolled through the gate into the west as the red sun was setting and the prairie cocks were crowing.

The boys talked their plans all over again while the strong young horse spattered through the mud. Slowly the night fell, and as they rode under the branches of the oaks, Jack took courage to say:

"I wish Miss Yardwell had been here, Harry."

"It's no use talking about her; she don't care two straws for me; if she had she would have written to me, at least."

"Her mother may have been dying."

"Even that needn't keep her from letting me know or sending some word. She didn't care for me—she was just trying to convert me."

"She wasn't the kind of a girl who flirts. By jinks! You should see her look right through the boys that used to try to walk home with her after prayer meeting. They never tried it a second time. She's a wonder that way. One strange thing about her, she never acts like other girls. You know what I mean? She's different. She's going to be a singer, and travel around giving concerts—she told me so once."

Harold was disposed to be fair. "I don't want anybody to feel sorry for me. I suppose she felt that way, and tried to help me." Here he paused and his voice changed. "But when I'm a cattle king out West and can buy her the best home in Des Moines—maybe she won't pity me so much. Anyhow, there's nothing left for me but to emigrate. There's no use stayin' around here. Out there is the place for me now."

Jack put Harold down at the station and turned over to him all the money he had in the world. Harold took it, saying:

"Now you'll get this back with interest, old man. I need it now, but I won't six months from now. I'm going to strike a job before long—don't you worry."

Their good-by was awkward and constrained, and Harold felt the parting more keenly than he dared to show. Jack rode away crying—a brother could not have been more troubled. It seemed that the bitterness of death was in this good-by.

CHAPTER VII

ON THE WING

When Harold arose the next morning his cheeks were still red with the touch of the wind and sun and he looked like a college student just entering upon a vacation. His grace and dignity of bearing set him apart from the rough workmen with whom he ate, and he did not exchange a single word with anyone but the landlord. As soon as breakfast was over he went out into the town.

Roseville had only one street, and it was not difficult to learn that Pratt had not yet appeared upon the scene. It was essentially a prairie village; no tree broke the smooth horizon line. A great many emigrants were in motion, and their white-topped wagons suggested the sails of minute craft on the broad ocean as they came slowly up the curve to the East and fell away down the slope to the West. To all of these Harold applied during the days that followed, but received no offer which seemed to promise so well as that of Mr. Pratt, so he waited. At last he came, a tall, sandy-bearded fellow, who walked beside a four-horse team drawing two covered wagons tandem. Behind him straggled a bunch of bony cattle and some horses, herded by a girl and a small boy. The girl rode a mettlesome little pony, sitting sidewise on a man's saddle.

"Wal—I d'n know," the old man replied in answer to Harold's question. "I did 'low fer to get some help, but Jinnie she said she'd bring 'em along fer fifty cents a day, an' she's boss, stranger. If she's sick o' the job, why, I'll make out with ye. Jinnie, come here."

Jinnie rode up, eyeing the stranger sharply. "What's up, Dad?"

"Here's another young fellow after your job."

"Well, if he'll work cheap he can have it," replied the girl promptly. "I don't admire to ride in this mud any longer."

Pratt smiled. "I reckon that lets you in, stranger, ef we can come to terms. We ain't got any money to throw away, but we'll do the best we kin."

"I'll tell you what you do. You turn that pony and saddle over to me when we get through, and I'll call it square."

"Well, I reckon you won't," said the girl, throwing back her sunbonnet as if in challenge. "That's my pony, and nobody gets him without blood, and don't you forget it, sonny."

She was a large-featured girl, so blonde as to be straw-colored, even to the lashes of her eyes, but her teeth were very white, and her lips a vivid pink. She had her father's humorous smile, and though her words were bluff, her eyes betrayed that she liked Harold at once.

Harold smiled back at her. "Well, I'll take the next best, that roan there."

The boy burst into wild clamor: "Not by a darn sight, you don't. That's my horse, an' no sucker like you ain't goin' to ride him, nuther."

"Why don't *you* ride him?" asked Harold.

The boy looked foolish. "I'm goin' to, some day."

"He can't," said the girl, "and I don't think you can."

Pratt grinned. "Wal, you see how it is, youngster, you an' me has got to get down to a money basis. Them young uns claim all my stawk."

Harold said: "Pay me what you can," and Pratt replied: "Wal, throw your duds into that hind wagon. We've got to camp somewhere 'fore them durn critters eat up all the fences."

As Harold was helping to unhitch the team the girl came around and studied him with care.

"Say, what's your name?"

"Moses," he instantly replied.

"Moses what?"

"Oh, let it go at Mose."

"Hain't you got no other name?"

"I did have but the wind blew it away."

"What was it?"

"Moses N. Hardluck."

"You're terrible cute, ain't you?"

"Not so very, or I wouldn't be working for my board."

"You hain't never killed yourself with hard work, by the looks o' them hands."

"Oh, I've been going to school."

"A'huh! I thought you had. You talk pretty hifalutin' fer a real workin' man. I tell ye what I think—you're a rich man's son, and you've run away."

"Come, gal, get that coffee bilin'," called the mother. Mrs. Pratt was a wizened little woman, so humped by labor and chills and fever that she seemed deformed. Her querulousness was not so much ill-natured as plaintive.

"He *says* his name is Mose Hardluck," Harold heard the girl say, and that ended all further inquiry. He became simply "Mose" to them.

There was a satisfying charm to the business of camping out which now came to be the regular order of living to him. By day the cattle, thin and poor, crawled along patiently, waiting for feeding time to come, catching at such bunches of dry grass as came within their reach, and at their heels rode Harold on an old black mare, his clear voice urging the herd forward. At noon and again at night Pratt halted the wagons beside the road and while the women got supper or dinner Harold helped Pratt take care of the stock, which he was obliged to feed. "I started a little airly," he said at least a score of times in the first week. "But I wanted to get a good start agin grass come."

Harold was naturally handy at camping, and his ready and skillful hands became very valuable around the camp fire. He was quick and cheerful, and apparently tireless, and before the end of the week Jennie said:

"Say, Mose, you can ride my horse if you want to."

"Much obliged, but I guess I'll hang on to the black mare."

At this point Dannie, not to be outdone, chirped shrilly: "You can break my horse if you want to."

So a few days later Harold, with intent to check the girl in her growing friendliness, as well as to please himself, replied: "I guess I'll break Dan's colt."

He began by caressing the horse at every opportunity, leaning against him, or putting one arm over his back, to let him feel the weight of his body. At last he leaped softly up and hung partly over his back. Naturally the colt shied and reared, but Harold dropped off instantly and renewed his petting and soothing. It was not long before the pony allowed him to mount, and nothing remained but to teach him to endure the saddle and the bridle. This was done by belting him and checking him to a pad strapped upon his back. He struggled fiercely to rid himself of these fetters. He leaped in the air, fell, rolled over, backing and wheeling around and around till Dan grew dizzy watching him.

A bystander once said: "Why don't you climb onto him and stay with him till he gets sick o' pitchin'; that's what a broncho buster would do."

"Because I don't want him 'busted'; I want him taught that I'm his friend," said Harold.

In the end "Jack," as Harold called the roan, walked up to his master and rubbed his nose against his shoulder. Harold then stripped away the bridle and pad at once, and when he put them on next day Jack winced, but did not plunge, and Harold mounted him. A day or two later the colt worked under the saddle like an old horse. Thereafter it was a matter of making him a horse of finished education. He was taught not to trot, but to go directly from the walk to the "lope." He acquired a swift walk and a sort of running trot—that is, he trotted behind and rose in front with a wolflike action of the fore feet. He was guided by the touch of the rein on the neck or by the pressure of his rider's knee on his shoulder.

He was taught to stand without hitching and to allow his rider to mount on either side. This was a trick which Harold learned of a man who had been with the Indians. "You see," he said, "an Injun can't afford to have a horse that will only let him climb on from the nigh side, he has to get there in a hurry sometimes, and any side at all will do him."

It was well that Jack was trained early, for as they drew out on the open prairie and the feed became better the horses and cattle were less easy to drive. Each day the interest grew. The land became wilder and the sky brighter. The grass came on swiftly, and crocuses and dandelions broke from the sod on the sunny side of smooth hills. The cranes, with their splendid challenging cries, swept in wide circles through the sky. Ducks and geese moved by in myriads, straight on, delaying not. Foxes barked on the hills at sunset, and the splendid chorus of the prairie chickens thickened day by day.

It was magnificent, and Harold was happy. True, it was not all play. There were muddy roads to plod through and treacherous sloughs to cross. There were nights when camp had to be pitched in rain, and mornings when he was obliged to rise stiff and sore to find the cattle strayed away and everything wet and grimy. But the sunshine soon warmed his back and dried up the mud under his feet. Each day the way grew drier and the flowers more abundant. Each day signs of the wild life thickened. Antlers of elk, horns of the buffalo, crates of bones set around shallow water holes, and especially the ever-thickening game trails furrowing the hills filled the boy's heart with delight. This was the kind of life he wished to see. They were now beyond towns, and only occasionally small settlements relieved the houseless rolling plains. Soon the Missouri, that storied and muddy old stream, would offer itself to view.

"Mose" was now indispensable to the Pratt "outfit." He built fires, shot game, herded the cattle, greased the wagons, curried horses, and mended harness. He never complained and never grew sullen. Although he talked but little, the family were fond of him, but considered him a "singular critter." He had lost his pallor. His skin was a clear brown, and being dressed in rough clothing, wide hat, and gauntlet gloves, he made a bold and dashing herder, showing just the right kind of wear and tear. Occasionally, when a chance to earn a few dollars offered, Pratt camped and took a job, and Harold shared in the wages.

He spent a great deal of his pocket money in buying cartridges for his revolver. He shot at everything which offered a taking mark, and became so expert that Dan bowed down before him, and Mrs. Pratt considered him dangerous.

"It ain't natural fer to be so durned sure-pop on game," she said one day. "Doggone it, I'd want 'o miss 'em once in a while just fer to be aigged on fer to try again. First you know, you'll be obliged fer to shoot standin' on your haid like these yere champin' shooters that go 'round the kentry givin' shows, you shorely will, Mose."

Mose only laughed. "I want to be just as good a shot as anybody," he said, turning to Pratt.

"You'll be it ef you don't wear out your gun a-doin' of it," replied the boss.

These were splendid days. Each sundown they camped nearer to the land of the buffalo, and when the work was done and the supper eaten, Mose took his pipe and his gun and walked away to some ridge, there to sit while the yellow light faded out of the sky. He was as happy as one of his restless nature could properly hope to be, but sometimes when he thought of Mary his heart ached a little; he forgot her only when his imagination set wing into the sunset sky.

One other thing troubled him a little. Rude, plain Jennie was in love with him. Daily intercourse with a youngster half as attractive as Mose would have had the same effect upon her, for she was at that age when propinquity makes sentiment inevitable. She could scarcely keep her eyes from him during hours in camp, and on the drive she rode with him four times as long as he wished for. She bothered him, and yet she was so good and generous he could not rebuff her; he could only endure.

She had one accomplishment: she could ride like a Sioux, either astride or womanwise, with a saddle or without, and many a race they had as the roads grew firm and dry. She was scrawny and flat-chested, but agile as a boy when occasion demanded. She was fearless, too, of man or beast, and once when her father became crazy with liquor (which was his weakness) she went with Mose to bring him from a saloon, where he stood boasting of his powers as a fighter with the bowie knife.

As they entered Jennie walked straight up to him: "Dad, you come home. Come right out o' yere."

He looked at her for a moment until his benumbed brain took in her words and all their meaning; then he said: "All right, Jinnie,

just wait a second till I have another horn with these yer gents—
—"

"Horn nawthin," she said in reply, and seized him by the arm. "You come along."

He submitted without a struggle, and on the way out grew plaintive. "Jinnie, gal," he kept saying, "I'm liable to get dry before mornin', I shore am; ef you'd only jest let me had one more gill—
—"

"Oh, shet up, Dad. Ef you git dry I'll bring the hull crick in fer ye to drink," was her scornful reply.

After he was safe in bed Jennie came over to the wagon where Mose was smoking.

"Men are the blamedest fools," she began abruptly; "'pears like they ain't got the sense of a grayback louse, leastways some of 'em. Now, there's dad, filled up on stuff they call whisky out yer, and consequence is he can't eat any grub for two days or more. Doggone it, it makes me huffy, it plum does. Mam has put up with it fer twenty years, which is just twenty more than I'd stand it, and don't you forget it. When I marry a man it will be a man with sense 'nough not to pizen hisself on rot-gut whisky."

Without waiting for a reply she turned away and went to bed in the bottom of the hinder wagon. Mose smoked his pipe out and rolled himself in his blanket near the smoldering camp fire.

Pratt was feeble and very long faced and repentant at breakfast. His appetite was gone. Mrs. Pratt said nothing, but pressed him to eat. "Come, Paw, a gill or two o' cawfee will do ye good," she said. "Cawfee is a great heatoner," she said to Mose. "When I'm so misorified of a moarnin' I can't eat a mossel o' bacon or pork, I kin take a gill o' cawfee an' it shore helps me much."

Pratt looked around sheepishly. "I do reckon I made a plum ejot of myself last night."

"As ush'll," snapped Jennie. "You wanted to go slicin' every man in sight up, just fer to show you could swing a bowie knife when you was on airth the first time."

"Now that's the quare thing, Mose; a peacebbler man than me don't live; Jinnie says I couldn't lick a hearty bedbug, but when I git red liquor into my insides I'm a terror to near neighbours, so they say. I can't well remember just what do take place 'long towards the fo'th drink."

"Durn lucky you can't. You'd never hole up your head again. A plummer fool you never see," said Jennie, determined to drive his shame home to him.

Pratt sighed, understood perfectly the meaning of all this vituperation. "Well, Mam, we'll try again. I think I'm doin' pretty good when I go two munce, don't you?"

"It's more'n that, Paw," said Mrs. Pratt, eager to encourage him at the right moment. "It's sixty-four days. You gained four days on it this time."

Pratt straightened up and smiled. "That so, Mam? Wal, that shorely is a big gain."

He took Mose aside after breakfast and solemnly said:

"Wimern-folk is a heap better'n men-folks. Now, me or you couldn't stand in wimern-folks what they put up with in men-folks. 'Pears like they air finer built, someway." After a pause he said with great earnestness: "Don't you drink red liquor, Mose; it shore makes a man no account."

"Don't you worry, Cap. I'm not drinkin' liquor of any color."

CHAPTER VIII

THE UPWARD TRAIL

Once across the Missouri the trail began to mount. "Here is the true buffalo country," thought Mose, as they came to the treeless hills of the Great Muddy Water. On these smooth buttes Indian sentinels had stood, morning and evening, through a thousand years, to signal the movement of the wild herds, and from other distant hills columns of smoke by day, or the flare of signal fires at night, had warned the chieftains of the approach of enemies. Down these grassy gulches, around these sugar-loaf mesas, the giant brown cattle of the plains had crawled in long, dark, knobby lines. On the green bottoms they had mated and fed and fought in thousands, roaring like lions, their huge hoofs flinging the alkaline earth in showers above their heads, their tongues curling, their tails waving like banners.

Mose was already deeply learned in all these dramas. All that he had ever heard or read of the wild country remained in his mind. He cared nothing about the towns or the fame of cities, but these deep-worn trails of shaggy beasts filled him with joy. Their histories were more to him than were the wars of Cyrus and Hannibal. He questioned all the men he met, and their wisdom became his.

Slowly the movers wound their way up the broad, sandy river which came from the wilder spaces of the West. The prairie was gone. The tiger lily, the sweet Williams, the pinks, together with the luxuriant meadows and the bobolinks, were left behind. In their stead, a limitless, upward shelving plain outspread, covered with a short, surly, hairlike grass and certain sturdy, resinous plants supporting flowers of an unpleasant odor, sticky and weedy. Bristling cacti bulged from the sod; small Quaker-gray sparrows and larks were the only birds. In the swales blue joint grew rank. The only trees were cottonwoods and cutleaf willow, scattered scantily along the elbows in the river.

At last they came to the home of the prairie dog and the antelope—the buffalo could not be far away! So wide was the earth, so all-embracing the sky, they seemed to blend at the horizon line, and lakes of water sprang into view, filling a swale in the sod—mystic and beautiful, only to vanish like cloud shadows.

The cattle country was soon at hand. Cowboys in sombreros and long-heeled boots, with kerchiefs knotted about their necks, careered on swift ponies in and out of the little towns or met the newcomers on the river road. They rode in a fashion new to Mose, with toes pointed straight down, the weight of their bodies a little on one side. They skimmed the ground like swallows, forcing their ponies mercilessly. Their saddles were very heavy, with high pommels and leather-covered stirrups, and Mose determined to have one at once. Some of them carried rifles under their legs in a long holster.

Realizing that those were the real "cow-punchers," the youth studied their outfits as keenly as a country girl scrutinizes the new gown of a visiting city cousin. He changed his manner of riding (which was more nearly that of the cavalry) to theirs. He slung a red kerchief around his neck, and bought a pair of "chaps," a sort of fringed leather leggings. He had been wearing his pistol at his side, he now slewed it around to his hip. He purchased also a pair of high-heeled boots and a "rope" (no one called it a "lariat"), and began to acquire the technicalities of the range. A horse that reared and leaped to fling its rider was said to "pitch." Any firearm was a "gun," and any bull, steer, or heifer, a "cow." In a few days all these distinctions had been mastered, and only the closest observer was able to "cut out" Mose as a "tenderfoot."

Pratt was bound for his brother's ranch on the Big Sandy River, and so pushed on steadily, although it was evident that he was not looked upon with favor. He had reached a section of country where the cattlemen eyed his small outfit with contempt and suspicion. He came under the head of a "nester," or "truck farmer," who was likely to fence in the river somewhere and homestead some land. He was another menace to the range, and was to be discouraged. The mutter of war was soon heard.

One day a couple of whisky-heated cowboys rode furiously up behind Mose and called out:

"Where in h—l ye think ye're goin', you dam cow milker?"

Mose was angry on the instant and sullenly said: "None of your business."

After threatening to blow his liver into bits they rode on and repeated their question to Pratt, who significantly replied: "I'm a-goin' to the mouth o' the Cannon Ball ef I don't miss it. Any objection?"

"You bet we have, you rowdy baggage puller. You better keep out o' here; the climate's purty severe."

Pratt smiled grimly. "I'm usen to that, boys," he replied, and the cowboys rode on, cursing him for a fool.

At last, late in July, the mouth of the Cannon Ball was reached. One afternoon they cut across a peninsular body of high land and came in sight of a wide green flat (between two sluggish, percolating streams) whereon a cluster of gray log buildings stood.

"I reckon that's Jake's," said Pratt as they halted to let the horses breathe. A minute, zig-zag line of deep green disclosed the course of the Cannon Ball, deep sunk in the gravelly soil as it came down to join the Big Sandy. All about stood domed and pyramidal and hawk-headed buttes. On the river bank huge old cottonwoods, worn and leaning, offered the only shadow in a land flooded with vehement, devouring light. The long journey was at an end.

Daniel raised a peculiar halloo, which brought a horseman hurrying out to meet him. The brother had not forgotten their boyish signal. He rode up swiftly and slid from his horse without speaking.

Jake resembled his brother in appearance, but his face was sterner and his eyes keener. He had been made a bold, determined man by the pressure of harsher circumstances. He shook his brother by the hand in self-contained fashion.

"Wal, Dan'l, I'm right glad you got h'yer safe. I reckon this is Miss Jinnie—she's a right hearty girl, ain't she? Mrs. Pratt, I'm heartily glad to see ye. This yer little man must be the tit-man. What's your name, sonny?"

"Dan. H. Pratt," piped the boy.

"Ah—hah! Wal, sir, I reckon you'll make a right smart of a cowboy yet. What's this?" he said, turning to Mose. "This ain't no son-in-law, I reckon!"

At this question all laughed, Jennie most immoderately of all.

"Not yit, Uncle Jake."

Mose turned red, being much more embarrassed than Jennie. He was indeed enraged, for it hurt his pride to be counted a suitor of this ungainly and ignorant girl. Right there he resolved to flee at the first opportunity. Distressful days were at hand.

"You've been a long time gettin' here, Dan."

"Wal, we've had some bad luck. Mam was sick for a spell, and then we had to lay by an' airn a little money once in a while. I'm glad I'm here—'peared like we'd wear the hoofs off'n our stawk purty soon." Jake sobered down first. "Wal, now I reckon you best unhook right h'yer for a day or two till we get a minute to look around and see where we're at." So, clucking to the tired horses the train entered upon its last half mile of a long journey.

Jake's wife, a somber and very reticent woman, with a slender figure and a girlish head, met them at the door of the cabin. Her features were unusually small for a woman of her height, and, as she shook hands silently, Mose looked into her sad dark eyes and liked her very much. She had no children; the two in which she had once taken a mother's joy slept in two little mounds on the hill just above the house. She seemed glad of the coming of her sister-in-law, though she did not stop to say so, but returned to the house to hurry supper forward.

After the meal was eaten the brothers lit their pipes and sauntered out to the stables, where they sat down for a long talk. Mose followed them silently and sat near to listen.

"Now, Dan'l," Jake began, "I'm mighty glad you've come and brought this yer young feller. We need ye both bad! It's like this"—he paused and looked around; "I don't want the wimern folks to hear," he explained. "Times is goin' to be lively here, shore. They's a big fight on 'twixt us truck farmers and the cattle ranchers. You see, the cattlemen has had the free range so long they naturally 'low they own it, and they have the nerve to tell us fellers to keep off. They explain smooth enough that they ain't got nawthin' agin me pussonally—you understand—only they 'low me settlin' h'yer will bring others, which is shore about right, fer h'yer you be, kit an' caboodle. Now you comin' in will set things a-whoopin', an' it ain't no Sunday-school picnic we're a-facin'. We're goin' to plant some o' these men before this is settled. The hull cattle business is built up on robbing the Government. I've said so, an' they're down on me already."

As Jake talked the night fell, and the boy's hair began to stir. A wolf was "yapping" on a swell, and a far-off heron was uttering his booming cry. Over the ridges, which cut sharply into the fleckless dull-yellow sky, lay unknown lands out of which almost any variety of fierce marauder might ride. Surely this was the wild country of which he had read, where men could talk so glibly of murder and violent death.

"When I moved in here three years ago," continued Jake, "they met me and told me to get out. I told 'em I weren't takin' a back track that year. One night they rode down a-whoopin' and a-shoutin', and I natcherly poked my gun out'n the winder and handed out a few to 'em—an' they rode off. Next year quite a little squad o' truck farmers moved into the bend just below, an' we got together and talked it over and agreed to stand by. We planted two more o' them, and they got one on us. They control the courts, and so we have got to fight. They've got a judge that suits 'em now, and this year will be hot—it will, sure."

Dan'l Pratt smoked for a full minute before he said: "You didn't write nothin' of this, Jake."

Jake grinned. "I didn't want to disappoint you, Dan. I knew your heart was set on comin'."

"Wal, I didn't 'low fer to hunt up no furss," Dan slowly said; "but the feller that tramps on me is liable to sickness."

Jake chuckled. "I know that, Dan; but how about this young feller?"

"He's all right. He kin shoot like a circus feller, and I reckon he'll stay right by."

Mose, with big heart, said, "You bet I will."

"That's the talk. Well, now, let's go to bed. I've sent word to Jennison—he's our captain—and to-morrow we'll settle you on the mouth o' the creek, just above here. It's a monstrous fine piece o' ground; I know you'll like it."

Mose slept very little that night. He found himself holding his breath in order to be sure that the clamor of a coyote was not a cowboy signal of attack. There was something vastly convincing in Jake Pratt's quiet drawl as he set forth the cause for war.

Early the next morning, Jennison, the leader of the settlers, came riding into the yard. He was tall, grim lipped and curt spoken. He had been a captain in the Union Army of Volunteers, and was plainly a man of inflexible purpose and resolution.

"How d'e do, gentlemen?" he called pleasantly, as he reined in his foaming broncho. "Nice day."

"Mighty purty. Light off, cap'n, an' shake hands with my brother Dan'l."

Jennison dismounted calmly and easily, dropping the rein over the head of his wild broncho, and after shaking hands all around, said:

"Well, neighbor, I'm right glad to see ye. Jake, your brother, has been savin' up a homestead for ye—and I reckon he's told you that a mighty purty fight goes with it. You see it's this way: The man that has the water has the grass and the circle, for by fencing in the river here controls the grass for twenty miles. They can range the whole country; nobody else can touch 'em. Williams, of the Circle Bar, controls the river for twenty miles here, and has fenced it in. Of course he has no legal right to more than a section or two of it—all the rest is a steal—the V. T. outfit joins him on the West, and so on. They all stand to keep out settlement—any kind—and they'll make a fight on you—the thing for you to do is move right in on the flat Jake has picked out for you, and meet all comers."

To this Pratt said: "'Pears to me, captain, that I'd better see if I can't make some peaceabler arrangement."

"We've tried all peaceable means," replied Jennison impatiently. "The fact is, the whole cattle business as now constituted is a steal. It rests on a monopoly of Government land. It's got to go. Settlement is creeping in and these big ranges which these 'cattle kings' have held, must be free. There is a war due between the sheepmen and the cattlemen, too, and our lay is to side in with the sheepmen. They are mainly Mexicans, but their fight is our feast."

As day advanced men came riding in from the Cannon Ball and from far below on the Big Sandy, and under Jennison's leadership the wires of the Williams fence were cut and Daniel Pratt moved to the creek flat just above his brother's ranch. Axes rang in the cottonwoods, and when darkness came, the building of a rude, farmlike cabin went on by the light of big fires. Mose, in the thick of it, was a-quiver with excitement. The secrecy, the haste, the glory of flaring fires, the almost silent swarming of black figures filled his heart to the brim with exultation. He was satisfied, rapt with it as one in the presence of heroic music.

But the stars paled before the dawn. The coyotes changed their barking to a solemn wail as though day came to rob them of some irredeemable joy. A belated prairie cock began to boom, and then tired, sleepy, and grimy, the men sat down to breakfast at Jacob Pratt's house. The deed had been done. Daniel had entered the lion's den.

"Now," said Jennison grimly, "we'll just camp down here in Jake's barn to sleep, and if you need any help, let us know."

The Pratts continued their work, and by noon a habitable shack was ready for Mrs. Pratt and the children. In the afternoon Mose and Daniel slept for a few hours while Jake kept watch. The day ended peacefully, but Jennison and one or two others remained to see the newcomer through a second night.

They sat around a fire not far from the cabin and talked quietly of the most exciting things. The question of Indian outbreaks came up and Jennison said: "We won't have any more trouble with the Indians. The Regulars has broken their backs. They can't do anything now but die."

"They hated to give up this land here," said a small, dark man. "I used to hear 'em talk it a whole lot. They made out a case."

"Hank lived with 'em four years," Jennison explained to Daniel Pratt.

"The Indians are a good deal better than we give 'em credit for bein'," said another man. "I lived next 'em in Minnesota and I never had no trouble."

Jennison said decisively: "Oh, I guess if you treat 'em right they treat you right. Ain't that their way, Hank?"

"Well, you see it's like this," said the hairy little man; "they're kind o' suspicious nacherly of the white man—they can't understand what he says, and they don't get his drift always. They make mistakes that way, but they mean all right. Of course they have young plug-uglies amongst 'em jest the same as 'mongst any other c'munity, but the majority of 'em druther be peaceful with their neighbors. What makes 'em wildest is seein' the buffalo killed off. It's like you havin' your water right cut off."

As the talk went on, Mose squatted there silently receiving instruction. His eyes burned through the dusk as he listened to the dark little man who spoke with a note of authority and decision in his voice. His words conveyed to Mose a conception of the Indian new to him. These "red devils" were people. In this man's talk they were husbands and fathers, and sons, and brothers. They loved these lands for which the cattlemen and sheepmen were now about to battle, and they had been dispossessed by the power of the United States Army, not by law and justice. A desire to know more of them, to see them in their homes, to understand their way of thinking, sprang up in the boy's brain.

He edged over close to the plainsman and, in a pause in the talk, whispered to him: "I want you to tell me more about the Indians."

The other man turned quickly and said: "Boy, they're my friends. In a show-down I'm on their side; my father was a half-breed."

The night passed quietly and nearly all the men went home, leaving the Pratts to meet the storm alone, but Jennison had a final word. "You send your boy to yon butte, and wave a hat any time during the day and we'll come, side arms ready. I'll keep an eye on the butte all day and come up and see you to-night. Don't let 'em get the drop on ye."

It was not until the third day that Williams, riding the line in person, came upon the new settler. He sat upon his horse and swore. His face was dark with passion, but after a few minutes' pause he drew rein and rode away.

"Another butter maker," he said to his men as he slipped from the saddle at his own door, "some ten miles up the river."

"Where?"

"Next to Pratt's. I reckon it's that brother o' his he's been talking about. They cut my wires and squatted on the Rosebud flat."

"Give the word and we'll run 'em out," said one of his men. "Every son-of-a-gun of 'em."

Williams shook his head. "No, that won't do. W've got to go slow in rippin' these squatters out o' their holes. They anchor right down to the roots of the tree of life. I reckon we've got to let 'em creep in; we'll scare 'em all we can before they settle, but when they settle we've got to go around 'em. If the man was a stranger we might do something, but Jake Pratt don't bluff—besides, boys, I've got worse news for you."

"What's that?"

"A couple of Mexicans with five thousand sheep crossed Lizard Creek yesterday."

The boys leaped to their feet, variously crying out: "Oh, come off! It can't be true."

"It is true—I saw 'em myself," insisted Williams.

"Well, that means war. Does the V. T. outfit know it?"

"I don't think so. We've got to stand together now, or we'll be overrun with sheep. The truck farmers are a small matter compared to these cursed greasers."

"I guess we'd better send word up the river, hadn't we?" asked his partner.

"Yes, we want to let the whole county know it."

Cheyenne County was an enormous expanse of hilly plain, if the two words may be used together. Low heights of sharp ascent, pyramid-shaped buttes, and wide benches (cut here and there by small creek valleys) made up its surface, which, broadly considered, was only the vast, treeless, slowly-rising eastern slope of the Rocky Mountains. At long distances, on the flat, sandy river, groups of squat and squalid ranch buildings huddled as if to escape the wind. For years it has been a superb range for cattle, and up till the coming of the first settlements on the Cannon Ball, it had been parceled out among a few big firms, who cut Government timber, dug Government stone, and pastured on Government grass. When the wolves took a few ponies, the ranchers seized the opportunity to make furious outcry and bring in the Government troops to keep the Indians in awe, and so possessed the land in serenity. Nothing could be more perfect, more commodious.

But for several years before the coming of the Pratts certain other ominous events were taking place. Over the mountains from the West, or up the slope from New Mexico, enormous herds of small, greasy sheep began to appear. They were "walking" for better pasture, and where they went they destroyed the grasses and poisoned the ground with foul odors. Cattle and horses would not touch any grass which had been even touched by these ill-smelling woolly creatures. There had been ill-feeling between sheepmen and cattlemen from the first, but as water became scarcer and the range more fully stocked, bitterness developed into hatred and warfare. Sheep herders were considered outcasts, and of no social account. To kill one was by some considered a kindness, for it ended the misery of a man who would go crazy watching the shifting, crawling maggots anyway. It was bad enough to be a cow milker, but to be a sheep herder was living death.

These herds thickened from year to year. They followed the feed, were clipped once, sometimes twice, and then were headed back to winter in the south, dying in myriads on the way—only to reappear augmented in numbers the succeeding year. They were worthless as mutton, and at first were never shipped, but as the flocks were graded up, the best were culled and sent to Eastern markets. They menaced the cattlemen in the West and South, while the rancher made slow but inexorable advance on the East. As the cattleman came to understand this his face grew dark and sullen, but thus far no herd had entered the Big Sandy Range, though Williams feared their coming and was ready to do battle.

At the precise time that Daniel Pratt was entering Cheyenne County from the East, a Mexican sheepman was moving toward the Cannon Ball from the Southwest, walking behind ten thousand sheep, leaving a dusty, bare and stinking trail behind him. Williams' report drew the attention of the cattlemen, and the Pratts were for the time forgotten.

A few days after Daniel's assault on the fences of the big ranch, a conference of cattlemen met and appointed a committee to wait upon the owner of the approaching flock of sheep. The Pratts heard of this, and, for reasons of their own, determined to be present. Mose, eager to see the outcome of these exciting movements, accompanied the Pratts on their ride over the hills.

They found the man and his herders encamped on the bank of a little stream in a smooth and beautiful valley. He had a covered wagon and a small tent, and a team of hobbled horses was feeding near. Before the farmers had time to cross the stream the cattlemen came in sight, riding rapidly, and the Pratts waited for them to come up. As they halted on the opposite bank of the stream the sheep owner came out of his tent with a rifle in his arm and advanced calmly to meet them.

"Good evening, gentlemen," he called pleasantly, but the slant of his chin was significant. He was a tall, thin man with a long beard. He wore an ordinary sombrero, with wide, stiff brim, a gray shirt, and loose, gray trousers. At his belt, and significantly in front and buttoned down, hung two splendid revolvers. Aside from these weapons, he looked like a clergyman camping for the summer.

Hitching their horses to the stunted willow and cottonwood trees, the committee approached the tent, and Williams, of Circle Bar, became spokesman: "We have come," he said, "to make a statement. We are peaceably disposed, but would like to state our side of the case. The range into which you are walking your sheep is already overstocked with cattle and horses, and we are going to suffer, for you know very well cattle will not follow sheep. The coming of your flock is likely to bring others, and we can't stand it. We have come to ask you to keep off our range. We have been to big expense to build sheds and fences, and we can't afford to have sheep thrown in on us."

To this the sheepman made calm reply. He said: "Gentlemen, all that you have said is true, but it does not interest me. This land belongs as much to me as to you. By law you can hold only one quarter section each by squatters' right. That right I shall respect, but no more. I shall drive my sheep anywhere on grounds not actually occupied by your feeding cattle. Neither you nor I have much more time to do this kind of thing. The small settler is coming westward. Until he comes I propose to have my share of Government grass."

The meeting grew stormy. Williams, of Circle Bar, counselled moderation. Others were for beginning war at once. "If this man is looking for trouble he can easily find it," one of them said.

The sheepman grimly replied: "I have the reputation in my country of taking care of myself." He drew a revolver and laid it affectionately in the hollow of his folded left arm. "I have two of these, and in a mix-up with me, somebody generally gets hurt."

There was deadly serenity in the stranger's utterance, and the cowboys allowed themselves to be persuaded into peace measures, though some went so far as to handle guns also. They withdrew for a conference, and Jake said: "Stranger, we're with you in this fight; we're truck farmers at the mouth o' the Cannon Ball. My name is Pratt."

The sheepman smiled pleasantly. "Mighty glad to know you, Mr. Pratt. My name is Delmar."

"This is my brother Dan," said Jake, "and this is his herder."

When Mose took the small, firm hand of the sheepman and looked into his face he liked him, and the stranger returned his liking. "Your fight is mine, gentlemen," he said. "These cattlemen are holding back settlement for their own selfish purposes."

Williams, returning at this point, began speaking, but with effort, and without looking at Delmar. "We don't want any fuss, so I want to make this proposition. You take the north side of the Cannon Ball above the main trail, and we'll keep the south side and all the grass up to the trail. That'll give you range enough for your herd and will save trouble. We've had all the trouble we want. I don't want any gun-work myself."

To this the stranger said: "Very well. I'll go look at the ground. If it will support my sheep I'll keep them on it. I claim to be a reasonable man also, and I've had troubles in my time, and now with a family growing up on my hands I'm just as anxious to live peaceable with my fellow-citizens as any man, but I want to say to you that I'm a mean man when you try to drive me."

Thereupon he shook hands with Williams and several others of the older men. After most of the cattlemen had ridden away, Jake said, "Well, now, we'll be glad to see you over at our shack at the mouth o' the Cannon Ball." He held out his hand and the sheepman shook it heartily. As he was saying good-by the sheep owner's eyes dwelt keenly on Mose. "Youngster, you're a good ways from home and mother."

Mose blushed, as became a youth, and said: "I'm camping in my hat these days."

The sheepman smiled. "So am I, but I've got a wife and two daughters back in Santy Fay. Come and see me. I like your build. Well, gentlemen, just call on me at any time you need me. I'll see that my sheep don't trouble you."

"All right; you do the same," replied the Pratts.

"You fellows hold the winning hand," said Delmar; "the small rancher will sure wipe the sheepman out in time. I've got sense enough to see that. You can't fight the progress of events. Youngster, you belong to the winning side," he ended, turning to Mose, "but it's the unpopular side just now."

All this was epic business into which to plunge a boy of eighteen whose hot blood tingled with electric fire at sight of a weapon in the hands of roused and resolute men. He redoubled his revolver practice, and through Daniel's gossip and especially through the boasting of Jennie, his skill with the revolver soon became known to Delmar, who invited him to visit him for a trial of skill. "I used to shoot a little myself," he said; "come over and we'll try conclusions."

Out of this friendly contest the youth emerged very humble. The old sheepman dazzled him with his cunning. He shot equally well from either hand. He could walk by a tree, wheel suddenly, and fire both revolvers over his shoulders, putting the two bullets within an inch of each other. "That's for use when a man is sneaking onto you from behind," he explained. "I never used it but once, but it saved my life." He could fire two shots before Mose could get his pistol from his holster. "A gun is of no use, youngster, unless you can get it into action before the other man. Sling your holster in front and tie it down when you're going to war, and never let a man come to close quarters with you. The secret of success is to be just a half second ahead of the other man. It saves blood, too."

His hands were quick and sure as the rattlesnake's black, forked tongue. He seemed not to aim—he appeared to shoot from his fist rather than from the extended weapon, and when he had finished Mose said:

"I'm much obliged, Mr. Delmar; I see I didn't know the a b c's— but you try me again in six months."

The sheepman smiled. "You've got the stuff in you, youngster. If you ever get in a serious place, and I'm in reaching distance, let me know and I'll open a way out for you. Meanwhile, I can make use of you as you are. I need another man. My Mexicans are no company for me. Come over and help me; I'll pay you well and you can have the same fare that I eat myself. I get lonesome as the old boy."

Thus it came about that Mose, without realizing it, became that despised, forlorn thing, a sheep herder. He made a serious social mistake when he "lined up" with the truck farmers, the tenderfeet and the "greaser" sheep herders, and cut out "a great gob of trouble" for himself in Cheyenne County.

He admired Delmar most fervidly, and liked him. There was a quality in his speech which appealed to the eagle's heart in the boy. The Pratts no longer interested him; they had settled down into farmers. They had nothing for him to do but plow and dig roots, for which he had no love. He had not ridden into this wild and splendid country to bend his back over a spade. One day he accepted Delmar's offer and rode home to get his few little trinkets and to say good-by.

Another reason why he had accepted Delmar's offer lay in the growing annoyance of Jennie's courtship. She made no effort to conceal her growing passion. She put herself in his way and laid hands on him with unblushing frankness. Her love chatter wearied him beyond measure, and he became cruelly short and evasive. Her speech grew sillier as she lost her tomboy interests, and Mose avoided her studiously.

That night as he rode up Daniel was at the barn. To him Mose repeated Delmar's offer.

Pratt at once said: "I don't blame ye fer pullin' out, Mose. I done the best I could, considerin'. Co'se I can't begin fer to pay ye the wages Delmar can, but be keerful; trouble is comin', shore pop, and I'd hate to have ye killed, on the wimmen's account. They 'pear to think more o' you than they do o' me."

Jennie's eyes filled with tears when Mose told her of his new job. She looked very sad and wistful and more interesting than ever before in her life as she came out to say good-by.

"Well, Mose, I reckon you're goin' for good?"

"Not so very far," he said, in generous wish to ease her over the parting.

"You'll come 'round once in a while, won't ye?"

"Why, sure! It's only twenty miles over to the camp."

"Come over Sundays, an' we'll have potpie and soda biscuits fer ye," she said, with a feminine reliance on the power of food.

"All right," he replied with a smile, and abruptly galloped away.

His heart was light with the freedom of his new condition. He considered himself a man now. His wages were definite, and no distinction was drawn between him and Delmar himself. Besides, the immense flock of sheep interested him at first.

His duties were simple. By day he helped to guide the sheep gently to their feeding and in their search for water; by night he took his turn at guarding from wolves. His sleep was broken often, even when not on guard. They were such timid folk, these sheep; their fears passed easily into destructive precipitances.

But the night watch had its joys. As the sunlight died out of the sky and the blazing stars filled the deep blue air above his head, the world grew mysterious and majestic, as well as menacing. The wolves clamored from the buttes, which arose on all sides like domes of a sleeping city. Crickets cried in the grass, drowsily, and out of the dimness and dusk something vast, like a passion too great for words, fell upon the boy. He turned his face to the unknown West. There the wild creatures dwelt; there were the beings who knew nothing of books or towns and toil. There life was governed by the ways of the wind, the curve of the streams, the height of the trees—there—just over the edge of the plain, the mountains dwelt, waiting for him.

Then his heart ached like that of a young eagle looking from his natal rock into the dim valley, miles below. At such times the youth knew he had not yet reached the land his heart desired. All this was only resting by the way.

At such times, too, in spite of all, he thought of Mary and of Jack; they alone formed his attachments to the East. All else was valueless. To have had them with him in this land would have put his heart entirely at rest.

CHAPTER IX

WAR ON THE CANNON BALL

The autumn was very dry, and as the feed grew short on his side of the Cannon Ball, Delmar said to his boss herder, "Drive the herd over the trail, keeping as close to the boundary as you can. The valley through which the road runs will keep us till November, I reckon."

Of this Mose knew nothing, and when he saw the sheep drifting across the line he set forth to turn them. The herder shouted, "Hold on, Mose; let 'em go."

Mose did as he was ordered, but looked around nervously, expecting a charge of cattlemen. Delmar laughed. "Don't worry; they won't make any trouble."

A couple of days later a squad of cowboys came riding furiously over the hill. "See here!" they called to Mose, "you turn that stinkin' river of sheep back over the line."

Mose shouted a reply: "I'm not the boss; go talk to him. And, say! you'd better change your tune when you whistle into his ear."

"Oh, hell!" said one contemptuously. "It's that tenderfoot of Pratt's." They rode to the older herder, who laughed at them. "Settle with the 'old man,'" he said. "I'm under orders to feed these sheep and I'm goin' to do it."

"You take them sheep back on your range or you won't have any to feed," said one of the cowboys.

The herder blew a whiff from his lips as if blowing away thistle down. "Run away, little ones, you disturb my siesta."

With blistering curses on him and his sheep, the cowboys rode to the top of the hill, and there, turning, fired twice at the herder, wounding him in the arm. The Mexican returned the fire, but to no effect.

When Mose reported this, Delmar's eyebrows drew down over his hawklike eyes. "That's all right," he said ominously. "If they want war they'll get it."

A few days later he rode over toward the Circle Bar Ranch house. On the way he overtook Williams, riding along alone. Williams did not hear Delmar till he called sharply, "Throw up your hands."

Williams quickly complied. "Don't shoot—for God's sake!" he called, with his hands quivering above his head. He had heard of Delmar's skill with weapons.

"Mr. Williams," Delmar began with sinister formality, "your men have been shooting my herders."

"Not by my orders, Mr. Delmar; I never sanction——"

"See here, Williams, you are responsible for your cowboys, just as I am for my Mexicans. It's low-down business for you to shoot my men who are working for me at fifteen dollars a month. I'm the responsible party—I'm the man to kill. I want to say right here that I hold you accountable, and if your men maim one of my herders or open fire on 'em again I'll hunt you down and kill you like a wolf. Now ride on, and if you look back before you top that divide I'll put a bullet through you. Good-day."

Williams rode away furiously and was not curious at all; he topped the divide without stopping. Delmar smiled grimly as he wheeled his horse and started homeward.

On the same day, as Mose was lying on the point of a grassy mesa, watching the sheep swarming about a water hole in the valley below, he saw a cloud of dust rising far up to the north. While he wondered, he heard a wild, rumbling, trampling sound. Could it be a herd of buffalo? His blood thrilled with the hope of it. His sheep were forgotten as the roar increased and wild yells came faintly to his ears. As he jerked his revolver from its holder, around the end of the mesa a herd of wild horses swept, swift as antelope, with tails streaming, with eyes flashing, and behind them, urging them on, whooping, yelling, shooting, came a band of cowboys, their arms flopping, their kerchiefs streaming.

A gasping shout arose from below. "The sheep! the sheep!" Mose turned and saw the other herders rushing for their horses. He realized then the danger to the flock. The horses were sweeping like a railway train straight down upon the gray, dusty, hot river of woolly flesh. Mose shuddered with horror and pity—a moment later and the drove, led by a powerful and vicious brown mare, drove like a wedge straight into the helpless herd, and, leaping, plunging, kicking, stumbling, the powerful and swift little bronchos crossed, careering on down the valley, leaving hundreds of dead, wounded, and mangled sheep in their path. The cowboys swept on after them with exultant whooping, firing their revolvers at the Mexican herders, who stood in a daze over their torn and mangled herd.

When Mose recovered from his stupefaction, his own horse was galloping in circles, his picket rope dragging, and the boss herder was swearing with a belated malignity which was ludicrous. He swept together into one steady outpour all the native and alien oaths he had ever heard in a long and eventful career among profane persons. When Mose recovered his horse and rode up to him, Jose was still swearing. He was walking among the wounded sheep, shooting those which he considered helplessly injured. His mouth was dry, his voice husky, and on his lips foam lay in yellow flecks. He ceased to imprecate only when, by repetition, his oaths became too inexpressive to be worth while.

Mose's heart was boyishly tender for any animal, and to see the gentle creatures mangled, writhing and tumbling, uttering most piteous cries, touched him so deeply that he wept. He had no inclination to swear until afterward, when the full knowledge that it was a trick and not an accident came to him. He started at once for the camp to carry the black news.

Delmar did not swear when Mose told him what had happened. He saddled his horse, and, buckling his revolvers about him said, "Come on, youngster; I'm going over to see about this."

Mose felt the blood of his heart thicken and grow cold. There was a deadly resolution in Delmar's deliberate action. Prevision of a bloody fray filled the boy's mind, but he could not retreat. He could not let his boss go alone into an enemy's country; therefore he rode silently after.

Delmar galloped steadily on toward the Circle Bar Ranch house. Mile after mile was traversed at steady gallop till the powerful little ponies streamed with salty sweat. At last Delmar drew rein and allowed Mose to ride by his side.

"You needn't be alarmed," he said in a kindly tone; "these hounds won't shoot; they're going to evade it, but I shall hold 'em to it— trust me, my boy."

As they topped a ridge and looked down into Willow Creek, where the Ranch house stood, several horsemen could be seen riding in from the opposite side, and quite a group of men waited Delmar's approach, and every man was armed. Each face wore a look of constraint, though one man advanced hospitably. "Good afternoon, gentlemen; ride your horses right into the corral, and the boys'll take the saddles off."

"Where is Williams?" asked Delmar as he slid from his horse.

"Gone to town; anything I can do for you? I'm his boss."

"You tell Mr. Williams," said Delmar, with menacing calm, "I came to tell him that a drove of horses belonging partly to you and partly to Hartley, of The Horseshoe, were stampeded through my sheep yesterday, killing over two hundred of them."

Conrad replied softly: "I know, I know! I just heard of it. Too bad! but you understand how it is. Herds get going that way, and you can't stop 'em nor head 'em off."

"Your men didn't try to head 'em off."

"How about that, boys?" inquired Conrad, turning to the younger men.

A long, freckled, grinning ape stepped forward.

"Well, it was this way: we was a-tryin' to head the herd off, and we didn't see the sheep till we was right into 'em——"

"That's a lie!" said Mose. "You drove the horses right down the valley into the sheep. I saw you do it."

"You call me a liar and I'll blow your heart out," shouted the cowboy, dropping his hand to his revolver.

"Halt!" said Delmar. "Easy now, you young cockalorum. It ain't useful to start shooting where Andrew Delmar is."

Conrad spoke sharply: "Jim, shut up." Turning to Mose, "Where did it happen?"

"In Boulder Creek, just south of the road."

Conrad turned to Delmar in mock surprise. "*South* of the road! Your sheep must o' strayed over the line, Mr. Delmar. As they was on our side of the range I don't see that I can do anything for you. If they'd been on the north side——"

"That'll do," interrupted Delmar. "I told you that so long as the north side fed my sheep I would keep them there to accommodate your stockmen. I give notice now that I shall feed where I please, and I shall be with my sheep night and day, and the next man that crosses my sheep will leave his bones in the grass with the dead sheep, and likely a horse or two besides." He stepped toward Conrad. "Williams has had his warning; I give you yours. I hold you responsible for every shot fired at my men. If one of my men is shot I'll kill you and Williams at sight. Good-day."

"What'll *we* do?" called one of the cowboys.

Delmar turned, and his eyes took on a wild glare.

"I'll send you to hell so quick you won't be able to open your mouth. Throw up your hands!" The man's hands went up. "Why, I'd ear-mark ye and slit each nostril for a leather button——"

Conrad strove for peace. "Be easy on him, Delmar; he's a crazy fool, anyway; he don't know you."

"He will after this," said Delmar. "I'll trouble you, Mr. Conrad, to collect all the guns from your men." Mose drew his revolver. "My boy here is handy too. I don't care to be shot in the back as I ride away. Drop your guns, every scab of ye!"

"I'll be d——d if I do."

"Drop it!" snapped out Delmar, and the tone of his voice was terrible to hear. Mose's heart stopped beating; he held his breath, expecting the shooting to begin.

Conrad was white with fear as he said: "Give 'em up, boys. He's a desperate man. Don't shoot, you fools!"

One by one, with a certain amount of bluster on the part of two, the cowboys dropped their guns, and Delmar said: "Gather 'em in, Mose."

Mose leaped from his horse and gathered the weapons up. Delmar thrust the revolvers into his pockets, and handed one Winchester to Mose.

"You'll find your guns on that rise beside yon rock," said Delmar, "and when we meet again, it will be Merry War. Good-day!"

An angry man knows no line of moderation. Delmar, having declared war, carried it to the door of the enemy. Accompanying the sheep himself, he drove them into the fairest feeding-places beside the clearest streams. He spared no pains to irritate the cattlemen, and Mose, who alone of all the outsiders realized to the full his terrible skill with weapons, looked forward with profound dread to the fight which was sure to follow.

He dreaded the encounter for another reason. He had no definite plan of action to follow in his own case. A dozen times a day he said to himself: "Am I a coward?" His stomach failed him, and he ate so sparingly that it was commented upon by the more hardened men. He was the greater troubled because a letter from Jack came during this stormy time, wherein occurred this paragraph: "Mary came back to the autumn term. Her mother is dead, and she looks very pale and sad. She asked where you were and said: 'Please tell him that I hope he will come home safe, and that I am sorry I could not see him before he went away.'"

All the bitterness in his heart long stored up against her passed away in a moment, and sitting there on the wide plain, under the burning sun, he closed his eyes in order to see once more, in the cold gray light of the prison, that pale, grave girl with the glorious eyes. He saw her, too, as Jack saw her, her gravity turned into sadness, her pallor into the paleness of grief and ill health. He admitted now that no reason existed why she should write to him while her mother lay dying. All cause for hardness of heart was passed away. The tears came to his eyes and he longed for the sight of her face. For a moment the boy's wild heart grew tender.

He wrote her a letter that night, and it ran as well as he could hope for, as he re-read it next day on his way to the post office twenty miles away.

"DEAR MARY: Jack has just sent me a long letter and has told me what you said. I hope you will forgive me. I thought you didn't want to see me or write to me. I didn't know your mother was sick. I thought you ought to have written to me, but, of course, I understand now. I hope you will write in answer to this and send your picture to me. You see I never saw you in daylight and I'm afraid I'll forget how you look.

"Well, I'm out in the wild country, but it ain't what I want. I don't like it here. The cowboys are all the time rowin'. There ain't much game here neither. I kill an antelope once in a while, or a deer down on the bottoms, but I haven't seen a bear or a buffalo yet. I want to go to the mountains now. This country is too tame for me. They say you can see the Rockies from a place about one hundred miles from here. Some day I'm going to ride over there and take a look. I haven't seen any Indians yet. We are likely to have shooting soon.

"If you write, address to Running Bear, Cheyenne County, and I'll get it. I'll go down again in two weeks. Since Jack wrote I want to see you awful bad, but of course it can't be done, so write me a long letter.

"Yours respectfully,

"HAROLD EXCELL.

"Address your letter to Mose Harding, they don't know my real name out here. I'll try to keep out of trouble."

He arrived in Running Bear just at dusk, and went straight to the post office, which was in an ill-smelling grocery. Nothing more forlornly disreputable than "the Beast" (as the cowboys called the town) existed in the State. It was built on the low flat of the Big Sandy, and was composed of log huts (beginning already to rot at the corners) and unpainted shanties of pine, gray as granite, under wind and sun. There were two "hotels," where for "two bits" one could secure a dish of evil-smelling ham and eggs and some fried potatoes, and there were six saloons, where one could secure equally evil-minded whisky at ten cents a glass. A couple of rude groceries completed the necessary equipment of a "cow-town."

There was no allurement to vice in such a place as this so far as Mose was concerned, but a bunch of cowboys had just ridden in for "a good time," and to reach the post office he was forced to pass them. They studied him narrowly in the dusk, and one fellow said:

"That's Delmar's sheep herder; let's have some fun with him. Let's convert him."

"Oh, let him alone; he's only a kid."

"Kid! He's big as he'll ever be. I'm goin' to string him a few when he comes out."

Mose's breath was very short as he posted his letter, for trouble was in the air. He tried his revolvers to see that they were free in their holsters, and wiped the sweat from his hands and face with his big bandanna. He entered into conversation with the storekeeper, hoping the belligerent gang would ride away. They had no such intention, but went into a saloon next door to drink, keeping watch for Mose. One of them, a slim, consumptive-chested man, grew drunk first. He was entirely harmless when sober, and served as the butt of all jokes, but the evil liquor paralyzed the small knot of gray matter over his eyes and set loose his irresponsible lower centers. He threw his hat on the ground and defied the world in a voice absurdly large and strenuous.

His thin arms swung aimlessly, and his roaring voice had no more heart in it than the blare of a tin horn. His eyes wandered from face to face in the circle of his grinning companions who egged him on.

His insane, reeling capers vastly amused them. One or two, almost as drunk as he, occasionally wrestled with him, and they rolled in the dust like dirty bear cubs. They were helpless so far as physical struggle went, but, unfortunately, shooting was a second nature to them, and their hands were deadly.

As Mose came out to mount his horse the crowd saw him, and one vicious voice called out:

"Here, Bill, here's a sheep walker can do you up."

The crowd whooped with keen delight, and streaming over, surrounded Mose, who stood at bay not far from his horse in the darkness—a sudden numbness in his limbs.

"What do you want o' me?" he asked. "I've nothing to do with you." He knew that this crowd would have no mercy on him and his heart almost failed him.

"Here's a man wants to lick you," replied one of the herders.

The drunken man was calling somewhere in the crowd, "Where is he? Lemme get at him." The ring opened and he reeled through and up to Mose, who was standing ominously quiet beside his horse. Bill seized him by the collar and said: "You want 'o fight?"

"No," said Mose, too angry at the crowd to humor the drunken fool. "You take him away or he'll get hurt."

"Oh, he will, will he?"

"Go for him, Bill," yelled the crowd in glee.

The drunken fool gave Mose a tug. "Come 'ere!" he said with an oath.

"Let go o' me," said Mose, his heart swelling with wrath.

The drunken one aimlessly cuffed him. Then the blood-red film dropped over the young eagle's eyes. He struck out and his assailant went down. Then his revolvers began to speak and the crowd fell back. They rolled, leaped, or crawled to shelter, and when the bloody mist cleared away from his brain, Mose found himself in his saddle, his swift pony galloping hard up the street, with pistols cracking behind him. His blood was still hot with the murderous rage which had blinded his eyes. He did not know whether he had begun to shoot first or not, he did not know whether he had killed any of the ruffians or not, but he had a smarting wound in the shoulder, from which he could feel the wet, warm blood trickling down.

Once he drew his horse to a walk, and half turned him to go back and face the mob, which he could hear shouting behind him, but the thought of his wound, and the fear that his horse had also been hit, led him to ride on. He made a detour on the plain, and entered a ravine which concealed him from the town, and there alighted to feel of his horse's limbs, fearing each moment to come upon a wound, but he was unhurt, and as the blood had ceased to flow from his own wound, the youth swung into his saddle and made off into the darkness.

He heard no sound of his pursuers, but, nevertheless, rode on rapidly, keeping the west wind in his face and watching sharply for fences. At length he found his way back to the river trail and the horse galloped steadily homeward. As he rode the boy grew very sad and discouraged. He had again given away to the spirit of murder. Again he had intended to kill, and he seemed to see two falling figures; one, the man he had smitten with his fist, the other one whose revolver was flashing fire as he fell.

Then he thought of Mary and the sad look in her eyes when she should hear of his fighting again. She would not be able to get at the true story. She would not know that these men attacked him first and that he fought in self-defense. He thought of his father, also, with a certain tenderness, remembering how he had stood by him in his trial. "Who will stand by me now?" he asked himself, and the thought of the Pratts helped him. Delmar, he felt sure, would defend him, but he knew the customs of the cattle country too well to think the matter ended there. He must hereafter shoot or be shot. If these men met him again he must disable them instantly or die. "Hadn't I better just keep right on riding?" he kept asking some sense within him, but decided at last to return to Delmar.

It was deep night when he reached the camp, and his horse was covered with foam. Delmar was sitting by the camp fire as he came in from the dark.

"Hello, boy, what's up?"

Mose told him the whole story in a few incoherent phrases. The old man examined and dressed his wound, but remained curiously silent throughout the story. At last he said: "See here, my lad; let me tell you, this is serious business. I don't mean this scratch of a bullet—don't you be uneasy about that; but this whole row is mine. They haven't any grudge against you, but you're a sheep herder for me, and that is bad business just now. If you've killed a man they'll come a-rippin' up here about daylight with a warrant. You can't get justice in this country. You'll face a cowboy jury and it'll go hard with you. There's just one thing to do: you've got to git right close to where the west winds come from and do it quick. Throw the saddles on Bone and Rusty, and we'll hit the trail. I know a man who'll take care of you."

He whistled a signal and one of the herders came in: "Send Pablo here," he said. "Now, roll up any little trinkets that you want to take with you," he said a few minutes later as they were saddling the two bronchos. "You can't afford to stay here and face this thing; I had no business to set you on the wrong side. I knew better all the time, but I liked you, and——"

The herder came in. "Pablo, I'm going across country on a little business. If anybody comes asking for me or Mose here, say you don't know where we went, but that you expect us back about noon. Be ready to shoot to-day; some of these cowboys may try to stampede you again while I'm gone."

"You better stay and look after the sheep," began Mose as they started away, "you can't afford——"

"Oh, to hell with the sheep. I got you into this scrape and I'll see you out of it."

As they galloped away, leading Mose's worn pony, Delmar continued: "You're too young to start in as a killer. You've got somebody back in the States who thinks you're out here making a man of yourself, and I like you too well to see you done up by these dirty cow-country lawyers. I'm going to quit the country myself after this fall shipment, and I want you to come down my way some time. You better stay up here till spring."

They rode steadily till daylight, and then Delmar said: "Now I think you're perfectly safe, for this reason: These cusses know you came into the country with Pratt, and they'll likely ride over and search the Cannon Ball settlement. I'll ride around that way and detain 'em awhile and make 'em think you're hiding out, while you make tracks for upper country. You keep this river trail. Don't ride too hard, as if you was runnin' away, but keep a steady gait, and give your horse one hour out o' four to feed. Here's a little snack: don't waste time, but slide along without sleeping as long as you can.

"You'll come in sight of the mountains about noon, and you'll see a big bunch o' snowpeaks off to the left. Make straight for that, and after you go about one day bear sharp to the left, begin to inquire for Bob Reynolds on the Arickaree—everybody knows Bob. Just give him this note and tell him the whole business; he'll look out for you. Now, good-by, boy. I'm sorry—but my intentions were good."

Mose opened his heart at last. "I don't like to desert you this way, Mr. Delmar," he said; "it ain't right; I'd rather stay and fight it out."

"I won't have it," replied Delmar.

"You're going to have a lot of trouble."

"Don't you worry about me, and don't you feel streaked about pulling your freight. You started wrong on the Cannon Ball. Bob will put you right. The cattlemen will rule there for some years yet, and you keep on their side. Now, good-by, lad, and take care of yourself."

Mose's voice trembled as he took Delmar's hand and said: "Good-by, Mr. Delmar, I'm awfully obliged to you."

"That's all right—now git."

Mose, once more on his own horse, galloped off to the West, his heart big with love for his stern benefactor. Delmar sat on his horse and watched the boy till he was diminished to a minute spot on the dim swells of the plain. Then he wiped a little moisture from his eye with the back of his brown, small hand, and turned his horse's head to the East.

CHAPTER X

THE YOUNG EAGLE MOUNTS

After the momentary sorrow of parting from his good friend, Delmar, the youth's heart began to expand with joy. He lifted his arms and shook them as the young eagle exults. He was alone on the wide swells of plain enacting a part of the wild life of which he had read, and for which he had longed. He was riding a swift horse straight toward the mystic mountains of the West, leaving behind him the miserable wars of the sheep herders and the cattlemen. Every leap of his sturdy pony carried him deeper into the storied land and farther from the tumult and shame of the night at Running Bear.

He was not one to morbidly analyze, not even to feel remorse. He put the past behind him easily. Before him small grasshoppers arose in clapping, buzzing clouds. Prairie dogs squeaked and frisked and dived needlessly into their dens. Hawks sailed like kites in the glorious, golden, hazy air, and on the firm sod the feet of his pony steadily drummed. Once a band of antelope crossed a swale, running in silence, jerkily, like a train of some singular automatons, moved by sudden, uneven impulses of power. The deep-worn buffalo trails seemed so fresh the boy's heart quickened with the thought that he might by chance come suddenly upon a stray bunch of them feeding in some deep swale.

He had passed beyond fences, and his course was still substantially westward. His eyes constantly searched the misty purple-blue horizon for a first glimpse of the mountains, though he knew he could not possibly come in sight of them so soon. He rode steadily till the sun was overhead, when he stopped to let the pony rest and feed. He had a scanty lunch in his pocket, which he ate without water. Saddling up an hour or two later he continued his steady onward "shack" toward the West.

Once or twice he passed in sight of cattle ranches, but he rode on without stopping, though he was hungry and weary. Once he met a couple of cowboys who reined out and rode by, one on either side of him, to see what brands were on his horse. He was sufficiently waywise to know what this meant. The riders remained studiously polite in their inquiries:

"Where ye from, stranger?"

"Upper Cannon Ball."

"Eh—hah. How's the feed there this year?"

"Pretty good."

"Where ye aimin' at now, if it's a fair question?"

"Bob Reynolds' ranch."

"He's over on the head water of the South Fork, ain't he?"

"Yes."

"Well, it's a good piece yet. So long," they said in change of manner.

"So long."

They rode away, still filled with curiosity concerning the boy whose horse plainly showed hard riding. "He shore wants to git there," said one to the other.

Late in the afternoon the youth pulled in his horse and studied with the closest care a big cloud looming in the sky. All day snowy thunderheads had been emerging into view near the horizon, blooming like gigantic roses out of the deep purple of the sky, but this particular cloud had not changed its sharp, clean-cut outline for an hour, and, as he looked, a veil of vapor suddenly drifted away from it, and Mose's heart leaped with exultation, as though a woman's hand had been laid on his shoulder. That cloud-like form was a mountain! It could be nothing else, for while all around it other domes shifted line and mass, this one remained constant, riding through the mist as the moon endures in the midst of the flying vapor of the night.

Thereafter he rode with his eyes on that sunlit mass. The land grew wilder. Sharp hills broke the smooth expanses, and on these hills groves of dwarf pine appeared in irregular clumps like herds of cattle. He began to look for a camping place, for he was very tired. For an hour he led his spent horse, still moving toward the far-off shining peak, which glowed long after darkness had fallen on the plains. At last it grew too dim to guide him farther, and slipping the saddle from his horse, he turned him loose to feed upon the bunch grass.

As the light faded from the sky so the exultation and sense of freedom went out of the boy's heart. His mind went back to the struggle in the street. He felt no remorse, no pity for the drunken fools, but he was angry and discouraged and disgusted with himself. He had ended in failure and in flight where he should have won success and respect. He did not directly accuse himself; he had done as well as he could; he blamed "things," and said to himself, "it's my luck," by which he meant to express a profound feeling of dejection and weakness as of one in the grasp of inimical powers. By the working of unfriendly forces he was lying there under the pines, hungry, tired, chilled, and lone as a wolf. Jack was far away, Mary lost forever to him, and the officers of the law again on his trail. It was a time to make a boy a man, a bitter and revengeful man.

The night grew chill, and he was forced to walk up and down, wrapped in his saddle blanket to keep warm. Fuel was scarce, and his small fire sufficed only to warm him in minute sections, and hunger had thinned his blood. He was tired and sleepy, too, but dared not lie down for fear of being chilled. It would not do to be ill here alone in this land.

It was the loneliest night he had ever known in his life. On the hills near by the coyotes kept up ventriloquistic clamor, and from far off the bawling of great bulls and the bleating of the calves brought news of a huge herd of cattle, but these sounds only made his solitary vigil the more impressive. The sleepy chirp of the crickets and the sound of his horse nipping the grass, calmly careless of the wolves, were the only aids to sleep; all else had the effect to keep his tense nerves vibrating. As the cold intensified, the crickets ceased to cry, and the pony, having filled his stomach, turned tail to the wind and humped his back in drowse. At last, no friendly sounds were left in all the world, and shivering, sore, and sullen, the youth faced the east waiting for the dawn.

As the first faint light came into the east he turned his face to the west, anxiously waiting till the beautiful mountain should blossom from the dark. At last it came stealing forth, timid, delicate, blushing like a bride from nuptial chamber, ethereal as an angel's wing, persistent as a glacial wall. As it broadened and bloomed, the boy threw off his depression like a garment. Briskly saddling his shivery but well-fed horse he set off, keeping more and more to the left, as his instructions ran. But no matter in which direction he rode, his eyes were on the mountain. "There is where I end," was his constantly repeated thought. It would have been easy for him to have turned aside.

Shortly after sunrise he came upon a ranch set deep in a gully and sheltered by piñons. Smoke was curling from the stovepipe, but no other sign of life could be detected. He rode directly up to the door, being now too hungry and cold to pass by food and shelter, no matter what should follow.

A couple of cowboys, armed and armored, came out lazily but with menace in their glances.

"Good morning," said Mose.

"Howdy, stranger, howdy," they repeated with instant heartiness. "Git off your hoss and come in."

"Thanks, I believe I will. Can you tell me which-a-way is Bob Reynolds' ranch?" he asked.

Both men broke into grins. "Well, you've putt' nigh hit it right hyer. This is one o' his 'line camps.' The ranch house is about ten miles furder on—but slide off and eat a few."

One man took his horse while the other showed him into a big room where a huge stack of coals on a rude hearth gave out a cheerful heat. It was an ordinary slab shack with three rooms. A slatternly woman was busy cooking breakfast in a little lean-to at the back of the larger room, a child was wailing in a crib, and before the fire two big, wolfish dogs were sleeping. They arose slowly to sniff lazily at Mose's garments, and then returned to their drowse before the fire.

"Stranger, you look putt' nigh beat out," said the man who acted as host; "you look pale around the gills."

"I am," said Mose; "I got off my course last night, and had to make down under a piñon. I haven't had anything to eat since yesterday noon."

"Wal, we'll have some taters and sow-belly in a giff or two. Want 'o wash?"

Mose gladly took advantage of the opportunity to clean the dust and grime from his skin, though his head was dizzy with hunger.

The food was bacon, eggs, and potatoes, but it was fairly well cooked, and he ate with great satisfaction.

The men were very much interested in him, and tried to get at the heart of his relation to Reynolds, but he evaded them. They were lanky Missourians, types already familiar to him, and he did not care to make confidants of them. The woman was a graceless figure, a silent household drudge, sullenly sad, and gaunt, and sickly.

Mose offered to pay for his breakfast, but the boss waved it aside and said: "Oh, that's all right; we don't see enough people pass to charge, for a breakfast. Besides, we're part o' the Reynolds' outfit, anyway."

As Mose swung into the saddle his heart was light. Away to the south a long low cloud of smoke hung. "What is that?" he asked.

"That's the bull-gine on the Great Western; we got two railroads now."

"Which is two too many," said the other man. "First you know the cattle business will be wiped out o' 'Rickaree County just as it is bein' wiped out in Cheyenne and Runnin' Bear. Nesters and cow milkers are comin' in, and will be buildin' fences yet."

"Not in my day," said the host.

"Well, so long," said Mose, and rode away.

The Reynolds' ranch house was built close beside a small creek which had cut deep into the bottom of a narrow valley between two piñon-covered hills. It squat in the valley like a tortoise, but was much more comfortable than most ranch houses of the county. It was surrounded by long sheds and circular corrals of pine logs, and looked to be what it was, a den in which to seek shelter. A blacksmith's forge was sending up a shower of sparks as Mose rode through the gate and up to the main stable.

A long-bearded old man tinkering at some repairs to a plow nodded at the youth without speaking.

"Is Mr. Reynolds at home?" asked Mose.

"No, but he'll be here in a second—jest rode over the hill to look at a sick colt. Git off an' make yuself comfortable."

Mose slipped off his horse and stood watching the queer old fellow as he squinted and hammered upon a piece of iron, chewing furiously meanwhile at his tobacco. It was plain his skill was severely taxed by the complexity of the task in hand.

As he stood waiting Mose saw a pretty young woman come out of the house and take a babe from the ground with matronly impatience of the dirt upon its dress.

The old man followed the direction of the young man's eyes and mumbled: "Old man's girl.... Her child."

Mose asked no questions, but it gave a new and powerful interest to the graceful figure of the girl.

Occasionally the old man lifted his eyes toward the ridge, as if looking for some one, and at last said, "Old man—comin'."

A horseman came into view on the ridge, sitting his horse with the grace and ease of one who lives in the saddle. As he zig-zagged down the steep bank, his pony, a vicious and powerful roan "grade," was on its haunches half the time, sliding, leaping, trotting. The rider, a smallish man, with a brown beard, was dressed in plain clothing, much the worse for wind and sun. He seemed not to observe the steepness and roughness of the trail.

As he rode up and slipped from his horse Mose felt much drawn to him, for his was a kindly and sad face. His voice, as he spoke, was low and soft, only his eyes, keen and searching, betrayed the resolute plainsman.

"Howdy, stranger?" he said in Southern fashion. "Glad to see you, sir."

Mose presented his note from Delmar.

"From old Delmar, eh? How did you leave him? In good health and spirits, I hope."

He spoke in the rhythmical way of Tennesseans, emphasizing the auxiliary verbs beyond their usual value. After reading the letter he extended his hand. "I am very glad to meet you, sir. I am indeed. Bill, take care of Mr.——" He paused, and looked at the latter.

"Mose—Mose Harding," interpolated Mose.

"Put in Harding's horse. Come right in, Mr. Harding; I reckon dinner is in process of simmering by this time."

"Call me Mose," said the youth. "That's what Delmar called me."

Reynolds smiled. "Very good, sir; Mose it shall be."

They entered the front door into the low-ceiled, small sitting room where a young girl was sitting sewing, with a babe at her feet.

"My daughter, Mrs. Craig," said Reynolds gently. "Daughter, this young man is Mr. Mose Harding, who comes from my old friend Delmar. He is going to stay with us for a time. Sit down, Mose, and make yourself at home."

The girl blushed painfully, and Mose flushed sympathetically. He could not understand the mystery, and ignored her confusion as far as possible. The room was shabby and well worn. A rag carpet covered the floor. The white plastered walls had pictures cut from newspapers and magazines pinned upon them to break the monotony. The floor was littered also with toys, clothing, and tools, which the baby had pulled about, but the room wrought powerfully upon the boy's heart, giving him the first real touch of homesickness he had felt since leaving the Burns' farm that bright March day, now so far away it seemed that it was deep in the past. For a few moments he could not speak, and the girl was equally silent. She gathered up the baby's clothes and playthings, and passed into another room, leaving the young man alone.

His heart was very tender with memories. He thought of Mary and of his sister Maud, and his throat ached. The wings of the young eagle were weary, and here was safety and rest, he felt that intuitively, and when Reynolds returned with his wife, a pleasant-featured woman of large frame, tears were in the boy's eyes.

Mrs. Reynolds wiped her fingers on her apron and shook hands with him cordially. "I s'pose you're hungry as a wolf. Wal, I'll hurry up dinner. Mebbe you'd like a biscuit?"

Mose professed to be able to wait, and at last convinced the hospitable soul. "Wal, I'll hurry things up a little," she said as she went out. Reynolds, as he took a seat, said: "Delmar writes that you just got mixed up in some kind o' fuss down there. I reckon you had better tell me how it was."

Mose was glad to unburden his heart. As the story proceeded, Reynolds sat silently looking at the stove hearth, glancing at the youth only now and again as he reached some dramatic point. The girl came back into the room, and as she listened, her timidity grew less painful. The boy's troubles made a bond of sympathy between them, and at last Mose found himself telling his story to her. Her beautiful brown eyes grew very deep and tender as he described his flight, his hunger, and his weariness.

When he ended, she drew a sigh of sympathetic relief, and Reynolds said: "Mm! you have no certain knowledge, I reckon, whether you killed your man or not?"

"I can't remember. It was dark. We fired a dozen shots. I am afraid I hit; I am too handy with the revolver to miss."

"Mm, so Delmar says. Well, you're out of the State, and I have no belief they will take the trouble to look you up. Anyhow, I reckon you better stay with us till we see how the fuss ends. You certainly are a likely young rider, an' I can use you right hyere till you feel like goin' farther."

A wave of grateful emotion rushed over the boy, blinding his eyes with tears, and before he could speak to thank his benefactor, dinner was called. The girl perceived the tears in his eyes, and as they went out to dinner she looked at him with a comradeship born of the knowledge that he, too, had suffered.

He returned her glance with one equally frank and friendly, and all through the meal he addressed himself to her more often than to her parents. She was of the most gentle, and patient, and yielding type. Her beautiful lips and eyes expressed only sweetness and feminine charm, and her body, though thin and bent, was of girlish slimness.

Reynolds warmed to the boy wondrously. As they arose from the table he said:

"We'll ride over to the round-up to-morrow, and I'll introduce you to the cow boss, and you can go right into the mess. I'll turn my horse over to you; I'm getting mighty near too old to enjoy rustlin' cattle together, and I'll just naturally let you take my place."

CHAPTER XI

ON THE ROUND-UP

Mose was awakened next morning by the whirring of the coffee mill, a vigorous and cheerful sound. Mrs. Reynolds and Cora were busily preparing breakfast, and their housewifely movements about the kitchen below gave the boy a singular pleasure. The smell of meat in the pan rose to his nostrils, and the cooing laughter of the baby added a final strand in a homely skein of noises. No household so homelike and secure had opened to him since he said good-by to his foster parents in Rock River.

He dressed and hurried down and out to the barn. Frost lay white on the grass, cattle were bawling somewhere in the distance. The smoke of the kitchen went up into the sky straight as a poplar tree. The beautiful plain, hushed and rapt, lay waiting for the sun.

As he entered the stable, Mose found Reynolds looking carefully at Jack. "That looks a gentle horse; I can't see a mean thing about him. I don't reckon he's a cow hoss, is he?"

"No, I don't suppose he is a regular cow horse, but he'll soon learn."

"I must trade you outen that hoss. I certainly am 'blieged to do so. I'm growin' old, boy. I don't take the pleasu' in a broncho that I once did. I certainly am tired of hosses I can't touch with my hand. Fo' fo'ty yeahs I have handled these locoed hosses—they ah all locoed in my judgment—and I am plum tired of such. I shall send to Missouri aw Tennessee and get me a hoss I can trust. Meanwhile, you leave me yo' hoss an' take my bald-face pinto there; he is the fastest hoss on the range an' a plum devil, but that won't mattah to you, for you ah young an' frisky."

Mose hated to yield up his gentle and faithful horse even for a short time, but could not decently refuse. He shifted his saddle to the pinto with Reynolds' help.

"Whoa, there, Wild Cat," called the rancher, as the wicked eyes began to roll. "He'll get usen to ye after a day or two," he said reassuringly.

Mose's horsemanship was on trial, and though nervous and white, he led the pinto out and prepared to mount.

"If he wants to gambol a little, just let him go, only keep his head up," said Reynolds with careless glance.

Cora came out of the house and stood looking on, while Mose tightened the cinch again, and grasping the pommel with both hands put his toe in the stirrup. The pinto leaped away sidewise, swift as a cat, but before he could fairly get into motion Mose was astride, with both feet in the stirrups. With a series of savage sidewise bounds, the horse made off at a tearing pace, thrusting his head upon the bit in the hope to jerk his rider out of his seat. Failing of this he began to leap like a sheep. Just as he was about to let up on this Mose sank the rowels into him with a wild yell, and hotly lashed him from side to side with the end of his rope. For a few rods the horse continued to leap with stiffened legs and upraised back, then abandoned all tricks and ran up the hill like a scared antelope.

When Reynolds caught up with his new "hand" he smiled and said: "I reckon you can be trusted to look out fo' yo'sef," and the heart of the youth glowed with pleasure.

Again he felt the majesty and splendor of the life into which he had penetrated. The measureless plain, dimpled and wrinkled, swept downward toward the flaming eastern sky unmarked of man. To the west, cut close across their snow tops by the plain's edge, three enormous and snow-armored peaks arose, the sunlight already glittering on the thin, new-fallen snows.

Coyotes, still at vigil on the hills, slid out of sight at the coming of the horsemen. The prairie dogs peered sleepily from their burrows. Cattle in scattered bands snuffed and stared or started away hulking, yet swift, the bulls sullen and ferocious, the calves wild as deer. There were no fences, no furrows, no wagon tracks, no sign of sheep. It was the cow country in very truth.

On the way Reynolds said very little. Occasionally as they drew their ponies to a walk he remarked upon the kindliness of the horse, and said, "I hope you'll like my horse as well as I like youah's."

It was nearly twelve o'clock when they topped a treeless ridge and came in sight of the round-up. Below them, in the midst of a wide, grassy river flat, stood several tents and a covered wagon. Nearby lay a strong circular corral of poplar logs filled with steers.

At some distance from the corral a dense mass of slowly revolving cattle moved, surrounded by watching horsemen. Down from the hills and up the valley came other horsemen, hurrying forward irregular bands of cows and calves. A small fire near the corral was sending up a pale strand of smoke, and at the tail of the wagon a stovepipe, emitting a darker column, told that dinner was in preparation. Over the scene the cloudless September sky arched. Dust arose under the heels of the herds, and the bawling roar of bulls, the call of agonized cows, and the answering bleat of calves formed the base of the shrill whoopings and laughter of the men. Nothing could be wilder, more stirring, more picturesque, except a camp of Sioux or Cheyennes in the days of the buffalo.

In a few minutes Mose was in the midst of the turmoil. Everyone greeted Reynolds with affection, and he replied in the stately phrases which had made him famous, "How do you do, gentlemen. I certainly am glad to see you enjoyin' this fine fall day. Captain Charlesworth, allow me to present my young friend, Moses Harding."

Captain Charlesworth, a tall man with a squint eye and a humorous glance, came up to shake hands as Mose slipped from his broncho.

Reynolds went on: "Captain Charlesworth is cow boss, an' will see that you earn yo' bo'd. Cap'n, this young man comes from my good friend, Cap'n Delmar, of Sante Fe. You know Delmar?"

"I should think so," said the boss. "It seems this youngster kin ride, seem's he's on Wild Cat."

Reynolds smiled: "I reckon you can consider him both able and willin', captain."

"Well, slip off an' eat. I'll take care o' the cayuses."

On the ground, scattered among the tents, and in the shade of the cook wagon, were some twenty or thirty herders. For the most part they were slender, bronzed, and active, of twenty-five or thirty, with broad white hats (faded and flapping in the brim), gray or blue woolen shirts (once gay with red lacing), and dark pantaloons, tucked into tall boots with long heels. Spurs jingled at the heels of their tall boots, and most of them wore bandannas of silk or cotton looped gracefully about their necks. A few of the younger ones wore a sort of rude outside trouser of leather called "chaps," and each of them carried a revolver slung at the hip. They were superb examples of adaptation to environment, alert, bold, and graceful of movement.

A relay of them were already at dinner, with a tin plate full of "grub" and a big tin cup steaming with coffee before each man. They sat almost anywhere to eat, on saddles, wagon tongues—any convenient place. Some of them, more orderly, were squatted along a sort of table made of folded blankets piled through the center of a tent. Here Reynolds took a seat, and Mose followed, shrinking a little from the keen scrutiny of the men. The fact that Reynolds vouched for him, however, was introduction, and the cook made a place for him readily enough, and brought him a plate and a cup.

"Boys," said Reynolds, "this young feller is just come to town. His name is Mose Harding, and he can ride a hoss all right, all right. He's a-goin' to make a hand here in my place; treat him fair."

There was a moment's awkward pause, and then Mose said: "I'm going to try to do my share."

As he had time to look around he began to individualize the men. One of the first to catch his eye was an Indian who sat near the door of the tent. He was dressed like the other men, but was evidently a full-blood. His skin was very dark, not at all red or copper colored, and Mose inferred that he was a Ute. His eyes were fixed on Mose with intent scrutiny, and when the boy smiled the Indian's teeth gleamed white in ready good nature, and they were friends at once. The talk was all about the work on hand, the tussles with steers, the number of unbranded calves, the queries concerning shipment, etc.

Dinner was soon over, and "Charley," as the cow boss was called by his men, walked out with Mose toward the corral. "Kin ye rope?" he asked.

"No, not for a cent."

"Let him hold the herd foh a day or two," suggested Reynolds. "Give him time to work in."

"All right, s'pose you look after him this afternoon."

Together Reynolds and Mose rode out toward the slowly "milling" herd, a hungry, hot, and restless mob of broadhorns, which required careful treatment. As he approached, the dull roar of their movement, their snuffling and moaning, thrilled the boy. He saw the gleaming, clashing horns of the great animals uplift and mass and change, and it seemed to him there were acres and acres of them.

Reynolds called out to two sweating, dusty, hoarse young fellows: "Go to grub, boys."

Without a word they wheeled their horses and silently withdrew, while Reynolds became as instantly active.

His voice arose to a shout: "Now, lively, Mose, keep an eye on the herd, and if any cow starts to break out—lively now—turn him in."

A big bay steer, lifting his head, suddenly started to leave the herd. Mose spurred his horse straight at him with a yell, and turned him back.

"That's right," shouted Reynolds.

Mose understood more of it than Reynolds realized. He took his place in the cordon, and aided in the work with very few blunders. The work was twofold in character. Fat cattle were to be cut out of the herd for shipment, unbranded calves were to be branded, and strays tallied and thrown back to their own feeding grounds. Into the crush of great, dusty, steaming bodies, among tossing, cruel, curving horns the men rode to "cut out" the beeves and to rope the calves. It was a furious scene, yet there was less excitement than Mose at first imagined. Occasionally, as a roper returned, he paused on the edge of the herd long enough to "eat" a piece of tobacco and pass a quiet word with a fellow, then spurring his horse, re-entered the herd again. No matter how swift his action, his eyes were quiet.

It was hard work; dusty, hot, and dangerous also. To be unhorsed in that struggling mass meant serious injury if not death. The youth was glad of heart to think that he was not required to enter the herd.

That night, when the horse herd came tearing down the mesa, Reynolds said: "Now, Mose, you fall heir to my shift of horses, too. Let me show them to you. Each man has four extra horses. That wall-eyed roan is mine, so is the sorrel mare with the star face.

That big all-over bay, the finest hoss in the whole outfit, is mine, too, but he is unbroken. He shore is a hard problem. I'll give him to you, if you can break him, or I'll trade him for your Jack."

"I'll do it," cried Mose, catching his breath in excitement as he studied the splendid beast. His lithe, tigerlike body glittered in the sun, though his uplifted head bore a tangled, dusty mat of mane. He was neglected, wary, and unkempt, but he was magnificent. Every movement of his powerful limbs made the boy ache to be his master.

Thus Mose took his place among the cowboys. He started right, socially, this time. No one knew that he had been a sheep herder but Reynolds, and Reynolds did not lay it up against him. He was the equal of any of them in general horsemanship, they admitted that at the end of the second day, though he was not so successful in handling cattle as they thought he should be. It was the sense of inefficiency in these matters which led him to give an exhibition of his skill with the revolver one evening when the chance offered. He shot from his horse in all conceivable positions, at all kinds of marks, and with all degrees of speed, till one of the boys, accustomed to good shooting, said:

"You kin jest about shoot."

"That's right," said the cow boss; "I'd hate to have him get a grutch agin me."

Mose warmed with pardonable pride. He was taking high place in their ranks, and was entirely happy during these pleasant autumn days. On his swift and wise little ponies he tore across the sod in pursuit of swift steers, or came rattling down a hillside, hot at the heels of a wild-eyed cow and calf, followed by a cataract of pebbles. Each day he bestrode his saddle till his bones cried out for weariness, and his stomach, walls ground together for want of food, but when he sat among his fellows to eat with keenest pleasure the beef and beans of the pot wrestler's providing, he was content. He had no time to think of Jack or Mary except on the nights when he took his trick at watching the night herd. Then, sometimes in the crisp and fragrant dusk, with millions of stars blazing overhead, he experienced a sweet and powerful longing for a glimpse of the beautiful girlish face which had lightened his days and nights in prison.

The herders were rough, hearty souls, for the most part, often obscene and rowdy as they sat and sang around the camp fire. Mose had never been a rude boy; on the contrary, he had always spoken in rather elevated diction, due, no doubt, to the influence of his father, whose speech was always serious and well ordered. Therefore, when the songs became coarse he walked away and smoked his pipe alone, or talked with Jim the Ute, whose serious and dignified silence was in vivid contrast.

Some way, coarse speech and ribald song brought up, by the power of contrast, the pure, sweet faces of Mary and his sister Maud. Two or three times in his boyhood he had come near to slaying pert lads who had dared to utter coarse words in his sister's presence. There was in him too much of the essence of the highest chivalry to permit such things.

It happened, therefore, that he spent much time with "Ute Jim," who was a simple and loyal soul, thoughtful, and possessing a sense of humor withal. Mose took great pleasure in sitting beside the camp fire with this son of the plains, while he talked of the wild and splendid life of the days before the white man came. His speech was broken, but Mose pieced it out by means of the sign language, so graceful, so dignified, and so dramatic, that he was seized with the fervid wish to acquire a knowledge of it. This he soon did, and thereafter they might be seen at any time of day signaling from side to side of the herd, the Indian smiling and shaking his head when the youth made a mistake.

Jim believed in his new friend, and when questions brought out the history of the dispossession of his people he grew very sorrowful. His round cheeks became rigid and his eyes were turned away. "Injun no like fight white man all time. Injun gotta fight. White man crowd Injun back, back, no game, no rain, no corn. Injun heap like rivers, trees, all same—white man no like 'um, go on hot plain, no trees, no mountains, no game."

But he threw off these somber moods quickly, and resumed his stories of himself, of long trips to the snowpeaks, which he seemed to regard in the light of highest daring. The high mountains were not merely far from the land of his people; they were mythic places inhabited by monstrous animals that could change from beast to fowl, and talk—great, conjuring creatures, whose powers were infinite in scope. As the red man struggled forward in his story, attempting to define these conceptions, the heart of the prairie youth swelled with a poignant sense of drawing near a great mystery. The conviction of Jim's faith for the moment made him more than half believe in the powers of the mountain people. Day by day his longing for the "high country" grew.

At the first favorable moment he turned to the task of subduing the splendid bay horse for which he had traded his gentle Jack. One Sunday, when he had a few hours off, Mose went to Alf, the chief "roper," and asked him to help him catch "Kintuck," as Reynolds called the bay.

"All right," said Alf; "I'll tie him up in a jiffy."

"Can you get him without marking him all up?"

"I don't believe it. He's going to thrash around like h—l a-blazin'; we'll have to choke him down."

Mose shook his head. "I can't stand that. I s'pose it'll skin his fetlocks if you get him by the feet."

"Oh, it may, may not; depends on how he struggles."

Mose refused to allow his shining, proud-necked stallion to be roped and thrown, and asked the boys to help drive him into a strong corral, together with five or six other horses. This was done, and stripping himself as for a race, Mose entered the coral and began walking rapidly round and round, following the excited animals. Hour after hour he kept this steady, circling walk, till the other horses were weary, till Kintuck ceased to snort, till the blaze of excitement passed out of his eyes, till he walked with a wondering backward glance, as if to ask: "Two-legged creature, why do you so persistently follow me?"

The cowboys jeered at first, but after a time they began to marvel at the dogged walk of the youth. They gathered about the walls of the corral and laid bets on the outcome. At the end of the third hour Kintuck walked with a mechanical air, all the fire and fury gone out of him. He began to allow his pursuer to approach him closely, almost near enough to be touched. At the end of the four hours he allowed Mose to lay his hand on his nose, and Mose petted him and went to dinner. Odds stood in Mose's favor as he returned to the corral. He was covered with dust and sweat, but he was confident. He began to speak to the horse in a gentle, firm voice. At times the stallion faced him with head lifted, a singular look in his eyes, as though he meditated leaping upon his captor. At first Mose took no notice of these actions, did not slacken his pace, but continued to press the bay on and on. At last he began to approach the horse with his hand lifted, looking him in the eyes and speaking to him. Snorting as if with terror, the splendid animal faced him again and again, only to wheel at the last moment.

The cowboys were profanely contemptuous. "Think of taking all that trouble."

"Rope him, and put a saddle on him and bust him," they called resoundingly.

Mose kept on steadily. At last, when all the other horses had been turned loose, Kintuck, trembling, and with a curious stare in his eyes, again allowed Mose to lay his hand on his nose. He shrank away, but did not wheel. It was sunset, and the horse was not merely bewildered, he was physically tired. The touch of his master's hand over his eyes seemed to subjugate him, to take away his will. When Mose turned to walk away the horse followed him as though drawn by some magnetic force, and the herders looked at each other in amazement. Thereafter he had but to be accustomed to the bridle and saddle, and to be taught the duties of a cow horse. He had come to love his master.

This exploit increased the fame of "Dandy Mose," as the cowboys came to call him, because of the nature of his dress. He was bronzed now, and a very creditable brown mustache added to the maturity of his face. He was gaunt with hard riding, and somber and reticent in manner, so that he seemed to be much older than his years. Before the beef round-up was ended, he could rope a steer fairly well, could cut out or hold the herd as well as the best, and in pistol practice he had no equal.

He was well pleased with himself. He loved the swift riding, the night watches, the voices of wolves, the turmoil of the camp, the rush of the wild wide-horned herd, and the pounding roar of the relay horses as they came flying into camp of a morning. It all suited well with the leaping blood of his heart and the restless vigor of his limbs. He thought of his old home very little—even Mary was receding into the mist of distance.

When the beef herd was ready to be driven to the shipping point, Reynolds asked him if he wished to go. He shook his head. "No, I'll stay here." He did not say so, but he was still a little afraid of being called to account for his actions in Running Bear. He saw the herd move off with regret, for he would have enjoyed the ride exceedingly. He cared little for the town, though he would have liked the opportunity to make some purchases. He returned to the Reynolds ranch to spend the autumn and the winter in such duties as the stock required.

As the great peaks to the west grew whiter and whiter, looming ever larger at dawn, the heart of the boy grew restless. The dark cañons allured him, the stream babbled strange stories to him—tales of the rocky spaces from which it came—until the boy dreamed of great white doors that opened on wondrous green parks.

One morning when Cora called the men to breakfast Mose and Jim did not respond. A scrawl from Mose said: "We've gone to the mountains. I'll be back in the spring. Keep my outfit for me, and don't worry."

PART II

CHAPTER XII

THE YOUNG EAGLE FLUTTERS THE DOVE-COTE

The little town of Marmion was built on the high, grassy, parklike bank of the Cedar River; at least, the main part of the residences and stores stood on the upper level, while below, beside the roaring water, only a couple of mills and some miserable shacks straggled along a road which ran close to the sheer walls of water-worn limestone.

The town was considered "picturesque" by citizens of the smaller farm villages standing bleakly where the prairie lanes intersected. To be able to live in Marmion was held to be eminent good fortune by the people roundabout, and the notion was worth working for. "If things turn out well we will buy a lot in Marmion and build a house there," husbands occasionally said to their wives and daughters, to console them for the mud, or dirt, or heat, or cold of the farm life. One by one some of those who had come into the country early, and whose land had grown steadily in value as population increased, were able to rent their farms to advantage and "move into town." Thus the streets gradually lengthened out into the lanes, and brick blocks slowly replaced the battlemented wooden stores of earlier frontier construction.

To Harold Excell, fresh from the wide spaces of the plains, the town appeared smothered in leaves, and the air was oppressively stagnant. He came into the railway station early one July morning, tired and dusty, with a ride of two days and a night in an ordinary coach. As he walked slowly up the street toward the center of the sleeping village, the odor of ripe grain and the familiar smell of poplar and maple trees went to his heart. His blood leaped with remembered joys. Under such trees, in the midst of such fragrance, he had once walked with his sister and with Jack. His heart swelled with the thought of the Burns' farm, and the hearty greeting they would give him could he but ride up to the door.

And Mary! How would she seem to him now? Four years was a long time at that period of a girl's life, but he was certain he would recognize her. He had not written to her of his coming, for he wished to announce himself. There were elements of adventure and surprise in the plan which pleased him. He had not heard from her for nearly a year, and that troubled him a little; perhaps she had moved away or was married. The thought of losing her made him shiver with sudden doubt of the good sense of his action. Anyhow, he would soon know.

The clerk of the principal hotel was sleeping on a cot behind the counter, and Mose considerately decided not to wake him. Taking a seat by the window, he resumed his thinking, while the morning light infiltrated the sky. He was only twenty-two years of age, but in his own thought he had left boyhood far behind. As a matter of fact he looked to be five years older than he was. His face was set in lines indicating resolution and daring, his drooping mustache hid the boyish curves of his lips, and he carried himself with a singular grace, self-confident, decisive, but not assertive. The swing of his shoulders had charm, and he walked well. The cowboy's painful hobble had not yet been fastened upon him.

Sitting there waiting the dawn, his face became tired, somber, almost haggard, with self-accusing thought. He was not yet a cattle king, he was, in fact, still a cowboy. The time had gone by when a hired hand could easily acquire a bunch of cattle and start in for himself—and yet, though he had little beyond his saddle and a couple of horses, he was in Marmion to look upon the face of the girl who had helped him to keep "square" and clean in a land where dishonesty and vice were common as sage brush. He had sworn never to set foot in Rock River again, and no one but Jack knew of his visit to Marmion.

Now that he was actually in the town where Mary lived he was puzzled to know how to proceed. He had wit enough to know that in Marmion a girl could not receive visits from a strange young man and escape the fire of infuriate gossip. He feared to expose her to such comment, and yet, having traveled six hundred miles to see her, he was not to be deterred by any other considerations, especially by any affecting himself.

He knew something, but not all, of the evil fame his name conveyed to the citizens in his native state. As "Harry Excell, *alias* Black Mose," he had figured in the great newspapers of Chicago, and Denver, and Omaha. Imaginative and secretly admiring young reporters had heaped alliterative words together to characterize his daring, his skill as a marksman and horseman, and had also darkly hinted of his part in desperate stage and railway robbery in the Farther West. To all this—up to the time of his return—Harold had replied, "These chaps must earn a living some way, I reckon." He was said to have shot down six men in his first "scrimmage." "No one presumes to any impertinent inquiries when 'Black Mose' rides into town."

Another enterprising newspaper youth had worked out the secret history of "Black Mose": "He began his career of crime early; at sixteen years of age he served in State's prison for knifing a rival back in the States." This report enabled the Rock River Call to identify Harold Excell with "Black Mose," to the pain and humiliation of Pastor Excell.

Harold paid very little heed to all this till his longing to see Mary grew intolerable—even now, waiting for the Sabbath day to dawn, he did not fully realize the black shadow which streamed from his name and his supposititious violences. He divined enough of it to know that he must remain unknown to others, and he registered as "M. Harding, Omaha."

He was somewhat startled to find himself without appetite, and pushing away his tough steak and fried potatoes, he arose and returned to the street. The problem before him required delicacy of handling, and he was not one to assume a tactful manner. The closer he came to the meeting the more difficult it became. He must see her without causing comment, and without Jack's aid he saw no way of doing it. He had written to Jack, asking him to meet him, and so he waited.

He was a perilously notable figure in spite of his neat black suit and quiet ways. His wide hat sat upon his head with a negligence which stopped short of swagger, and his coat revealed the splendid lines of his muscular shoulders. He had grown to a physical manhood which had the leopard's lithe grace and the lion's gravity. His dimpled and clean-shaven chin was strong, and the line of his lips firm. His eyes were steady and penetrating, giving an impression of reticence. His hands were slender and brown, and soft in the palms as those of a girl. The citizens marveled over him as he moved slowly through the streets, thinking himself quite indistinguishable among the other young men in dark suits and linen collars.

Waiting was most difficult, and to remain indoors was impossible, so he walked steadily about the town. As he returned from the river road for the fifth time, the bells began to ring for church, filling him with other memories of his youth, of his father and his pulpit, and brought to his mind also the sudden recollection of one of Jack's letters, wherein he mentioned Mary's singing in the choir. If she were at home she would be singing yet, he argued, and set forth definitely to find her.

To inquire was out of the question—so he started in at the largest church with intent to make the rounds. After waiting till the choir was about to begin the first hymn, he slipped in and took a seat near the door, his heart beating loudly and his breath much quickened.

The interior was so familiar, it seemed for the moment to be his father's church in Rock River. The odors, sounds, movements were quite the same. The same deaf old men, led by determined, sturdy old women, were going up the aisle to the front pews. The pretty girls, taking their seats in the middle pews (where their new hats could be enjoyed by the young men at the rear) became Dot, and Alice, and Nettie—and for the moment the cowboy was very boyish and tender. The choir assembling above the pulpit made him shiver with emotion. "Perhaps one of them will be Mary and I won't know her," he said to himself. "I will know her voice," he added.

But, as the soprano took her place, his heart ceased to pound—she was small, and dark, and thin. He arose and slipped out to continue his search.

They were singing as he entered the next chapel, and it required but a moment's listening to convince himself that Mary was not there. The third church was a small stone building of odd structure, and while he hesitated before its door, a woman's voice took up a solo strain, powerful, exultant, and so piercingly sweet that the plainsman shivered as if with sudden cold. Around him the softly moving maples threw dappling shadows on the walk. The birds in the orchards, the insects in the grass, the clouds overhead seemed somehow involved in the poetry and joy of that song. The wild heart of the young trailer became like that of a child, made sweet and tender by the sovereign power of a voice.

He did not move till the clear melody sank into the harmony of the organ, then, with bent head and limbs unwontedly infirm, he entered the lovely little audience room. He stumbled into the first seat in the corner, his eyes piercing the colored dusk which lay between him and the singer. It was Mary, and it seemed to him that she had become a princess, sitting upon a throne. Accustomed to see only the slatternly women of the cow towns, or the thin, hard-worked, and poorly-dressed wives and daughters of the ranchers, he humbled himself before the beauty and dignity and refinement of this young singer.

She was a mature woman, full-bosomed, grave of feature, introspective of glance. Her graceful hat, her daintily gloved hands, her tasteful dress, impressed the cowboy with a feeling that all art and poetry and refinement were represented by her. For the moment his own serenity and self-command were shaken. He cowered in his seat like a dust-covered plowman in a parlor, and when Mary looked in his direction his breath quickened and he shrank. He was not yet ready to have her recognize him.

The preacher, a handsome and scholarly young fellow, arose to speak, and Harold was interested in him at once. The service had nothing of the old-time chant or drawl or drone. In calm, unhesitating speech the young man proceeded, from a text of Hebrew scripture, to argue points of right and wrong among men, and to urge upon his congregation right thinking and right action. He used a great many of the technical phrases of carpenters and stonemasons and sailors. He showed familiarity also with the phrases of the cattle country. Several times a low laugh rippled over his congregation as he uttered some peculiarly apt phrase or made use of some witty illustration. To the cowboy this sort of preaching came with surprise. He thought: "The boys would kieto to this chap all right." He was not eager to have them listen to Mary singing.

Sitting there amid the little audience of thoughtful people, his brain filled with new conceptions of the world and of human life. Nothing was clearly defined in the tumult of opposing pictures. At one moment he thought of his sister and his family, but before he could imagine her home or decide on how to see her, a picture of his father, or Jack, or the peaceful Burns' farm came whirling like another cloud before his brain, and all the time his eyes searched Mary's calm and beautiful face. He saw her smile, too, when the preacher made a telling application of a story. How would she receive him after so many years? She had not answered his last letter; perhaps she was married. Again the chilly wind from the cañon of doubt blew upon him. If she was, why that ended it. He would go back to the mountains and never return.

The minister finished at last and Mary arose again to sing. She was taller, Harold perceived, and more matronly in all ways. As she sang, the lonely soul of the plainsman was moved to an ecstasy which filled his throat and made his eyes misty with tears. He thought of his days in the gray prison, and of this girlish voice singing like an angel to comfort him. She did not seem to be singing to him now. She sang as a bird sings out of abounding health and happiness, and as she sang, the mountains retreated into vast distances. The rush of the cattle on the drive was fainter than the sigh of the wind, and the fluting of the Ute lover was of another world. For the moment he felt the majesty and the irrevocableness of human life.

He stood in a shadowed corner at the close of the service and watched her come down the aisle. As she drew near his breath left him, and the desire to lay his hand on her arm became so intense that his fingers locked upon the back of his pew—but he let her pass. She glanced at him casually, then turned to smile at some word of the preacher walking just behind her. Her passing was like music, and the fragrance of her garments was sweeter than any mountain flower. The grace of her walk, the exquisite fairness of her skin subdued him, who acknowledged no master and no mistress. She walked on out into the Sabbath sunshine and he followed, only to see her turn up the sidewalk close to the shoulder of the handsome young minister.

The lonely youth walked back to his hotel with manner so changed his mountain companions would have marveled at it. A visit which had seemed so simple on the Arickaree became each moment more complicated in civilization. The refined young minister with the brown pointed beard, so kindly and thoughtful and wholesome of manner, was a new sort of man to such as Harold Excell. He feared no rivalry among the youth of the village, but this scholar——

Jack met him at the hotel—faithful old Jack, whose freckled face beamed, and whose spectacled eyes were dim with gladness. They shook hands again and again, crying out confused phrases. "Old man, how are you?" "I'm all right, how are you?" "You look it."

"Where'd you find the red whiskers?" "They came in a box." "Your mustache is a wonder."

Ultimately they took seats and looked at each other narrowly and quietly. Then Harold said, "I'm Mr. Harding here."

Jack replied: "I understand. Your father knows, too. He wants to come up and see you. I said I'd wire, shall I?"

"Of course—if he wants to see me—but I want to talk to you first. I've seen Mary!"

"Have you? How did you manage?"

"I trailed her. Went to all the churches in town. She sings in a little stone church over here."

"I know. I've been up here to see her once or twice myself."

Harold seized him by the arm. "See here, Jack—I must talk with her. How can I manage it without doing her harm?"

"That's the question. If these people should connect you with 'Black Mose' they'd form a procession behind you. Harry, you don't know, you can't imagine the stories they've got up about you. They've made you into a regular Oklahoma Billy the Kid and train robber. The first great spread was that fight you had at Running Bear, that got into the Omaha papers in three solid columns about six months after it happened. Of course I knew all about it from your letters—no one had laid it to you then, but now everybody knows you are 'Black Mose,' and if you should be recognized you couldn't see Mary without doing her an awful lot of harm. You must be careful."

"I know all that," replied Harold gloomily. "But you must arrange for me to see her right away, this afternoon or to-night."

"I'll manage it. They know me here and I can call on her and take a friend, an old classmate, you see, without attracting much attention—but it isn't safe for you to stay here long, somebody is dead-sure to identify you. They've had two or three pictures of you going around that really looked like you, and then your father coming up may let the secret out. We must be careful. I'll call on Mary immediately after dinner and tell her you are here."

"Is she married? Some way she seemed like a married woman."

"No, she's not married, but the young preacher you heard this morning is after her, they say, and he's a mighty nice chap."

There was no more laughter on the gentle, red-bearded face of young Burns. Had Harold glanced at him sharply at that moment, he would have seen a tremor in Jack's lips and a singular shadow in his eyes. His voice indeed did affect Harold, though he took it to be sympathetic sadness only.

Jack brightened up suddenly. "I can't really believe it is you, Harry. You've grown so big and burly, and you look so old." He smiled. "I wish I could see some of that shooting they all tell about, but that *would* let the cat out."

Harold could not be drawn off to discuss such matters.

"Come out to the ranch and I'll show you. But how are we to meet father? If he is seen talking with me it may start people off——"

"I'll tell you. We'll have him come up and join you on the train and go down to Rock River together. I don't mean for you to get off, you can keep right on. Now, you mustn't wear that broad hat; you wear a grape-box straw hat while you're here. Take mine and I'll wear a cap."

He took charge of Harold's affairs with ready and tactful hand. He was eager to hear his story, but Harold refused to talk on any other subject than Mary. At dinner he sat in gloomy silence, disregarding his friend's pleasant, low-voiced gossip concerning old friends in Rock River.

After Jack left the hotel Harold went to his room and took a look at himself in the glass. He was concerned to see of what manner of man he really was. He was not well-satisfied with himself; his face and hands were too brown and leathery, and when he thought of his failure as a rancher his brow darkened. He was as far from being a cattle king as when he wrote that boyish letter four years before, and he had sense enough to know that a girl of Mary's grace and charm does not lack for suitors. "Probably she is engaged or married," he thought. Life seemed a confusion and weariness at the moment.

As soon as he heard Jack on the stairs he hurried to meet him.

"What luck? Have you seen her?"

Jack closed the door before replying, "Yes."

"What did she say?"

"She turned a little paler and just sat still for a minute or two. You know she isn't much of a talker. Then she said, 'Was he at church to-day?' I said 'Yes'; then she said, 'I think I saw him. I saw a stranger and was attracted by his face, but of course I never thought it could be Harold.' She was completely helpless for a while, but as I talked she began to see her way. She finally said, 'He has come a long way and I must see him. I *must* talk with him, but people must not know who he is.' I told her we were going to be very careful for her sake."

"That's right, we must," Harold interrupted.

"She didn't seem scared about herself. 'It won't harm me,' she said, 'but father is hard to manage when anything displeases him. We must be careful on Harold's account.'"

Harold's throat again contracted with emotion. "She never thinks of herself; that's her way."

"Now we've just got to walk boldly up the walk, the two of us together, and call on her. I'll introduce you to her father or she will; he knows me. We will talk about our school days while the old gentleman is around. He will drift away after a time, naturally. If he doesn't I'll take him out for a walk."

This they did. Made less of a cowboy by Jack's straw hat, Harold went forth on a trail whose course was not well-defined in his mind, though now that Jack had arranged details so deftly that Mary was not in danger of being put to shame, his native courage and resolution came back to him. In the full springtide of his powerful manhood Mary's name and face had come at last to stand for everything worth having in the world, and like a bold gambler he was staking all he had on a single whirl of the wheel.

Their meeting was so self-contained that only a close observer could have detected the tension. Mary was no more given to externalizing her emotions than he. She met him with a pale, sweet, dignified mask of face. She put out her hand, and said, "I am glad to see you, Mr. Harding," but his eyes burned down into hers with such intensity that she turned to escape his glance.

"Father, you know Mr. Burns, and this is his friend, Mr. Harding, whom I used to know."

Jack came gallantly to the rescue. He talked crops, politics, weather, church affairs, and mining. He chattered and laughed in a way which would have amazed Harold had he not been much preoccupied. He was unprepared for the change in Mary. He had carried her in his mind all these years as a little slip of a maiden, wrapt in expression, somber of mood, something half angel and half child, and always she walked in a gray half light, never in the sun. Now here she faced him, a dignified woman, with deep, serene eyes, and he could not comprehend how the pale girl had become the magnetic, self-contained woman. He was thrown into doubt and confusion, but so far from showing this he sat in absolute silence, gazing at her with eyes which made her shiver with emotion.

Talk was purposeless and commonplace at first, a painful waiting. Suddenly they missed Jack and the father. They were alone and free to speak their most important words. Harold seized upon the opportunity with most disconcerting directness.

"I've come for you, Mary," he said, as if he had not hitherto uttered a word, and his voice aroused some mysterious vibration within her bosom. "I'm not a cattle king; I have nothing but two horses, a couple of guns, and a saddle—but all the same, here I am. I got lonesome for you, and at last I took the back trail to find out whether you had forgot me or not."

His pause seemed to require an answer and her lips were dry as she said in a low voice, "No, I did not forget, but I thought you had forgotten *me*."

"A man don't forget such a girl as you are, Mary. You were in my mind all the time. Your singing did more for me than anything else. I've tried to keep out of trouble for your sake. I haven't succeeded very well as you know—but most of the stories about me are lies. I've only had two fights and they were both in self-defense and I don't think I killed anybody. I never know exactly what I'm doing when I get into a scrap. But I've kept out of the way of it on your account. I never go after a man. It's pretty hard not to shoot out there where men go on the rampage so often. It's easier, now than it used to be, for they are afraid of me."

He seemed to come to a halt in that direction, and after a moment's pause took a new start. "I saw you at church to-day, and I saw you walk off with the minister, and that gave me a sudden jolt. It seemed to me you—liked him mighty well——"

She was sitting in silence and apparent calmness, but she flushed and her lips set close together. It was evident that no half-explanations would suffice this soul of the mountain land.

He arose finally and stood for an instant looking at her with piercing intentness. His deep excitement had forced him to physical action.

"I could see he was the man for you, not me. Right there I felt like quitting. I went back to my hotel doing more thinking to the square minute than ever before in my life, I reckon. I ought to have pulled out for the mountains right then, but you see, I had caught a glimpse of you again, and I couldn't. The smell of your dress——" he paused a moment. "You are the finest girl God ever made and I just couldn't go without seeing you, at least once more."

He was tense, almost rigid with the stress of his sudden passion. She remained silent with eyes fixed upon him, musing and somber. She was slower to utter emotion than he, and could not speak even when he had finished.

He began to walk up and down just before her, his brows moodily knitted. "I'm not fit to ask a girl like you to marry me, I know that. I've served time in jail, and I'm under indictment by the courts this very minute in two States. I'm no good on earth but to rope cattle. I can't bring myself to farm or sell goods back here, and if I could you oughtn't to have anything to do with me—but all the same you're worth more to me than anything else. I don't suppose there has been an hour of my life since I met you first that I haven't thought of you. I dreamed of you—when I'm riding at night—I try to think——"

He stopped abruptly and caught up her left hand. "You've got a ring on your finger—is that from the minister?"

Her eyes fled from his and she said, "Yes."

He dropped her hand. "I don't blame you any. I've made a failure of it." His tone was that of a bankrupt at fifty. "I don't know enough to write a letter—I'm only a rough, tough fool. I thought you'd be thinking of me just the way I was thinking of you, and there was nothing to write about because I wasn't getting ahead as I expected. So I kept waiting till something turned up to encourage me. Nothing did, and now I'm paid for it."

His voice had a quality which made her weep. She tried to think of some words of comfort but could not. She was indeed too deeply concerned with her own contending emotions. There was marvelous appeal in this powerful, bronzed, undisciplined youth. His lack of tact and gallantry, his disconcerting directness of look and speech shook her, troubled her, and rendered her weak. She was but a year younger than he, and her life had been almost as simple exteriorly, but at center she was of far finer development. She had always been introspective, and she had grown self-analytic. She knew that the touch of this young desperado's hand had changed her relation toward the world. As he talked she listened without formulating a reply.

When at last she began to speak she hesitated and her sentences were broken. "I am very sorry—but you see I had not heard from you for a long time—it would be impossible—for me to live on the plains so far away—even if—even if I had not promised Mr. King——"

"Well, that ends it," he said harshly, and his voice brought tears again. "I go back to my cow punching, the only business I know. As you say, the cow country is no place for a girl like you. It's a mighty hard place for women of any kind, and you ... Besides, you're a singer, you can't afford to go with me. It's all a part of my luck. Things have gone against me from the start."

He paused to get a secure hold on his voice. "Well, now, I'm going, but I don't want you to forget me; don't pray for me, just *sing* for me. I'll hear you, and it'll help keep me out of mischief. Will you do that?"

"Yes—if you—if it will help——"

Jack's voice, unusually loud, interrupted her, and when the father entered, there was little outward sign of the passionate drama just enacted.

"Won't you sing for us, Mary?" asked Jack a few minutes later.

Mary looked at Harold significantly and arose to comply. Harold sat with head propped on his palm and eyes fixed immovably upon her face while she sang, If I Were a Voice. The voice was stronger, sweeter, and the phrasing was more mature, but it was after all the same soul singing through the prison gloom, straight to his heart. She charged the words with a special, intimate, tender meaning. She conveyed to him the message she dared not speak, "Be true in spite of all. My heart is sore for you, let me comfort you."

He, on his part, realized that one who could sing like that had a wider mission in the world than to accompany a cowboy to the bleak plains of the West. To comfort him was a small part of her work in the world. It was her mission to go on singing solace and pleasure to thousands all over the nation.

When she had finished he arose and offered his hand with a singular calmness which moved the girl more deeply than any word he had said. "When you sing that song, think of me, sometimes, will you?"

"Yes—always," she replied.

"Good-by," he said abruptly. Dropping her-hand, he went out without speaking another word.

Jack, taking her hand in parting, found it cold and nerveless.

"May I see you again before we go?" he asked.

Her eyes lighted a little and her hand tightened in his. "Yes—I want to speak with you," she said, and ended in a whisper, "about him."

Jack overtook Harold but remained silent. When they reached their room, Harold dropped into a chair like one exhausted by a fierce race.

"This ends it, Jack, I'll never set foot in the States again; from this time on I keep to the mountains."

CHAPTER XIII

THE YOUNG EAGLE DREAMS OF A MATE

As the young men sat at supper that night a note was handed to Jack by the clerk. Upon opening it he found a smaller envelope addressed to "Mr. Harding." Harold took it, but did not open it, though it promised well, being quite thick with leaves. Jack read his note at a glance and passed it across the table. It was simple:

"DEAR MR. BURNS: Won't you please see that the inclosed note reaches Harold. I wish you could persuade him to come and see me once more before he goes. I shall expect to see *you* anyhow. Father does not suspect anything out of the ordinary as yet, and it will be quite safe.

"Your friend,

"MARY YARDWELL.

As soon as he decently could Harold went to his room and opened the important letter. In it the reticent-girl had uttered herself with unusual freedom. It was a long letter, and its writer must have gone to its composition at once after the door had closed upon her visitors. It began abruptly, too:

"DEAR FRIEND: My heart aches for you. From the time I first saw you in the jail I have carried your face in my mind. I can't quite analyze my feeling for you now. You are so different from the boy I knew. I think I am a little afraid of you, you scare me a little. You are of another world, a strange world of which I would like to hear. I have a woman's curiosity, I can't let you go away until you tell me all your story. I would like to say something on my own side also. Can't you come and see me once more? My father is going to be away at his farm all day to-morrow, can't you come with Mr. Burns and take dinner with me and tell me all about yourself—your life is so strange.

"There will be no one there (I mean at dinner) but Mr. Burns and you, and we can talk freely. Does being 'under indictment' mean that you are in danger of arrest? I want to understand all about that. You can't know how strange and exciting all these things are to me. My life is so humdrum here. You come into it like a great mountain wind. You take my words away as well as my breath. I am not like most women, words are not easy to me even when I write, though I write better than I talk—I think.

"Mr. King asked me to be his wife some months ago, and I promised to do so, but that is no reason why we should not be good friends. You have been too much in my life to go out of it altogether, though I had given up seeing you again, and then we always think of our friends as we last saw them, we can't imagine their development. Don't you find this so? You said you found me changed.

"I have little to tell you about myself. I graduated and then I spent one winter in Chicago to continue my music studies. I am teaching here summers to get pin money. It is so quiet here one grows to think all the world very far away, and the wild things among which you have lived and worked are almost unimaginable even when the newspapers describe them with the greatest minuteness.

"This letter is very rambling, I know, but I am writing as rapidly as I can, for I want to send it to you before you take the train. Please come to see me to-morrow. To-night I sing in the song service at the church. I hope you will be there. The more I think about your story the more eager to listen I become. There must be some basis of stirring deeds for all the tales they tell of you. My friends say I have a touch of the literary poison in my veins; anyhow I like a story above all things, and to hear the hero tell his own adventures will be the keenest delight.

"I am sorry I could not do more to make things easier for you to-day, but I come of men and women who are silent when they mean most. I am never facile of speech and to-day I was dumb. Perhaps if we meet on a clear understanding we will get along better. Come, anyhow, and let me know you as you are. Perhaps I have never really known you, perhaps I only imagined you.

> "Your friend,
>
> "MARY YARDWELL.

"P.S. The reason for the postscript is that I have re-read the foregoing letter and find it unsatisfactory in everything except the expression of my wish to see you. I had meant to say so much and I have said so little. I am afraid now that I shall not see you at all, so I add my promise. I shall always remember you and I *will* think of you when I sing, and I will sing If I Were a Voice every Sunday for you, especially when I am all alone, and I'll send it out to you by thought waves. You shall never fail of the best wishes of

"MARY YARDWELL.

Not being trained in psychologic subtleties, Harold took this letter to mean only what it said. He was not as profoundly moved by it as he would have been could he have read beneath the lines the tumult he had produced in the tranquil life of its writer. One skilled in perception of a woman's moods could have detected a sense of weakness, or irresolution, or longing in a girl whose nature had not yet been tried by conflicting emotions.

Jack perceived something of this when Harold gave him the letter to read. His admiration of Harold's grace and power, his love for every gesture and every lineament of his boyish hero, made it possible for him to understand how deeply Mary had been moved when brought face to face with a handsome and powerful man who loved as lions love. He handed the letter back with a smile: "I think you'd better stay over and see her."

"I intend to," replied Harold; "wire father to come up."

"Let's go walk. We may happen by the church where she sings," suggested Jack.

It was a very beautiful hour of the day. The west was filled with cool, purple-gray clouds, and a fresh wind had swept away all memory of the heat of the day. Insects filled the air with quavering song. Children were romping on the lawns. Lovers sauntered by in pairs or swung under the trees in hammocks. Old people sat reading or listlessly talking beside their cottage doors. A few carriages were astir. It was a day of rest and peace and love-making to this busy little community. The mills were still and even the water seemed to run less swiftly, only the fishes below the dam had cause to regret the day's release from toil, for on every rock a fisherman was poised.

The tension being a little relieved, Harold was able to listen to Jack's news of Rock River. His father was still preaching in the First Church, but several influential men had split off and were actively antagonizing the majority of the congregation. The fight was at its bitterest. Maud had now three children, and her husband was doing well in hardware. This old schoolmate was married, that one was dead, many had moved West. Bradley Talcott was running for State Legislator. Radbourn was in Washington.

Talking on quietly the two young men walked out of the village into a lane bordered with Lombardy poplars. Harold threw himself down on the grass beneath them and said:

"Now I can imagine I am back on the old farm. Tell me all about your folks."

"Oh, they're just the same. They don't change much. Father scraped some money together and built a new bedroom on the west side. Mother calls it 'the boys' room.' By 'boys' they mean you and me. They expect us to sleep there when you come back on a visit. They'll be terribly disappointed at not seeing you. Mother seems to think as much of you as she does of me."

There was charm in the thought of the Burns' farm and Mrs. Burns coming and going about the big kitchen stove, the smell of wholesome cooking about her clothing, and for the moment the desperado's brain became as a child's. There was sadness in the thought that he never again could see his loyal friends or the old walks and lanes.

Jack aroused him and they walked briskly back toward the little church which they found already quite filled with young people. The choir, including Mary, smiled at the audience and at each other, for the spirit of the little church was humanly cheerful.

The strangers found seats in a corner pew together with a pale young man and a very pretty little girl. Jack was not imaginative, but he could not help thinking of the commotion which would follow if those around him should learn that "Black Mose" was at that moment seated among them. Mary, seeing the dark, stern face of the plainsman, had some such thought also. There was something gloriously unfettered, compelling, and powerful in his presence. He made the other young men appear commonplace and feeble in her eyes, and threw the minister into pale relief, emphasizing his serenity, his scholarship, and his security of position.

Harold gave close attention to the young minister, who, as Mary's lover, became important. As a man of action he put a low valuation on a mere scholar, but King was by no means contemptible physically. Jack also perceived the charm of such a man to Mary, and acknowledged the good sense of her choice. King could give her a pleasant home among people she liked, while Harold could only ask her to go to the wild country, to a log ranch in a cottonwood gulch, there to live month after month without seeing a woman or a child.

A bitter and desperate melancholy fell upon the plainsman. What was the use? Such a woman was not for him. He had only the pleasure of the wild country. He would go back to his horses, his guns, and the hills, and never again come under the disturbing influence of this beautiful singer. She was not of his world; her smiles were not for him. When the others arose in song he remained seated, his sullen face set toward the floor, denying himself the pleasure of even seeing Mary's face as she sang.

Her voice arose above the chorus, guiding, directing, uplifting the less confident ones. When she sang she was certain of herself, powerful, self-contained. That night she sang with such power and sweetness that the minister turned and smiled upon her at the end. He spoke over the low railing which separated them: "You surpass yourself to-night."

Looking across the heads of the audience as they began to take seats Harold saw this smile and action, and his face darkened again.

For her solo Mary selected one which expressed in simple words the capabilities each humble soul had for doing good. If one could not storm the stars in song one could bathe a weary brow. If one could not write a mighty poem one could speak a word of cheer to the toiler by the way.

It was all poor stuff enough, but the singer filled it with significance and appeal. At the moment it seemed as if such things were really worth doing. Each word came from her lips as though it had never been uttered by human lips before, so simple, so musical, so finely enunciated, so well valued was it. To Harold, so long separated from any approach to womanly art, it appealed with enormous power. He was not only sensitive, he was just come to the passion and impressionability of full-blooded young manhood. Powers converged upon him, and simple and direct as he was, the effects were confusion and deepest dejection. He heard nothing but Mary's voice, saw nothing but her radiant beauty. To him she was more wonderful than any words could express.

At the end of the singing he refused to wait till she came down the aisle, but hurried out into the open air away from the crowd. As Jack caught up with him he said: "You go to bed; I've got to take a run out into the country or I can't sleep at all. Father will be up in the morning, I suppose. I'll get off in the six o'clock train to-morrow night."

Jack said nothing, not even in assent, and Mose set off up the lane with more of mental torment than had ever been his experience before. Hitherto all had been simple. He loved horses, the wild things, the trail, the mountains, the ranch duties, and the perfect freedom of a man of action. Since the door of his prison opened to allow him to escape into the West he had encountered no doubts, had endured no remorse, and had felt but little fear. All that he did was forthright, manly, single-purposed, and unhesitating.

Now all seemed changed. His horses, his guns, the joys of free spaces, were met by a counter allurement which was the voice of a woman. Strong as he was, stern as he looked, he was still a boy in certain ways, and this mental tumult, so new and strange to him, wearied him almost to tears. It was a fatigue, an ache which he could not shake off, and when he returned to the hotel he had settled nothing and was ready to flee from it all without one backward look. However, he slept soundlier than he thought himself capable of doing.

He was awakened early by Jack: "Harry, your father is here, and very anxious to see you."

Mose arose slowly and reluctantly. He had nothing to say to his father, and dreaded the interview, which he feared would be unpleasantly emotional. The father met him with face pale and hands trembling with emotion. "My son, my son!" he whispered. Mose stood silently wondering why his father should make so much fuss over him.

Mr. Excell soon recovered his self-command, and his voice cleared. "I had almost given up seeing you, Harold. I recognize you with difficulty—you have changed much. You seem well and strong—almost as tall as I was at your age."

"I hold my own," said Harold, and they all sat down more at ease. "I got into rough gangs out there, but I reckon they got as good as they sent."

"I suppose the newspapers have greatly exaggerated about your conflicts?"

Harold was a little disposed to shock his father. "Oh, yes, I don't think I really killed as many men as they tell about; I don't know that I killed any."

"I hope you did not lightly resort to the use of deadly weapons," said Mr. Excell sadly.

"It was kill or be killed," said Harold grimly. "It was like shooting a pack of howling wolves. I made up my mind to be just one shot ahead of anybody. There are certain counties out there where the name 'Black Mose' means something."

"I'm sorry for that, my son. I hope you don't drink?"

"Don't you worry about that. I can't afford to drink, and if I could I wouldn't. Oh, I take a glass of beer with the boys once in a while on a hot day, but it's my lay to keep sober. A drunken man is a soft mark." He changed the subject: "Seems to me you're a good deal grayer."

Mr. Excell ran his fingers through the tumbled heap of his grizzled hair. "Yes; things are troubling me a little. The McPhails are fighting me in the church, and intend to throw me out and ruin me if they can, but I shall fight them till the bitter end. I am not to be whipped out like a dog."

"That's the talk! Don't let 'em run you out. I got run out of Cheyenne, but I'll never run again. I was only a kid then. After you throw 'em down, come out West and round up the cowboys. They won't play any underhanded games on you, and mebbe you can do them some good—especially on gambling. They are sure enough idiots about cards."

They went down to breakfast together, but did not sit together.

Jack and Harold talked in low voices about Mr. Excell.

"The old man looks pretty well run down, don't he?" said Harold.

"He worries a whole lot about you."

"He needn't to. When does he go back?"

"He wants to stay all day—just as long as he can."

"He'd better pull right out on that ten o'clock train. His being here is sure to give me away sooner or later."

It was hard for the father to say good-by. He had a feeling that it was the last time he should ever see him, and his face was gray with suffering as he faced his son for the last time. Harold became not merely unresponsive, he grew harsher of voice each moment. His father's tremulous and repeated words seemed to him foolish and absurd—and also inconsiderate. After he was gone he burst out in wrath.

"Why can't he act like a man? I don't want anybody to snivel over me. Suppose I *am* to be shot this fall, what of it?"

This disgust and bitterness prepared him, strange to say, for his call upon Mary. He entered the house, master of himself and the situation. His nerves were like steel, and his stern face did not quiver in its minutest muscle, though she met him in most gracious mood, dressed as for conquest and very beautiful.

"I'm so glad you stayed over," she said. "I have been so eager to hear all about your life out there." She led the way to the little parlor once more and drew a chair near him.

"Well," he began, "it isn't exactly the kind of life your Mr. King leads."

There was a vengeful sneer in his voice which Mary felt as if he had struck her, but she said gently:

"I suppose our life does seem very tame to you now."

"It's sure death. I couldn't stand it for a year; I'd rot."

Mary was aware that some sinister change had come over him, and she paused to study him keenly. The tremulous quality of his voice and action had passed away. He was hard, stern, self-contained, and she (without being a coquette) determined that his mood should give way to hers. He set himself hard against the charm of her lovely presence and the dainty room. Mary ceased to smile, but her brows remained level.

"You men seem to think that all women are fond only of the quiet things, but it isn't true. We like the big deeds in the open air, too. I'd like to see a cattle ranch and take a look at a 'round-up,' though I don't know exactly what that means."

"Well, we're not on the round-up all the time," he said, relaxing a little. "It's pretty quiet part of the time; that is, quiet for our country. But then, you're always on a horse and you're out in the air on the plains with the mountains in sight. There's a lot of hard work about it, too, and it's lonesome sometimes when your're ridin' the lines, but I like it. When it gets a little too tame for me I hit the trail for the mountains with an Indian. The Ogallalahs are my friends, and I'm going to spend the winter with them and then go into the West Elk country. I'm due to kill a grizzly this year and some mountain sheep." He was started now, and Mary had only to listen. "Before I stop, I'm going to know all there is to know of the Rocky Mountains. With ol' Kintuck and my Winchester I'm goin' to hit the sunset trail and hit it hard. There's nothing to keep me now," he said with a sudden glance at her. "It don't matter where I turn up or pitch camp. I reckon I'd better not try to be a cattle king." He smiled bitterly and pitilessly at the poor figure he cut. "I reckon I'm a kind of a mounted hobo from this on."

"But your father and sister——"

"Oh, she isn't worryin' any about me; I haven't had a letter from her for two years. All I've got now is Jack, and he'd be no earthly good on the trail. He'd sure lose his glasses in a fight, and then he couldn't tell a grizzly from a two-year-old cow. So you see, there's nothing to hinder me from going anywhere. I'm footloose. I want to spend one summer in the Flat Top country. Ute Jim tells me it's fine. Then I want to go into the Wind River Mountains for elk. Old Talfeather, chief of the Ogallalahs, has promised to take me into the Big Horn Range. After that I'm going down into the southwest, down through the Uncompagre country. Reynolds says they're the biggest yet, and I'm going to keep right down into the Navajo reservation. I've got a bid from old Silver Arrow, and then I'm going to Walpi and see the Mokis dance. They say they carry live rattlesnakes in their mouths. I don't believe it: I'm going to see. Then I swing 'round to the Grand Cañon of the Colorado. They say that's the sorriest gash in the ground that ever happened. Reynolds gave me a letter to old Hance; he's the man that watches to see that no one carries the hole away. Then I'm going to take a turn over the Mohave desert into Southern California. I'm due at the Yosemite Valley about a year from next fall. I'll come back over the divide by way of Salt Lake."

He was on his feet, and his eyes were glowing. He seemed to have forgotten all women in the sweep of his imaginative journey.

"Oh, that will be grand! How will you do it?"

"On old Kintuck, if his legs don't wear off."

"How will you live?"

"Forage where I can. Turn to and help on a 'round-up,' or 'drive' where I can—shoot and fish—oh, I'll make it if it takes ten years."

"Then what?" Mary asked, with a curious intonation.

"Then I'll start for the Northwest," he replied after a little hesitation—"if I live. Of course the chances are I'll turn up my toes somewhere on the trail. A man is liable to make a miss-lick somewhere, but that's all in the game. A man had better die on the trail than in a dead furrow."

Mary looked at him with dreaming eyes. His strange moods filled her with new and powerful emotions. The charm of the wild life he depicted appealed to her as well as to him. It was all a fearsome venture, but after all it was glorious. The placid round of her own life seemed for the moment intolerably commonplace. There was epic largeness in the circuit of the plainsman's daring plans. The wonders of Nature which he catalogued loomed large in the misty knowledge she held of the West. She cried out:

"Oh, I wish I could see those wonderful scenes!"

He turned swiftly: "You can; I'll take you."

She shrank back. "Oh, no! I didn't mean that—I meant—some time——"

His face darkened. "In a sleeping car, I reckon. That time'll never come."

Then a silence fell on them. Harold knew that his plans could not be carried out with a woman for companion—and he had sense enough to know that Mary's words were born of a momentary enthusiasm. When he spoke it was with characteristic blunt honesty.

"No; right here our trails fork, Mary. Ever since I saw you in the jail the first time, you've been worth more to me than anything else in the world, but I can see now that things never can go right with you and me. I couldn't live back here, and you couldn't live with me out there. I'm a kind of an outlaw, anyway. I made up my mind last night that I'd hit the trail alone. I won't even ask Jack to go with me. There's something in me here"—he laid his hand on his breast—"that kind o' chimes in with the wind in the piñons and the yap of the ky-ote. The rooster and the church bells are too tame for me. That's all there is about it. Maybe when I get old and feeble in the knees I'll feel like pitchin' a permanent camp, but just now I don't; I want to be on the move. If I had a nice ranch, and you, I might settle down now, but then you couldn't stand even a ranch with nearest neighbors ten miles away." He turned to take his hat. "I wanted to see you—I didn't plan for anything else—I've seen you and so——"

"Oh, you're not going now!" she cried. "You haven't told me your story."

"Oh, yes, I have; all that you'd care to hear. It don't amount to much, except the murder charges, and they are wrong. It wasn't my fault. They crowded me too hard, and I had to defend myself. What is a man to do when it's kill or be killed? That's all over and past, anyway. From this time on I camp high. The roosters and church bells are getting too thick on the Arickaree."

He crushed his hat in his hand as he turned to her, and tears were in her eyes as she said:

"Please don't go; I expected you to stay to dinner with me."

"The quicker I get out o' here the better," he replied hoarsely, and she saw that he was trembling. "What's the good of it? I'm out of it."

She looked up at him in silence, her mind filled with the confused struggle between her passion and her reason. He allured her, this grave and stern outlaw, appealing to some primitive longing within her.

"I hate to see you go," she said slowly. "But—I—suppose it is best. I don't like to have you forget me—I shall not forget you, and I will sing for you every Sunday afternoon, and no matter where you are, in a deep cañon, or anywhere, or among the Indians, you just stop and listen and think of me, and maybe you'll hear my voice."

Tears were in her eyes as she spoke, and he took a man's advantage of her emotion.

"Perhaps if I come back—if I make a strike somewhere—if you'd say so——"

She shook her head sadly but conclusively. "No, no, I can't promise anything."

"All right—that settles it. Good-by."

And she had nothing better to say than just "Good-by, good-by."

CHAPTER XIV

THE YOUNG EAGLE RETURNS TO HIS EYRIE

It was good to face the West again. The wild heart of the youth flung off all doubt, all regret. Not for him were the quiet joys of village life. No lane or street could measure his flight. His were the gleaming, immeasurable walls of the Sangre de Cristo range, his the grassy mountain parks and the silent cañons, and the peaks. "To hell with the East, and all it owns," was his mood, and in that mood he renounced all claim to Mary.

He sat with meditative head against the windowpane, listless as a caged and sullen eagle, but his soul was far ahead, swooping above the swells that cut into the murky sky. His eyes studied every rod of soil as he retraced his way up that great wind-swept slope, noting every change in vegetation or settlement. Five years before he had crept like a lizard; now he was rushing straight on like the homing eagle who sees his home crag gleam in the setting sun.

The cactus looked up at him with spiney face. The first prairie dog sitting erect uttered a greeting to which he smiled. The first mirage filled his heart with a rush of memories of wild rides, and the grease wood recalled a hundred odorous camp fires. He was getting home.

The people at the stations grew more unkempt, untamed. The broad hats and long mustaches of the men proclaimed the cow country at last. It seemed as though he might at any moment recognize some of them. At a certain risk to himself he got off the train at one or two points to talk with the boys. As it grew dark he took advantage of every wait to stretch his legs and enjoy the fresh air, so different in its clarity and crisp dryness from the leaf-burdened, mist-filled atmosphere of Marmion. He lifted his eyes to the West with longing too great for words, eager to see the great peaks peer above the plain's rim.

The night was far spent when the brakeman called the name of the little town in which he had left his outfit, and he rose up stiff and sore from his cramped position.

Kintuck, restless from long confinement in a stall, chuckled with joy when his master entered and called to him. It was still dark, but that mattered little to such as Mose. He flung the saddle on and cinched it tight. He rolled his extra clothes in his blanket and tied it behind his saddle, and then, with one hand on his pommel, he said to the hostler, moved by a bitter recklessness of mind:

"Well, that squares us, stranger. If anybody asks you which-a-way 'Black Mose' rode jist say ye didn't notice." A leap, a rush of hoofs, and the darkness had eaten both horse and man.

It was a long ride, and as he rode the dawn came over the plains, swift, silent, majestic with color. His blood warmed in his limbs and his head lifted. He was at home in the wild once more, all ties were cut between him and the East. Mary was not for him. Maud had grown indifferent, Jack would never come West, and Mr. and Mrs. Burns were merely cheery memories. There was nothing now to look backward upon—nothing to check his career as hunter and explorer. All that he had done up to this moment was but careful preparation for great journeys. He resolved to fling himself into unknown trails—to know the mountains as no other man knew them.

Again he rode down into the valley of the Arickaree, and as the boys came rolling out with cordial shouts of welcome, his eyes smarted a little. He slipped from his horse and shook hands all around, and ended by snatching Pink and pressing her soft cheek against his lips—something he had never done before.

They bustled to get his breakfast, while Reynolds took care of Kintuck. Cora, blushing prettily as she set the table for him, said: "We're mighty glad to see you back, Mose. Daddy said you'd never turn up again, but I held out you would."

"Oh, I couldn't stay away from Kintuck and little Pink," he replied.

"How'd they feed ye back there?" inquired Mrs. Reynolds.

"Oh, fair to middlin'—but, of course, they couldn't cook like Ma Reynolds."

"Oh, you go hark!" cried Mrs. Reynolds, vastly delighted. "They've got so much more to do with."

It was good to sit there in the familiar kitchen and watch these simple, hearty women working with joy to feed him. His heart was very tender, and he answered most of their questions with unusual spirit, fending off, however, any reference to old sweethearts. His talk was all of absorbing interest to the women. They were hungry to know how people were living and dressing back there. It was so sweet and fine to be able to return to the East—and Mrs. Reynolds hoped to do so before she died. Cora drew from Mose the information that the lawns were beautifully green in Marmion, and that all kinds of flowers were in blossom, and that the birds were singing in the maples. Even his meagre descriptions brought back to the girl the green freshness of June.

"Oh, I'm so tired of these bare hills," she said wistfully. "I wish I could go East again, back to our old home in Missouri."

"I wish now I'd stayed here and sent you," said Mose.

She turned in surprise. "Why so, Mose?"

"Because I had so little fun out of it, while to you it would have been a picnic."

"You're mighty good, Mose," was all she said in reply, but her eyes lingered upon his face, which seemed handsomer than ever before, for it was softened by his love, his good friends, and the cheerful home.

In the days that followed Cora took on new youth and beauty. Her head lifted, and the swell of her bosom had more of pride and grace than ever before in her life. She no longer shrank from the gaze of men, even of strangers, for Mose seemed her lover and protector. Before his visit to the East she had doubted, but now she let her starved heart feed on dreams of him.

Mose had little time to give to her, for (at his own request) Reynolds was making the highest use of his power. "I want to earn every cent I can for the next three months," Mose explained, and he often did double duty. He was very expert now with the rope and could throw and tie a steer with the best of the men. His muscles seemed never to tire nor his nerves to fail him. Rain, all-night rides, sleeping on the ground beneath frosty blankets, nothing seemed to trouble him. He was never cheery, but he was never sullen.

One day in November he rode up to the home ranch leading a mule with a pack saddle fully rigged.

"What are you doing with that mule?" asked Reynolds as he came out of the house, followed by Pink.

"I'm going to pack him."

"Pack him? What do you mean?"

"I'm going to hit 'the long trail.'"

Cora came hurrying forward. "Good evening, Mose."

"Good evening, Cory. How's my little Pink?"

"What did you say about hittin' the trail, Mose?"

"Now I reckon you'll give an account of yourself," said Reynolds with a wink.

Mose was anxious to avoid an emotional moment; he cautiously replied: "Oh, I'm off on a little hunting excursion; don't get excited about it. I'm hungry as a coyote; can I eat?"

Cora was silenced but not convinced, and after supper, when the old people withdrew from the kitchen, she returned to the subject again.

"How long are you going to be gone this time?"

Mose saw the storm coming, but would not lie to avoid it.

"I don't know; mebbe all winter."

She dropped into a chair facing him, white and still. When she spoke her voice was a wail. "O Mose! I can't live here all winter without you."

"Oh, yes, you can; you've got Pink and the old folks."

"But I want *you*! I'll die here without you, Mose. I can't endure it."

His face darkened. "You'd better forget me; I'm a hoodoo, Cory; nobody is ever in luck when I'm around. I make everybody miserable."

"I was never really happy till you come," she softly replied.

"There are a lot of better men than I am jest a-hone'in to marry you," he interrupted her to say.

"I don't want them—I don't want anybody but you, and now you go off and leave me——"

The situation was beyond any subtlety of the man, and he sat in silence while she wept. When he could command himself he said:

"I'm mighty sorry, Cory, but I reckon the best way out of it is to just take myself off in the hills where I can't interfere with any one's fun but my own. Seems to me I'm fated to make trouble all along the line, and I'm going to pull out where there's nobody but wolves and grizzlies, and fight it out with them."

She was filled with a new terror: "What do you mean? I don't believe you intend to come back at all!" She looked at him piteously, the tears on her cheeks.

"Oh, yes, I'll round the circle some time."

She flung herself down on the chair arm and sobbed unrestrainedly. "Don't go—please!"

Mose felt a sudden touch of the same disgust which came upon him in the presence of his father's enforcing affection. He arose. "Now, Cory, see here; don't you waste any time on me. I'm no good under the sun. I like you and I like Pinkie, but I don't want you to cry over me. I ain't worth it. Now that's the God's truth. I'm a black hoodoo, and you'll never prosper till I skip; I'm not fit to marry any woman."

Singularly enough, this gave the girl almost instant comfort, and she lifted her head and dried her eyes, and before he left she smiled a little, though her face was haggard and tear stained.

Mose was up early and had his packs ready and Kintuck saddled when Mrs. Reynolds called him to breakfast. Cora's pale face and piteous eyes moved him more deeply than her sobbing the night before, but there was a certain inexorable fixedness in his resolution, and he did not falter. At bottom the deciding cause was Mary. She had passed out of his life, but no other woman could take her place—therefore he was ready to cut loose from all things feminine.

"Well, Mose, I'm sorry to see you go, I certainly am so," said Reynolds. "*But*, you ah you' own master. All I can say is, this old ranch is open to you, and shall be so long as we stay hyer— though I am mighty uncertain how long we shall be able to hold out agin this new land-boom. You had better not stay away too long, or you may miss us. I reckon we ah all to be driven to the mountains very soon."

"I may be back in the spring. I'm likely to need money, and be obliged to come back to you for a job."

On this tiny crumb of comfort Cora's hungry heart seized greedily. The little pink-cheeked one helped out the sad meal. She knew nothing of the long trail upon which her hero was about to set foot, and took possession of the conversation by telling of a little antelope which one of the cowboys had brought her.

The mule was packed and Mose was about to say good-by. The sun was still low in the eastern sky. Frost was on the grass, but the air was crisp and pleasant. All the family stood beside him as he packed his outfit on the mule and threw over it the diamond hitch. As he straightened up he turned to the waiting ones and said: "Do you see that gap in the range?"

They all looked where he pointed. Down in the West, but lighted into unearthly splendor by the morning light, arose the great range of snowy peaks. In the midst of this impassable wall a purple notch could be seen.

"Ever sence I've been here," said Mose, with singular emotion, "I've looked away at that range and I've been waiting my chance to see what that cañon is like. There runs my trail—good-by."

He shook hands hastily with Cora, heartily with Mrs. Reynolds, and kissed Pink, who said: "Bring me a little bear or a fox."

"All right, honey, you shall have a grizzly."

He swung into the saddle. "Here I hit the trail for yon blue notch and the land where the sun goes down. So long."

"Take care o' yourself, boy."

"Come back soon," called Cora, and covered her face with her shawl in a world-old gesture of grief.

In the days that followed she thought of him as she saw him last, a minute fleck on the plain. She thought of him when the rains fell, and prayed that he might not fall ill of fever or be whelmed by a stream. He seemed so little and weak when measured against that mighty and merciless wall of snow. Then when the cold white storms came and the plain was hid in the fury of wind and sleet, she shuddered and thought of him camped beside a rock, cold and hungry. She thought of him lying with a broken leg, helpless, while his faithful beasts pawed the ground and whinnied their distress. She spoke of these things once or twice, but her father merely smiled.

"Mose can take care of himself, daughter, don't you worry."

Months passed before they had a letter from him, and when it came it bore the postmark of Durango.

"DEAR FRIENDS: I should a-written before, but the fact is I hate to write and then I've been on the move all the time. I struck through the gap and angled down to Taos, a Pueblo Indian town, where I stayed for a while—then went on down the Valley to Sante Fee. Then I hunted up Delmar. He was glad to see me, but he looks old. He had a hell of a time after I left. It wasn't the way the papers had it—but he won out all right. He sold his sheep and quit. He said he got tired of shooting men. I stayed with him— he's got a nice family—two girls—and then I struck out into the Pueblo country. These little brown chaps interest me but they're a different breed o' cats from the Ogallalahs. Everybody talks about the Snake Dance at Moki, so I'm angling out that way. I'm going to do a little cow punchin' for a man in Apache County and go on to the Dance. I'm going through the Navajoe reservation. I stand in with them. They've heard of me some way—through the Utes I reckon."

The accounts of the Snake Dance contained mention of "Black Mose," who kept a band of toughs from interfering with the dance. His wonderful marksmanship was spoken of. He did not write till he reached Flagstaff. His letter was very brief. "I'm going into the Grand Cañon for a few days, then I go to work on a ranch south of here for the winter. In the spring I'm going over the range into California."

When they heard of him next he was deputy marshal of a mining town, and the Denver papers contained long despatches about his work in clearing the town of desperadoes. After that they lost track of him altogether—but Cora never gave him up. "He'll round the big circle one o' these days—and when he does he'll find us all waiting, won't he, pet?" and she drew little Pink close to her hungry heart.

PART III

CHAPTER XV

THE EAGLE COMPLETES HIS CIRCLE

All days were Sunday in the great mining camp of Wagon Wheel, so far as legal enactment ran, but on Saturday night, in following ancient habit, the men came out of their prospect holes on the high, grassy hills, or threw down the pick in their "overland tunnels," or deep shafts and rabbitlike burrows, and came to camp to buy provisions, to get their mail, and to look upon, if not to share, the vice and tumult of the town.

The streets were filled from curb to curb with thousands of men in mud-stained coats and stout-laced boots. They stood in the gutters and in the middle of the street to talk (in subdued voices) of their claims. There was little noise. The slowly-moving streams of shoppers or amusement seekers gave out no sudden shouting. A deep murmur filled the air, but no angry curse was heard, no whooping. In a land where the revolver is readier than the fist men are wary of quarrel, careful of abuse, and studiously regardful of others.

There were those who sought vice, and it was easily found. The saloons were packed with thirsty souls, and from every third door issued the click of dice and whiz of whirling balls in games of chance.

Every hotel barroom swarmed with persuasive salesmen bearing lumps of ore with which to entice unwary capital. All the talk was of "pay-streaks," "leads," "float," "whins," and "up-raises," while in the midst of it, battling to save souls, the zealous Salvation Army band paraded to and fro with frenzied beating of drums. Around and through all this, listening with confused ears, gazing with wide, solemn eyes, were hundreds of young men from the middle East, farmers' sons, cowboys, mountaineers, and miners. To them it was an awesome city, this lurid camp, a wonder and an allurement to dissipation.

To Mose, fresh from the long trail, it was irritating and wearying. He stood at the door of a saloon, superbly unconscious of his physical beauty, a somber dream in his eyes, a statuesque quality in his pose. He wore the wide hat of the West, but his neat, dark coat, though badly wrinkled, was well cut, and his crimson tie and dark blue shirt were handsomely decorative. His face was older, sterner, and sadder than when he faced Mary three years before. No trace of boyhood was in his manner. Seven years of life on the long trail and among the mountain peaks had taught him silence, self-restraint, and had also deepened his native melancholy. He had ridden into Wagon Wheel from the West, eager to see the great mining camp whose fame had filled the world.

As he stood so, with the light of the setting sun in his face, the melancholy of a tiger in his eyes, a woman in an open barouche rode by. Her roving glance lighted upon his figure and rested there. "Wait!" she called to her driver, and from the shadow of her silken parasol she studied the young man's absorbed and motionless figure. He on his part perceived only a handsomely dressed woman looking out over the crowd. The carriage interested him more than the woman. It was a magnificent vehicle, the finest he had ever seen, and he wondered how it happened to be there on the mountain top.

A small man with a large head stepped from the crowd and greeted the woman with a military salute. In answer to a question, the small man turned and glanced toward Mose. The woman bowed and drove on, and Mose walked slowly up the street, lonely and irresolute. At the door of a gambling house he halted and looked in. A young lad and an old man were seated together at a roulette table, and around them a ring of excited and amused spectators stood. Mose entered and took a place in the circle. The boy wore a look of excitement quite painful to see, and he placed his red and white chips with nervous, blundering, and ineffectual gestures, whereas the older man smiled benignly over his glasses and placed his single dollar chip each time with humorous decision. Each time he won. "This is for a new hat," he said, and the next time, "This is for a box at the theater." The boy, with his gains in the circle of his left arm, was desperately absorbed. No smile, no jest was possible to him.

Mose felt a hand on his shoulder, and turning, found himself face to face with the small man who had touched his hat to the woman in the carriage. The stranger's countenance was stern in its outlines, and his military cut of beard added to his grimness, but his eyes were surrounded by fine lines of good humour.

"Stranger, I'd like a word with you."

Mose followed him to a corner, supposing him to be a man with mines to sell, or possibly a confidence man.

"Stranger, where you from?"

"From the Snake country," replied Mose.

"What's your little game here?"

Mose was angered at his tone. "None of your business."

The older man flushed, and the laugh went out of his eyes. "I'll make it my business," he said grimly. "I've seen you somewhere before, but I can't place you. You want to get out o' town to-night; you're here for no man's good—you've got a 'graft.'"

Mose struck him with the flat of his left hand, and, swift as a rattlesnake's stroke, covered him with his revolver. "Wait right where you are," he said, and the man became rigid. "I came here as peaceable as any man," Mose went on, "but I don't intend to be ridden out of town by a jackass like you."

The other man remained calm. "If you'll kindly let me unbutton my coat, I'll show you my star; I'm the city marshal."

"Be quiet," commanded Mose; "put up your hands!"

Mose was aware of an outcry, then a silence, then a rush.

From beneath his coat, quick as a flash of light from a mirror, he drew a second revolver. His eyes flashed around the room. For a moment all was silent, then a voice called, "What's all this, Haney?"

"Keep them quiet," said Mose, still menacing the officer.

"Boys, keep back," pleaded the marshal.

"The man that starts this ball rolling will be sorry," said Mose, searching the crowd with sinister eyes. "If you're the marshal, order these men back to the other end of the room."

"Boys, get back," commanded the marshal. With shuffling feet the crowd retreated. "Shut the door, somebody, and keep the crowd out."

The doors were shut, and the room became as silent as a tomb.

"Now," said Mose, "is it war or peace?"

"Peace," said the marshal.

"All right." Mose dropped the point of his revolver.

The marshal breathed easier. "Stranger, you're a little the swiftest man I've met since harvest; would you mind telling me your name?"

"Not a bit. My friends call me Mose Harding."

"'Black Mose'!" exclaimed the marshal, and a mutter of low words and a laugh broke from the listening crowd. Haney reached out his hand. "I hope you won't lay it up against me." Mose shook his hand and the marshal went on: "To tell the honest truth, I thought you were one of Lightfoot's gang. I couldn't place you. Of course I see now—I have your picture at the office—the drinks are on me." He turned with a smile to the crowd: "Come, boys— irrigate and get done with it. It's a horse on me, sure."

Taking the mildest liquor at the bar, Mose drank to further friendly relations, while the marshal continued to apologize. "You see, we've been overrun with 'rollers' and 'skin-game' men, and lately three expresses have been held up by Lightfoot's gang, and so I've been facing up every suspicious immigrant. I've had to do it—in your case I was too brash—I'll admit that—but come, let's get away from the mob. Come over to my office, I want to talk with you."

Mose was glad to escape the curious eyes of the throng. While his life was in the balance, he saw and heard everything hostile, nothing more—now, he perceived the crowd to be disgustingly inquisitive. Their winks, and grins, and muttered words annoyed him.

"Open the door—much obliged, Kelly," said the marshal to the man who kept the door. Kelly was a powerfully built man, dressed like a miner, in broad hat, loose gray shirt, and laced boots, and Mose admiringly studied him.

"This is not 'Rocky Mountain Kelly'?" he asked.

Kelly smiled. "The same; 'Old Man Kelly' they call me now."

Mose put out his hand. "I'm glad to know ye. I've heard Tom Gavin speak of you."

Kelly shook heartily. "Oh! do ye know Tom? He's a rare lump of a b'y, is Tom. We've seen great times together on the plains and on the hills. It's all gone now. It's tame as a garden since the buffalo went; they've made it another world, b'y."

"Come along, Kelly, and we'll have it out at my office."

As the three went out into the street they confronted a close-packed throng. The word had passed along that the marshal was being "done," and now, singularly silent, the miners waited the opening of the door.

The marshal called from the doorstep: "It's all right. Don't block the street. Break away, boys, break away." The crowd opened to let them pass, fixing curious eyes upon Mose.

As the three men crossed the street the woman in the carriage came driving slowly along. Kelly and the marshal saluted gallantly, but Mose did not even bow.

She leaned from her carriage and called:

"What's that I hear, marshal, about your getting shot?"

"All a mistake, Madam. I thought I recognized this young man and was politely ordering him out of town when he pulled his gun and nailed me to the cross."

The woman turned a smiling face toward Mose. "He must be a wonder. Introduce me, please."

"Certain sure! This is Mrs. Raimon, Mose; 'Princess Raimon,' this is my friend, Mose Harding, otherwise known as 'Black Mose.'"

"Black Mose!" she cried; "are *you* that terrible man?"

She reached out her little gloved hand, and as Mose took it her eyes searched his face. "I think we are going to be friends." Her voice was affectedly musical as she added: "Come and see me, won't you?"

She did not wait for his reply, but drove on with a sudden assumption of reserve which became her very well.

The three men walked on in silence. At last, with a curious look at Kelly, the marshal said, "Young man, you're in luck. Anything you want in town is yours now. How about it, Kelly?"

"That's the thrue word of it."

"What do you mean?" asked Mose.

"Just this—what the princess asks for she generally gets. She's taken a fancy to you, and if you're keen as I think you are, you'll call on her without much delay."

"Who is she? How does she happen to be here?"

"She came out here with her husband—and stays for love of men and mines, I reckon. Anyhow, she always has a man hangin' on, and has managed to secure some of the best mines in the camp. She works 'em, too. She's a pretty high roller, as they call 'em back in the States, but she helps the poor, and pays her debts like a man, and it's no call o' mine to pass judgment on her."

The marshal's office was an old log shanty, one of the first to be built on the trail, and passing through the big front room in which two or three men were lounging, the marshal led his guests to his inner office and sleeping room. A fire was blazing in a big stone fireplace. Skins and dingy blankets were scattered about, and on the mantle stood a bottle and some dirty glasses.

"Sit down, gentlemen," said the marshal, "and have some liquor."

After they were served and cigars lighted, the marshal began:

"Mose, I want you to serve as my deputy."

Mose was taken by surprise and did not speak for a few moments. The marshal went on:

"I don't know that you're after a job, but I'm sure I need you. There's no use hemming and hawing—I've made a cussed fool of myself this evenin', and the boys are just about going to drink up my salary for me this coming week. I can't afford *not* to have you my deputy because you unlimbered your gun a grain of a second before me—beat me at my own trick. I need you—now what do you say?"

Mose took time to reply. "I sure need a job for the winter," he admitted, "but I don't believe I want to do this."

The marshal urged him to accept. "I'll call in the newspaper men and let them tell the whole story of your life, and of our little jamboree to-day—they'll fix up a yarn that'll paralyze the hold-up gang. Together we'll swoop down on the town. I've been planning a clean-out for some weeks, and I need you to help me turn 'em loose."

Mose arose. "I guess not; I'm trying to keep clear of gun-play these days. I've never hunted that kind of thing, and I won't start in on a game that's sure to give me trouble."

The marshal argued. "Set down; listen; that's the point exactly. The minute the boys know who you are we won't *need* to shoot. That's the reason I want you—the reporters will prepare the way. Wherever we go the 'bad men' will scatter."

But Mose was inexorable. "No, I can't do it. I took just such a job once—I don't want another."

Haney was deeply disappointed, but shook hands pleasantly. "Well, good-night; drop in any time."

Mose went out into the street once more. He was hungry, and so turned in at the principal hotel in the city for a "good square meal." An Italian playing the violin and his boy accompanying him on the harp, made up a little orchestra. Some palms in pots, six mirrors set between the windows, together with tall, very new, oak chairs gave the dining room a magnificence which abashed the bold heart of the trailer for a moment.

However, his was not a nature to show timidity, and taking a seat he calmly spread his damp napkin on his knee and gave his order to the colored waiter (the Palace Hotel had the only two colored waiters in Wagon Wheel) with such grace as he could command after long years upon the trail.

As he lifted his eyes he became aware of "the princess" seated at another table and facing him. She seemed older than when he saw her in the carriage. Her face was high-colored, and her hair a red-brown. Her eyes were half closed, and her mouth drooped at the corners. Her chin, supported on her left hand, glittering with jewels, was pushed forward aggressively, and she listened with indifference to the talk of her companion, a dark, smooth-featured man, with a bitter and menacing smile.

Mose was oppressed by her glance. She seemed to be looking at him from the shadow as a tigress might glare from her den, and he ate awkwardly, and his food tasted dry and bitter. Ultimately he became angry. Why should this woman, or any woman, stare at him like that? He would have understood her better had she smiled at him—he was not without experience of that sort, but this unwavering glance puzzled and annoyed him.

Putting her companion aside with a single gesture, the princess arose and came over to Mose's table and reached her hand to him. She smiled radiantly of a sudden, and said, "How do you do, Mr. Harding; I didn't recognize you at first."

Mose took her hand but did not invite her to join him. However, she needed no invitation, and taking a seat opposite, leaned her elbows on the table and looked at him with eyes more inscrutable than ever—despite their nearness. They were a mottled yellow and brown, he noticed, unusual and interesting eyes, but by contrast with the clear deeps of Mary's eyes they seemed like those of some beautiful wild beast. He could not penetrate a thousandth part of a hair line beyond the exterior shine of her glance. The woman's soul was in the unfathomable shadow beneath.

"I know all about you," she said. "I read a long article about you in the papers some months ago. You stood off a lot of bogus game wardens who were going to butcher some Shoshonees. I liked that. The article said you killed a couple of them. I hope you did."

Mose was very short. "I don't think any of them died at my hands, but they deserved it, sure enough."

She smiled again. "After seeing you on the street, I went home and looked up that slip—I saved it, you see. I've wanted to see you for a long time. You've had a wonderful life for one so young. This article raked up a whole lot of stuff about you—said you were the son of a preacher—is that so?"

"Yes, that part of it was true."

"Same old story, isn't it? I'm the daughter of a college professor— sectarian college at that." She smiled a moment, then became as suddenly grave. "I like men. I like men who face danger and think nothing of it. The article said you came West when a mere boy and got mixed up in some funny business on the plains and had to take a sneak to the mountains. What have you been doing since? I wish you'd tell me the whole story. Come to my house; it's just around the corner."

As she talked, her voice became more subtly pleasing, and the lines of her mouth took on a touch of girlish grace.

"I haven't time to do that," Mose said, "and besides, my story don't amount to much. You don't want to believe all they say of me. I've just knocked around a little like a thousand other fellows, that's all. I pull out to-night. I'm looking up an old friend down here on a ranch."

She saw her mistake. "All right," she said, and smiled radiantly. "But come some other time, won't you?" She was so winning, so frank and kindly that Mose experienced a sudden revulsion of feeling. A powerful charm came from her superb physique, her radiant color, and from her beautiful, flexile lips and sound white teeth. He hesitated, and she pressed her advantage.

"You needn't be afraid of me. The boys often drop in to see me of an evening. If I can be of any use to you, let me know. I'll tell you what you do. You take supper with me here to-morrow night. What say?"

Mose looked across at the scowling face of the woman's companion and said hesitatingly:

"Well, I'll see. If I have time—maybe I will."

She smiled again and impulsively reached her hand to him, and as he took it he was nearly won by her friendliness. This she did not know, and he was able to go out into the street alone. He could not but observe that the attendants treated him with added respect by reason of his acquaintance with the wealthiest and most powerful woman in the camp. She had made his loneliness very keen and hard to bear.

As he walked down the street he thought of Mary—she seemed to be a sister to the distant, calm and glorious moon just launching into the sky above the serrate wall of snowy peaks to the East. There was a powerful appeal in the vivid and changeful woman he had just met, for her like had never touched his life before.

As he climbed back up the hill toward the corral where he had left his horse, he was filled with a wordless disgust of the town and its people. The night was still and cool, almost frosty. The air so clear and so rare filled his lungs with wholesomely sweet and reanimating breath. His head cleared, and his heart grew regular in its beating. The moon was sailing in mid-ocean, between the Great Divide and the Christo Range, cold and sharp of outline as a boat of silver. Lizard Head to the south loomed up ethereal as a cloud, so high it seemed to crash among the stars. The youth drew a deep breath and said: "To hell with the town."

Kintuck whinnied caressingly as he heard his master's voice. After putting some grain before the horse, Mose rolled himself in his blanket and went to sleep with only a passing thought of the princess, her luxurious home, and her radiant and inscrutable personality.

CHAPTER XVI

AGAIN ON THE ROUND-UP

It was good to hear again the bawling of the bulls and the shouts of the cowboys, and to see the swirling herd and the flying, guarding, checking horsemen. Mose, wearied, weather-beaten, and somber-visaged, looked down upon the scene with musing eyes. The action was quite like that on the Arickaree; the setting alone was different. Here the valley was a wide, deliciously green bowl, with knobby hills, pine-covered and abrupt, rising on all sides. Farther back great snow-covered peaks rose to enormous heights. In the center of this superb basin the camps were pitched, and the roping and branding went on like the action of a prodigious drama. The sun, setting in orange-colored clouds, brought out the velvet green of the sward with marvelous radiance. The tents gleamed in the midst of the valley like flakes of pearl.

The heart of the wanderer warmed within him, and with a feeling that he was almost home he called to his pack horse "Hy-ak-boy!" and started down the hill. As he drew near the herd he noted the great changes which had come over the cattle. They were now nearly all grades of Hereford or Holstein. They were larger of body, heavier of limb, and less active than the range cattle of the plains, but were sufficiently speedy to make handling them a fine art.

As he drew near the camp a musical shout arose, and Reynolds spurred his horse out to meet him. "It's Mose!" he shouted. "Boy, I'm glad to see ye, I certainly am. Shake hearty. Where ye from?"

"The Wind River."

"What have you been doing up there?"

"Oh, knocking around with some Shoshones on a hunting trip."

"Well, by mighty, I certainly am glad to see ye. You look thin as a spring steer."

"My looks don't deceive me then. My two sides are rubbin' together. How are the folks?"

"They ah very well, thank you. Cora and Pink will certainly go plumb crazy when they see you a-comin'."

"Where's your house?"

"Just over that divide—but slip your packs off. Old Kintuck looks well; I knew him when you topped the hill."

"Yes, he's still with me, and considerable of a horse yet."

They drew up to the door of one of the main tents and slipped the saddles from the weary horses.

"Do ye hobble?"

"No—they stay with me," said Mose, slapping Kintuck. "Go on, boy, here's grass worth while for ye."

"By mighty, Mose!" said Reynolds, looking at the trailer tenderly, "it certainly is good for sore eyes to see ye. I didn't know but you'd got mixed up an' done for in some of them squabbles. I heard the State authorities had gone out to round up that band of reds you was with."

"We did have one brush with the sheriff and some game wardens, but I stood him off while my friends made tracks for the reservation. The sheriff was for fight, but I argued him out of it. It looked like hot weather for a while."

While they were talking the cook set up a couple of precarious benches and laid a wide board thereon. Mose remarked it.

"A table! Seems to me that's a little hifalutin'."

"So it is, but times are changing."

"I reckon the range on the Arickaree is about wiped out."

"Yes. We had a couple of years with rain a-plenty, and that brought a boom in settlement; everything along the river was homesteaded, and so I retreated—the range was overstocked anyhow. This time I climbed high. I reckon I'm all right now while I live. They can't raise co'n in this high country, and not much of anything but grass. They won't bother us no mo'. It's a good cattle country, but a mighty tough range to ride, as you'll find. I thought I knew what rough riding was, but when it comes to racin' over these granite knobs, I'm jest a little too old. I'm getting heavy, too, you notice."

"*Grub-pile! All down for grub!*" yelled the cook, and the boys came trooping in. They were all strangers, but not strange to

Mose. They conformed to types he already knew. Some were young lads, and the word having passed around that "Black Mose" was in camp, they approached with awe. The man whose sinister fame had spread throughout three States was a very great personage to them.

"Did you come by way of Wagon Wheel?" inquired a tall youth whom the others called "Brindle Bill."

"Yes; camped there one night."

"Ain't it a caution to yaller snakes? Must be nigh onto fifteen thousand people there now. The hills is plumb measly with prospect holes, and you can't look at a rock f'r less'n a thousand dollars. It shore is the craziest town that ever went anywhere."

"Bill's got the fever," said another. "He just about wears hisself out a-pickin' up and a-totein' 'round likely lookin' rocks. Seems like he was lookin' fer gold mines 'stid o' cattle most of the time."

"You're just in time for the turnament, Mose."

"For the how-many?"

"The turnament and bullfight. Joe Grassie has been gettin' up a bullfight and a kind of a show. He 'lows to bring up some regular fighters from Mexico and have a real, sure-'nough bullfight. Then he's offered a prize of fifty dollars for the best roper, and fifty dollars for the best shooter."

"I didn't happen to hear of it, but I'm due to take that fifty; I need it," said Mose.

"He 'lows to have some races—pony races and broncho busting."

"When does it come off?" asked Mose with interest.

"On the fourth."

"I'll be there."

After supper was over Reynolds said: "Are you too tired to ride over to the ranch?"

"Oh, no! I'm all right now."

"Well, I'll just naturally throw the saddles on a couple of bronchos and we'll go see the folks."

Mose felt a warm glow around his heart as he trotted away beside Reynolds across the smooth sod. His affection for the Reynolds family was scarcely second to his boyish love for Mr. and Mrs. Burns.

It was dark before they came in sight of the light in the narrow valley of the Mink. "There's the camp," said Reynolds. "No, I didn't build it; it's an old ranch; in fact, I bought the whole outfit."

Mrs. Reynolds had not changed at all in the three years, but Cora had grown handsomer and seemed much less timid, though she blushed vividly as Mose shook her hand.

"I'm glad to see you back," she said.

Moved by an unusual emotion, Mose replied: "You haven't pined away any."

"Pined!" exclaimed her mother. "Well, I should say not. You should see her when Jim Haynes——"

"Mother!" called the girl sharply, and Pink, now a beautiful child of eight, came opportunely into the room and drew the conversation to herself.

As Mose, with Pink at his knee, sat watching the two women moving about the table, a half-formed resolution arose in his brain. He was weary of wandering, weary of loneliness. This comfortable, homely room, this tender little form in his arms, made an appeal to him which was as powerful as it was unexpected. He had lived so long in his blanket, with only Kintuck for company, that at this moment it seemed as if these were the best things to do—to stay with Reynolds, to make Cora happy, and to rest. He had seen all phases of wild life and had carried out his plans to see the wonders of America. He had crossed the Painted Desert and camped beside the Colorado in the greatest cañon in the world. He had watched the Mokis while they danced with live rattlesnakes held between their lips. He had explored the cliff-dwellings of the Navajo country and had looked upon the sea of peaks which tumbles away in measureless majesty from Uncompahgre's eagle-crested dome. He had peered into the boiling springs of the Yellowstone, and had lifted his eyes to the white Tetons whose feet are set in a mystic lake, around which the loons laugh all the summer long. He knew the chiefs of a dozen tribes and was a welcome guest among them. In his own mind he was no longer young—his youth was passing, perhaps the time had come to settle down.

Cora turned suddenly from the table, where she stood arranging the plates and knives and forks with a pleasant bustle, and said:

"O Mose! we've got two or three letters for you. We've had 'em ever so long—I don't suppose they will be of much good to you now. I'll get them for you."

"They look old," he said as he took them from her hand. "They look as if they'd been through the war." The first was from his father, the second from Jack, and the third in a woman's hand—could only be Mary's. He stared at it—almost afraid to open it in the presence of the family. He read the one from his father first, because he conceived it less important, and because he feared the other.

"MY DEAR SON: I am writing to you through Jack, although he does not feel sure we can reach you. I want to let you know of the death of Mrs. Excell. She died very suddenly of acute pneumonia. She was always careless of her footwear and went out in the snow to hang out some linen without her rubber shoes. We did everything that could be done but she only lived six days after the exposure. Life is very hard for me now. I write also to say that as I am now alone and in bad health I shall accept a call to Sweetwater Springs, Colorado, for two reasons. One is that my health may be regained, and for the reason, also, my dear son, that I may be nearer you. If this reaches you and you can come to see me I hope you will do so. I am lonely now and I long for you. The parish is small and the pay meager, but that will not matter if I can see you occasionally. Maud and her little family are well. I go to my new church in April.

"Your father,

"SAMUEL EXCELL".

For a moment this letter made Mose feel his father's loneliness, and had he not held in his hand two other and more important letters he would have replied with greater tenderness than ever before in his life.

"Well, Mose, set up," said Mrs. Reynolds; "letters'll keep."

He was distracted all through the meal in spite of the incessant questioning of his good friends. They were determined to uncover every act of his long years of wandering.

"Yes," he said, "I've been hungry and cold, but I always looked after my horse, and so, when I struck a cow country I could whirl in and earn some money. It don't take much to keep me when I'm on the trail."

"What's the good of seein' so much?" asked Mrs. Reynolds.

He smiled a slow, musing smile. "Oh, I don't know. The more you see the more you want to see. Just now I feel like taking a little rest."

Cora smiled at him. "I wish you would. You look like a starved cat—you ought'o let us feed you up for a while."

"Spoil me for the trail," he said, but his eyes conveyed a message of gratitude for her sympathy, and she flushed again.

After supper Mrs. Reynolds said: "Now if you want to read your letters by yourself, you can." She opened a door and he looked in.

"A bed! I haven't slept in a bed for two years."

"Well, it won't kill ye, not for one night, I reckon," she said.

He looked around the little room, at the dainty lace curtains tied with little bows of ribbon, at the pictures and lambrequins, and it filled his heart with a sudden stress of longing. It made him remember the pretty parlor in which Mary had received him four years before, and he opened her letter with a tremor in his hands. It was dated the Christmas day of the year of his visit; it was more than three years belated, but he read it as if it were written the day before, and it moved him quite as powerfully.

"MY DEAR FRIEND: The impulse to write to you has grown stronger day by day since you left. Your wonderful life and your words appealed to my imagination with such power that I have been unable to put them out of my mind. Without intending to do so you have filled me with a great desire to see the West which is able to make you forget your family and friends and calls you on long journeys. I have sung for you every Sunday as I promised to do. Your friend Jack called to see me last night and we had a long talk about you. He is to write you also and gave me your probable address. You said you were not a good writer but I wish you would let me know where you are and what you are doing, for I feel a deep interest in you, although I can not make myself believe that you are not the Harold Excell I saw in Rock River. In reality you are not he, any more than I am the little prig who sang those songs to save your soul! However, I was not so bad as I seemed even then, for I wanted you to admire my voice.

"I hope this Christmas day finds you in a warm and sheltered place. It would be a great comfort to me if I could know you were not cold and hungry. Jack brought me a beautiful present— a set of George Eliot. I ought not to have accepted it but he seemed so sure it would please me I had not the heart to refuse. I would send something to you only I can't feel sure of reaching you, and neither does Jack.

"It may be of interest to you to know that Mr. King the pastor, in whose church I sang, has resigned his pastorate to go abroad for a year. His successor is a man with a family—I don't see how he will manage to live on the salary. Mr. King had independent means and was a bachelor."

Right there the youth stopped. Something told him that he had reached the heart of the woman's message. King had resigned to go abroad. Why? The tone of the letter was studiedly cold. Why? There were a few more lines to say that Jack was coming in to eat Christmas dinner with her and that she would sing If I Were a Voice. He was not super-subtle and yet something in this letter made his throat fill and his head a little *dizzy*. If it did not mean that she had broken with King, then truth could not be conveyed in lines of black ink.

He tore open Jack's letter. It was short and to the point.

"DEAR HARRY: If you can get away come back to Marmion and see Mary again. She wants to see you *bad*. I don't know what has happened but I *think* she has given King his walking papers—and all on account of you. *I know it.* It can't be anybody else. She talked of you the entire evening. O man! but she was beautiful. She sang for me but her mind was away in the mountains. I could see that. It was her interest in you made her so nice to me. Now that's the God's truth. Come back and get her.

"Yours in haste,

Mose tingled with the sudden joy of it. Jack's letter, so unlike his usual calm, was convincing. He sprang up, a smile on his face, his eyes shining with happiness, his blood surging through his heart, and then he remembered the letters were three years old! The gray cloud settled down upon him—his limbs grew cold, and the light went out of his eyes.

Three years! While he was camping in the Grand Cañon with the lizards and skunks she was waiting to hear from him. While he sat in the shade of the walls of Walpi, surrounded by hungry dogs and pot-bellied children, she was singing for him and wondering whether her letter had ever reached him. Three years! A thousand things could happen in three years. She may have died!—a cold shudder touched him—she might tire of waiting and marry some one else—or she might have gone away to the East, that unknown and dangerous jungle of cities.

He sprang up again. "I will go to see her!" he said to himself. Then he remembered. His horse was worn, he had no money and no suitable clothing. Then he thought: "I will write." It did not occur to him to telegraph, for he had never done such a thing in his life.

He walked out into the sitting-room, his letters in his hands.

"How far do you call it to Wagon Wheel?"

"About thirty miles, and all up hill."

"Will you loan me one of your bronchos?"

"Certain sure, my boy."

"I want to ride up there and send a couple of letters."

"Better wait till morning," said Reynolds. "Your letters have waited three years—I reckon they'll keep over night."

"That's so," said Mose with a smile.

Sleep came to him swiftly, in spite of his letters, for he was very tired, but he found the room close and oppressive when he arose in the morning. The women were already preparing breakfast and Reynolds sat by the fire pulling on his boots.

As they were walking out to the barn Reynolds plucked him by the sleeve and said:

"I reckon I've lost my chance to kill Craig."

"Why?"

"A Mexican took the job off my hands." His face expressed a sort of gloomy dissatisfaction. Then without looking at Mose he went on: "That's one reason daughter looks so pert. She's free of that skunk's clutches now—and can hold up her head. She's free to marry a decent man."

Mose was silent. Mary's letter had thrust itself between his lips and Cora's shapely head, and all thought of marriage with her was gone.

As they galloped up to the camp the boys were at work finishing the last bunch of calves. The camp wagon was packed and ready to start across the divide, but the cook flourished a newspaper and came running up.

"Here you are, posted like a circus."

Mose took the paper, and on the front page read in big letters:

BLACK MOSE!
Mysterious as Ever.
The Celebrated Dead Shot.
Visits Wagon Wheel, and Swiftly Disappears.

"Damn 'em!" said Mose, "can't they let me alone? Seems like they can't rest till they crowd me into trouble."

CHAPTER XVII

MOSE RETURNS TO WAGON WHEEL

As Mose threw the rope over the bald-faced pinto the boys all chuckled and drew near, for they knew the character of the horse. Reynolds had said, "Take your pick o' the bunch," and Mose, with the eye of a horseman, had roped the pinto because of his size, depth of chest, and splendid limbs.

As he was leading his captive out of the bunch the cook said to Mose, "Better not take that pinto; he's mean as a hornet."

"Is his wind all right?"

"He's one o' the best horses on the range, all right, but he shore is mean all the way through. He always pitches at the start like he was fair crazy."

"Does he go when he gets through?" asked Mose of Reynolds.

"Yes, he's a good traveler."

"I don't want to be delayed, that's all. If he'll go, I'll stay by him."

The boys nudged elbows while Mose threw the saddle on the cringing brute and cinched it till the pinto, full of suffering, drew great, quiet gulps of breath and groaned. Swift, practiced, relentless, Mose dragged at the latigo till the wide hair web embedded itself in the pony's hide. Having coiled the rope neatly out of the way, while the broncho stood with drooping head but with a dull red flame in his eyes, Mose flung the rein over the pony's head. Then pinto woke up. With a mighty sidewise bound he attempted to leave his rider, but Mose, studiedly imperturbable, with left hand holding the reins and right hand grasping the pommel, went with him as if that were the ordinary way of mounting. Immense power was in the stiff-legged leaping of the beast. His body seemed a ball of coiled steel springs. His "watch-eye" rolled in frenzy. It seemed he wished to beat his head against his rider's face and kill him. He rushed away with a rearing, jerking motion, in a series of jarring bounds, snapping his rider like the lash of a whip, then stopped suddenly, poised on his fore feet, with devilish intent to discharge Mose over his head. With the spurs set deep into the quivering painted hide of his mount Mose began plying the quirt like a flail. The boys cheered and yelled with delight. It was one of their chief recreations, this battle with a pitching broncho.

Suddenly the desperate beast paused and, rearing recklessly high in the air, fell backward hoping to crush his rider under his saddle. In the instant, while he towered, poised in the air, Mose shook his right foot free of the stirrup and swung to the left and alighted on his feet, while the fallen horse, stunned by his own fall, lay for an instant, groaning and coughing. Under the sting of the quirt, he scrambled to his feet only to find his inexorable rider again on his back, with merciless spurs set deep in the quick of his quivering sides. With a despairing squeal he set off in a low, swift, sidewise gallop, and for nearly an hour drummed along the trail, up hill and down, the foam mingling with the yellow dust on his heaving flanks.

When the broncho's hot anger had cooled, Mose gave him his head, and fell to thinking upon the future. He had been more than eight years in the range and on the trail and all he owned in the world was a saddle, a gun, a rope, and a horse. The sight of Cora, the caressing of little Pink, and Mary's letter had roused in him a longing for a wife and a shanty of his own.

The grass was getting sere, there was new-fallen snow on Lizard Head, and winter was coming. He had the animal's instinct to den up, to seek winter quarters. Certain ties other than those of Mary's love combined to draw him back to Marmion for the winter. If he could only shake off his burdening notoriety and go back to see her—to ask her advice—perhaps she could aid him. But to *sneak* back again—to crawl about in dark corners—that was impossible.

He was no longer the frank and boyish lover of adventure. Life troubled him now, conduct was become less simple, actions each day less easily determined. These women now made him ponder. Cora, who was accustomed to the range and whose interests were his own in many ways, the princess, whose money and influence could get him something to do in Wagon Wheel, and Mary, whose very name made him shudder with remembered adoration—each one now made him think. Mary, of all the group, was most certainly unfitted to share his mode of life, and yet the thought of her made the others impossible to him.

The marshal saw him ride up the street and throw himself from his horse before the post office and hastened toward him with his hand extended. "Hello! Mose, I've got a telegram for you from Sweetwater."

Mose took it without a word and opened it. It was from his father: "Wait for me in Wagon Wheel. I am coming."

The marshal was grinning. "Did you see the write-up in yesterday's Mother Lode?"

"Yes—I saw it, and cussed you for it."

"I knowd you would, but I couldn't help it. Billy, the editor, got hold of me and pumped the whole story out of me before I knew it. I don't think it does you any harm."

"It didn't do me any good," replied Mose shortly.

"Say, the princess wants to see you. She's on the street somewhere now, looking for you."

"Where's the telegraph office?" he abruptly asked.

The telegram from his father had put the idea into his head to communicate in that way with Mary and Jack.

The marshal led the way to a stage office wherein stood a counter and a row of clicking machines.

"What is the cost of a telegram to Marmion, Iowa?" asked Mose.

"One dollar, ten words. Each ad——"

Mose thrust his hand into his pocket and pulled out all his money, a handful of small change. His face grew bitter, his last dollar was broken into bits.

"Make it night rates for sixty," said the operator. "Be delivered to-morrow morning."

"Go ahead," said Mose, and set to work to compose a message. The marshal, with unexpected delicacy, sauntered out into the street.

Now that he was actually face to face with the problem of answering Mary's letter in ten words the youth's hand refused to write, and he stood looking at the yellow slip of paper with an intensity that was comical to the clerk. Plainly this cowboy was not accustomed to telegraphing.

Mose felt the waiting presence of the clerk and said:

"Can I set down here and think it over?"

"Why sure, take a seat at that table over there."

Under the pressure of his emotion Mose wrote "Dear Mary" and stopped. The chap at the other end of the line would read that and comment on it. He struck that out. Then it occurred to him that if he signed it "Harry" *this* operator would marvel, and if he signed "Mose" the other end of the line would wonder. He rose, crushing the paper in his hand, and went out into the street. There was only one way—to write.

This he did standing at the ink-bespattered shelf which served as writing desk in the post office.

> "DEAR MARY: I have just received your letter. It's a little late but perhaps it ain't too late. Anyhow, I'm banking on this finding you just the same as when you wrote. I wish I could visit you again but I'm afraid I couldn't do it a second time without being recognized, but write to me at once, and, if you say come, I'll come. I am poorer than I was four years ago, but I've been on the trail, I know the mountains now. There's no other place for me, but I get lonesome sometimes when I think of you. I'm no good at writing letters—can't write as well as I could when I was twenty, so don't mind my short letter, but if I could see you! Write at once and I'll borrow or steal enough money to pay my way to you—I don't expect to ever see you out here in the West."

While still pondering over his letter he heard the rustle of a woman's dress and turned to face the princess, in magnificent attire, her gloved hand extended toward him, her face radiant with pleasure.

"Why, my dear boy, where have you been?"

Mose shook hands, his letter to Mary (still unsealed) in his left hand. "Been down on the range," he mumbled in profound embarrassment.

She assumed a girlish part. "But you *promised* to come and see me."

He turned away to seal his letter and she studied him with admiring eyes. He was so interesting in his boyish confusion— graceful in spite of his irrelevant movements, for he was as supple, as properly poised, and as sinewy as a panther.

"You're a great boy," she said to him when he came back. "I like you, I want to do something for you. Get into my carriage, and let me tell you of some plans."

He looked down at his faded woolen shirt and lifted his hand to his greasy sombrero. "Oh, no! I can't do that."

She laughed. "You ought to be able to stand it if I can. I'd be rather proud of having 'Black Mose' in my carriage."

"I guess not," he said. There was a cadence in these three words to which she bowed her head. She surrendered her notion quickly.

"Come down to the Palace with me."

"All right, I'll do that," he replied without interest.

"Meet me there in half an hour."

"All right."

"Good-by till then."

He did not reply but took her extended hand, while the young fellow in the postal cage grinned with profound appreciation. After the princess went out this clerk said, "Pard, you've struck it rich."

Mose turned and his eyebrows lowered dangerously. "Keep to your letter punchin', young feller, and you'll enjoy better health."

Those who happened to be standing in the room held their breath, for in that menacing, steady glare they recognized battle.

The clerk gasped and stammered, "I didn't mean anything."

"That's all right. You're lately from the East, or you wouldn't get gay with strangers in this country. See if there is any mail for Mose Harding—or Harry Excell."

"Sorry, sir—nothing for Mr. Harding, nothing for Mr. Excell."

Mose turned back to the desk and scrawled a short letter to Jack Burns asking him to let him know at once where Mary was, and whether it would be safe for him to visit her.

As he went out in the street to mount his horse the marshal met him again, and Mose, irritated and hungry, said sharply:

"See here, pardner, you act most cussedly like a man keeping watch on me."

The marshal hastened to say, "Nothing of the kind. I like you, that's all. I want to talk with you—in fact I'm under orders from the princess to help you get a job if you want one. I've got an offer now. The Express Company want you to act as guard between here and Cañon City. Pay is one hundred dollars a month, ammunition furnished."

Mose threw out his hand. "I'll do it—take it all back."

The marshal shook hands without resentment, considering the apology ample, and together they sauntered down the street.

"Now, pardner, let me tell you how I size up the princess. She's a good-hearted woman as ever lived, but she's a little off color with the women who run the church socials here. She's a rippin' good business woman, and her luck beats h—l. Why last week she bought a feller's claim in fer ten thousand dollars and yesterday they tapped a vein of eighty dollar ore, runnin' three feet wide. She don't haff to live here—she's worth a half million dollars—but she likes mining and she likes men. She knows how to handle 'em too—as you'll find out. She's hail-fellow with us all—but I tell ye she's got to like a feller all through before he sees the inside of her parlor. She's stuck on you. We're good friends—she come to call on my wife yesterday, and she talked about you pretty much the hull time. I never saw her worse bent up over a man. I believe she'd marry you, Mose, I do."

"Takes two for a bargain of that kind," said Mose.

The marshal turned. "But, my boy, that means making you a half owner of all she has—why that last mine may go to a million within six months."

"That's all right," Mose replied, feeling the intended good will of the older man. "But I expect to find or earn my own money. I can't marry a woman fifteen years older'n I am for her money. It ain't right and it ain't decent, and you'll oblige me by shutting up all such talk."

The sheriff humbly sighed. "She is a good deal older, that's a fact—but she's took care of herself. Still, as you say, it's none o' my business. If she can't persuade you, I can't. Come in, and I'll introduce you to the managers of the National——"

"Can't now, I will later."

"All right, so long! Come in any time."

Mose stepped into a barber shop to brush up a little, for he had acquired a higher estimate of the princess, and when he entered the dining room of the Palace he made a handsome figure. Whatever he wore acquired distinction from his beauty. His hat, no matter how stained, possessed charm. His dark shirt displayed the splendid shape of his shoulders, and his cartridge belt slanted across his hip at just the right angle.

The woman waiting for him smiled with an exultant glint in her half-concealed eyes.

"Sit there," she commanded, pointing at a chair. "Two beers," she said to the waiter.

Mose took the chair opposite and looked at her smilelessly. He waited for her to move.

"Ever been East—Chicago, Washington?"

"No."

"Want to go?"

"No."

She smiled again. "Know anything about mining?"

"Not a thing."

She looked at him with a musing, admiring glance. "I've got a big cattle ranch—will you superintend it for me?"

"Where is it?"

She laughed and stammered a little. "Well—I mean I've been thinking of buying one. I'm kind o' tired of these mining towns; I believe I'd like to live on a ranch, with you to superintend it."

His face darkened again, and she hastened to say, "The cattle business is going to boom again soon. They're all dropping out of it fast, but *now* is the time to get in and buy."

The beer came and interrupted her. "Here's to good luck," she said. They drank, and as she daintily touched her lips with her handkerchief she lifted her eyes to him again—strange eyes with lovely green and yellow and pink lights in them not unlike some semi-precious stones.

"You don't like me," she said. "Why won't you let me help you?"

"You want a square-toed answer?" he asked grimly, looking her steadily in the eyes.

She paled a little. "Yes."

"There is a girl in Iowa—I make it my business to work for her."

Her eyes fell and her right hand slowly turned the mug around and around. When she looked up she seemed older and her eyes were sadder. "That need make no difference."

"But it does," he said slowly. "It makes all the difference there is."

She became suddenly very humble. "You misunderstand me—I mean, I'll help you both. How do you expect to live?"

His eyes fell now. He flushed and shifted uneasily in his chair. "I don't know." Then he unbent a little in saying, "That's what's bothering me right now."

She pursued her advantage. "If you marry you've got to quit all this trail business."

"Dead sure thing! And that scares me too. I don't know how I'd stand being tied down to a stake."

She laid a hand on his arm. "Now see here, Mose, you let me help you. You know all about cattle and the trail, you can shoot and throw a rope, but you're a babe at lots of other things. You've got to get to work at something, settle right down, and dig up some dust. Now isn't that so?"

"I reckon that's the size of it."

It was singular how friendly she now seemed in his eyes. There was something so frank and gentle in her voice (though her eyes remained sinister) that he began almost to trust her.

"Well, now, I tell you what you can do. You take the job I got for you with the Express Company and I'll look around and corral something else for you."

He could not refuse to take her hand upon this compact. Then she said with an attempt to be careless, "Have you a picture of this girl? I'd like to see how she looks."

His face darkened again. "No," he said shortly, "I never had one of her."

She recognized his unwillingness to say more.

"Well, good-by, come and see me."

He parted from her with a sense of having been unnecessarily harsh with a woman who wished to be his good friend.

He was hungry and that made him think of his horse which he returned to at once. After watering and feeding his tired beast he turned in at a coffeehouse and bought a lunch—not being able to afford a meal. Everywhere he went men pointed a timid or admiring thumb at him. They were unobtrusive about it, but it annoyed him at the moment. His mind was too entirely filled with perplexities to welcome strangers' greetings. "I *must* earn some money," was the thought which brought with it each time the offer of the Express Company. He determined each time to take it although it involved riding the same trail over and over again, which made him shudder to think of. But it was three times the pay of a cowboy and a single month of it would enable him to make his trip to the East.

After his luncheon he turned in at the office and sullenly accepted the job. "You're just the man we need," said the manager. "We've had two or three hold-ups here, but with you on the seat I shall feel entirely at ease. Marshal Haney has recommended you—and I know your record as a daring man. Can you go out to-morrow morning?"

"Quicker the better."

"I'd like to have you sleep here in the office. I'll see that you have a good bed."

"Anywhere."

After Mose went out the manager winked at the marshal and said:

"It's a good thing to have him retained on our side. He'd make a bad man on the hold-up side."

"Sure thing!" replied Haney.

While loitering on a street corner still busy with his problems Mose saw a tall man on a fine black horse coming down the street. The rider slouched in his saddle like a tired man but with the grace of a true horseman. On his bushy head sat a wide soft hat creased in the middle. His suit was brown corduroy.

Mose thought, "If that bushy head was not so white I should say it was father's. It *is* father!"

He let him pass, staring in astonishment at the transformation in the minister. "Well, well! the old man has woke up. He looks the real thing, sure."

A drum struck up suddenly and the broncho (never too tired to shy) gave a frenzied leap. The rider went with him, reins in hand, heels set well in, knees grasping the saddle.

Mose smiled with genuine pleasure. "I didn't know he could ride like that," and he turned to follow with a genuine interest.

He came up to Mr. Excell just as the marshal stepped out of the crowd and accosted him. For the first time in his life Mose was moved to joke his father.

"Marshal, that man is a dangerous character. I know him; put him out."

The father turned and a smile lit his darkly tanned face. "Harry——"

Mose made a swift sign, "Old man, how are ye?" The minister's manner pleased his son. He grasped his father's hand with a

- 164 -

heartiness that checked speech for the moment, then he said, "I was looking for you. Where you from?"

"I've got a summer camp between here and the Springs. I saw the notice of you in yesterday's paper. I've been watching the newspapers for a long time, hoping to get some word of you. I seized the first chance and came on."

Mose turned. "Marshal, I'll vouch for this man; he's an old neighbor of mine."

Mr. Excell slipped to the ground and Mose took the rein on his arm. "Come, let's put the horse with mine." They walked away, elbow to elbow. A wonderful change had swept over Mr. Excell. He was brown, alert, and vigorous—but more than all, his eyes were keen and cheerful and his smile ready and manly.

"You're looking well," said the son.

"I *am well*. Since I struck the high altitudes I'm a new man. I don't wonder you love this life."

"Are you preaching?"

"Yes, I speak once a week in the Springs. I ride down the trail from my cabin and back again the same day. The fact is I stayed in Rock River till I was nearly broken. I lost my health, and became morbid, trying to preach to the needs of the old men and women of my congregation. Now I am free. I am back to the wild country. Of course, so long as my wife lived I couldn't break away, but now I have no one but myself and my needs are small. I am happier than I have been for years."

As they walked and talked together the two men approached an understanding. Mr. Excell felt sure of his son's interest, for the first time in many years, and avoided all terms of affection. In his return to the more primitive, bolder life he unconsciously left behind him all the "soft phrases" which had disgusted his son. He struck the right note almost without knowing it, and the son, precisely as he perceived in his father a return to rugged manliness, opened his hand to him.

Together they took care of the horse, together they walked the streets. They sat at supper together and the father's joy was very great when at night they camped together and Mose so far unbent as to tell of his adventures. He did not confide his feeling for

Mary—his love was far too deep for that. A strange woman had reached it by craft, a father's affection failed of it.

CHAPTER XVIII

THE EAGLE GUARDS THE SHEEP

Mose did not enter upon his duties as guard with joy. It seemed like small business and not exactly creditable employment for a trailer and cow puncher. It was in his judgment a foolish expenditure of money; but as there was nothing better to do and his need of funds was imperative, he accepted it.

The papers made a great deal of it, complimenting the company upon its shrewdness, and freely predicted that no more hold-ups would take place along that route. Mose rode out of town on the seat with the driver, a Winchester between his knees and a belt of cartridges for both rifle and revolvers showing beneath his coat. He left the stable each morning at four A. M. and rode to the halfway house, where he slept over night, returning the following day. From the halfway house to the Springs there were settlers and less danger.

He was conscious of being an object of curious inquiry. Meeting stage coaches was equivalent to being fired at by fifty pistols. Low words echoed from lip to lip: "Black Mose," "bad man," "graveyard of his own," "good fellow when sober," etc. Sometimes, irritated and reckless, he lived up to his sinister reputation, and when some Eastern gentleman in brown corduroy timidly approached to say, "Fine weather," Mose turned upon him a baleful glare under which the questioner shriveled, to the delight of the driver, who vastly admired the new guard.

At times he was unnecessarily savage. Well-meaning men who knew nothing about him, except that he was a guard, were rebuffed in quite the same way. He was indeed becoming self-conscious, as if on exhibition, somehow—and this feeling deepened as the days passed, for nothing happened. No lurking forms showed in the shadow of the pines. No voice called "Halt!" It became more and more like a stage play.

He was much disturbed by Jack's letter which was waiting for him one night when he returned to Wagon Wheel.

"DEAR HARRY: I went up to see Mary a few weeks ago and found she had gone to Chicago. Her father died over a year ago and she decided soon after to go to the city and go on with her music.

She's in some conservatory there. I don't know which one. I tried hard to keep her on my own account but she wouldn't listen to me. Well, yes, she listened but she shook her head. She dropped King soon after your visit—whether you had anything to do with that or not I don't know—I think you did, but as you didn't write she gave you up as a bad job. She always used to talk of you and wonder where you were, and every time I called she used to sing If I Were a Voice. She never *said* she was singing it for you, but there were tears in her eyes—and in mine, too, old man. You oughtn't to be throwing yourself away in that wild, God-forsaken country. We discussed you most of the time. Once in a while she'd see a little note in the paper about you, and cut it out and send it to me. I did the same. We heard of you at Flagstaff, Arizona. Then that row you had with the Mormons was the next we knew, but we couldn't write. She said it was pretty tough to hear of you only in some scrape, but I told her your side hadn't been heard from and that gave her a lot of comfort. The set-to you had about the Indians' right to hunt pleased us both. That was a straight case. She said it was like a knight of the olden time.

"She was uneasy about you, and once she said, 'I wish I could reach him. That rough life terrifies me. He's in constant danger.' I think she was afraid you'd take to drinking, and I own up, old man, that worries *me*. If you only had somebody to look after you—somebody to work for—like I have. I'm going to be married in September. You know her—only she was a little girl when you lived here. Her name is Lily Blanchard.

"I wish I could help you about Mary. I'm going to write to one or two parties who may know her address. If she's in Chicago you could visit her without any trouble. They wouldn't get on to you there at all. If you go, be sure and come this way. Your father went to Denver from here—have you heard from him?"

There was deep commotion in the trailer's brain that night. The hope he had was too sacredly sweet to put into words—the hope that she still thought of him and longed for him. If Jack were right, then she had waited and watched for him through all those years of wandering, while he, bitter and unrelenting, and believing that she was King's wife, had refused to listen for her voice on Sunday evenings. If she had kept her promise, then on the trail, in cañons dark and deathly still, on the moonlit sand of the Painted Desert, on the high divides of the Needle Range, her thought had been winged toward him in song—and he had not listened.

His thought turned now, for the first time, toward the great city, which was to him a savage jungle of unknown things, a web of wire, a maze of streets, a swirling flood of human beings, of interest now merely and solely because Mary had gone to live therein. "I'm due to make another trip East," he said to himself with a grim straightening of the lips.

It was mighty serious business. To take Kintuck and hit the trail for the Kalispels over a thousand miles of mountain and plain, was simple, but to thrust himself amid the mad rush of a great city made his bold heart quail. Money was a minor consideration in the hills, but in the city it was a matter of life and death. Money he must now have, and as he could not borrow or steal it, it must be earned. In a month his wages would amount to one hundred dollars, but that was too slow. He saw no other way, however, so set his teeth and prepared to go on with the "fool business" of guarding the treasure wagon of the Express Company.

His mind reverted often to the cowboy tournament which was about to come off, after hanging fire for a month, during which Grassi wrestled with the problem of how to hold a bullfight in opposition to the laws of the State. "If I could whirl in and catch one of those purses," thought Mose, "I could leave at the end of August. If I don't I must hang on till the first of October."

He determined to enter for the roping contest and for the cowboy race and the revolver practice. Marshal Haney was delighted. "I'll attend to the business, but the entrance fees will be about twenty dollars."

This staggered Mose. It meant an expenditure of nearly one fourth his month's pay in entrance fees, not to speak of the expense of keeping Kintuck, for the old horse had to go into training and be grain-fed as well. However, he was too confident of winning to hesitate. He drew on his wages, and took a day off to fetch Kintuck, whom he found fat and hearty and very dirty.

The boys at the Reynolds ranch were willing to bet on Mose, and every soul determined to be there. Cora said quietly: "I know you'll win."

"Well, I don't expect to sweep the board, but I'll get a lunch while the rest are getting a full meal," he replied, and returned to his duties.

The weather did not change for the tournament. Each morning the sun arose flashing with white, undimmed fire. At ten o'clock great dazzling white clouds developed from hidden places behind huge peaks, and as they expanded each let fall a veil of shimmering white storms that were hail on the heights and sleet on the paths in the valleys. These clouds passed swiftly, the sun came out, the dandelions shone vividly through their coverlet of snow, the eaves dripped, the air was like March, and the sunsets like November.

Naturally, Sunday was the day fixed upon for the tournament, and early on that day miners in clean check shirts and bright new blue overalls began to stream away up the road which led to the race track, some two miles away, on the only level ground for a hundred miles. Swift horses hitched to light open buggies whirled along, loaded down with men. Horsemen galloped down the slopes in squadrons—and such horsemen!—cowboys from "Lost Park" and "the Animas." Prospectors like Casey and Kelly who were quite as much at home on a horse as with a pick in a ditch, and men like Marshal Haney and Grassi, who were all-round plainsmen, and by that same token born horsemen. Haney and Kelly rode with Reynolds and Mose, while Cora and Mrs. Reynolds followed in a rusty buggy drawn by a fleabitten gray cow pony, sedate with age.

Kintuck was as alert as a four-year-old. His rest had filled him to bursting with ambition to do and to serve. His muscles played under his shining skin like those of a trained athlete. Obedient to the lightest touch or word of his master, with ears in restless motion, he curvetted like a racer under the wire.

"Wouldn't know that horse was twelve years old, would you, gentlemen?" said Reynolds. "Well, so he is, and he has covered fifteen thousand miles o' trail."

Mose was at his best. With vivid tie flowing from the collar of his blue shirt, with a new hat properly crushed in on the crown in four places, with shining revolver at his hip, and his rope coiled at his right knee, he sat his splendid horse, haughty and impassive of countenance, responding to the greetings of the crowd only with a slight nod or a wave of the hand.

It seemed to him that the population of the whole State—at least its men—was assembled within the big stockade. There were a few women—just enough to add decorum to the crowd. They were for the most part the wives or sisters or sweethearts of those who were to contest for prizes, but as Mose rode around the course he passed "the princess" sitting in her shining barouche and waving a handkerchief. He pretended not to see her, though it gave him pleasure to think that the most brilliantly-dressed woman on the grounds took such interest in him. Another man would have ridden up to her carriage, but Mose kept on steadily to the judge's stand, where he found a group of cowboys discussing the programme with Haney, the marshal of the day.

Mose already knew his dangerous rival—a powerful and handsome fellow called Denver Dan, whose face was not unlike his own. His nose was straight and strong, his chin finely modeled, and his head graceful, but he was heavier, and a persistent flush on his nose and in his eyelids betrayed the effects of liquor. His hands were small and graceful and he wore his hat with a certain attractive insolence, but his mouth was cruel and his eyes menacing. When in liquor he was known to be ferocious. He was mounted on a superbly pointed grade broncho, and all his hangings were of costly Mexican workmanship and betrayed use.

"The first thing is a 'packing contest,'" read Haney.

"Oh, to h——l with that, I'm no packer," growled Dan.

"I try that," said Mose; "I let nothing get away to-day."

"Entrance fee one dollar."

"Here you are." Mose tossed a dollar.

"Then 'roping and holding contest.'"

"Now you're talking my business," exclaimed Dan.

"There are others," said Mose.

Dan turned a contemptuous look on the speaker—but changed his expression as he met Mose's eyes.

"Howdy, Mose?"

"So's to sit a horse," Mose replied in a tone which cut. He was not used to being patronized by men of Dan's set.

The crowd perceived the growing rivalry between the two men and winked joyously at each other.

At last all was arranged. The spectators were assembled on the rude seats. The wind, sweet, clear, and cool, came over the smooth grassy slopes to the west, while to the east, gorgeous as sunlit marble, rose the great snowy peaks with huge cumulus clouds—apparently standing on edge—peeping over their shoulders from behind. Mose observed them and mentally calculated that it would not shower till three in the afternoon.

In the track before the judge's stand six piles of "truck," each pile precisely like the others, lay in a row. Each consisted of a sack of flour, a bundle of bacon, a bag of beans, a box, a camp stove, a pick, a shovel, and a tent. These were to be packed, covered with a mantle, and caught by "the diamond hitch."

Mose laid aside hat and coat, and as the six pack horses approached, seized the one intended for him. Catching the saddle blanket up by the corners, he shook it straight, folded it once, twice—and threw it to the horse. The sawbuck followed it, the cinch flying high so that it should go clear. A tug, a grunt from the horse, and the saddle was on. Unwinding the sling ropes, he made his loops, and end-packed the box. Against it he put both flour and beans. Folding the tent square he laid it between. On this he set the stove, and packing the smaller bags around it, threw on the mantle. As he laid the hitch and began to go around the pack, the crowd began to cheer:

"Go it, Mose!"

"He's been there before."

"Well, I guess," said another.

Mose set his foot to the pack and "pinched" the hitch in front. Nothing remained now but the pick, shovel, and coffee can. The tools he crowded under the ropes on either side, tied the cans under the pack at the back and called Kintuck, "Come on, boy." The old horse with shining eyes drew near. Catching his mane, Mose swung to the saddle, Kintuck nipped the laden cayuse, and they were off while the next best man was still worrying over the hitch.

"Nine dollars to the good on that transaction," muttered Mose, as the marshal handed him a ten dollar gold piece.

"The next exercise on the programme," announced Haney, "will be the roping contest. The crowd will please be as quiet as possible while this is going on. Bring on your cows."

Down the track in a cloud of dust came a bunch of cattle of all shapes and sizes. They came snuffing and bawling, urged on by a band of cowboys, while a cordon of older men down the track stopped and held them before the judge's stand.

"First exercise—'rope and hold,'" called the marshal. "Denver Dan comes first."

Dan spurred into the arena, his rope swinging gracefully in his supple up-raised wrist.

"Which one you want?" he asked.

"The line-back yearling," called Haney.

With careless cast Dan picked up both hind feet of the calf—his horse set his hoofs and held the bawling brute.

"All right," called the judge. The rope was slackened and the calf leaped up. Dan then successively picked up any foot designated by the marshal. "Left hind foot! Right fore foot!" and so on with almost unerring accuracy. His horse, calm and swift, obeyed every word and every shift of his rider's body. The crowd cheered, and those who came after added nothing to the contest.

Mose rode into the inclosure with impassive face. He could only duplicate the deeds of those who had gone before so long as his work was governed by the marshal—but when, as in the case of others, he was free to "put on frills," he did so. Tackling the heaviest and wildest steer, he dropped his rope over one horn and caught up one foot, then taking a loose turn about his pommel he spoke to Kintuck. The steer reached the end of the rope with terrible force. It seemed as if the saddle must give way—but the strain was cunningly met, and the brute tumbled and laid flat with a wild bawl. While Kintuck held him Mose took a cigar from his pocket, bit the end off, struck a match and puffed carelessly and lazily. It was an old trick, but well done, and the spectators cheered heartily.

After a few casts of almost equal brilliancy, Mose leaped to the ground with the rope in his hand, and while Kintuck looked on curiously, he began a series of movements which one of Delmar's Mexicans had taught him. With the noose spread wide he kept it whirling in the air as if it were a hoop. He threw it into the air and sprang through it, he lowered it to the ground, and leaping into it, flung it far above his head. In his hand this inert thing developed snakelike action. It took on loops and scallops and retained them, apparently in defiance of all known laws of physics—controlled and governed by the easy, almost imperceptible motions of his steel-like wrist.

"Forty-five dollars more to the good," said Mose grimly as the decision came in his favor.

"See here—going to take all the prizes?" asked one of the judges.

"So long as you keep to my line of business," replied he.

The races came next. Kintuck took first money on the straightaway dash, but lost on the long race around the pole. It nearly broke his heart, but he came in second to Denver Dan's sorrel twice in succession.

Mose patted the old horse and said: "Never mind, old boy, you pulled in forty dollars more for me."

Reynolds had tears in his eyes as he came up.

"The old hoss cain't compete on the long stretches. He's like a middle-aged man—all right for a short dash—but the youngsters have the best wind—they get him on the mile course."

In the trained pony contest the old horse redeemed himself. He knelt at command, laid out flat while Mose crouched behind, and at the word "Up!" sprang to his feet and waited—then with his master clinging to his mane he ran in a circle or turned to right or left at signal. All the tricks which the cavalry had taught their horses, Mose, in years on the trail, had taught Kintuck. He galloped on three legs and waltzed like a circus horse. He seemed to know exactly what his master said to him.

A man with a big red beard came up to Mose as he rode off the track and said:

"What'll you take for that horse?"

Mose gave him a savage glance. "He ain't for sale."

The broncho-busting contest Mose declined.

"How's that?" inquired Haney, who hated to see his favorite "gig back" at a point where his courage could be tested.

"I've busted all the bronchos for fun I'm going to," Mose replied.

Dan called in a sneering tone: "Bring on your varmints. I'm not dodgin' mean cayuses to-day."

Mose could not explain that for Mary's sake he was avoiding all danger. There was risk in the contest and he knew it, and he couldn't afford to take it.

"That's all right!" he sullenly replied. "I'll be with you later in the game."

A wall-eyed roan pony, looking dull and stupid, was led before the stand. Saddled and bridled he stood dozing while the crowd hooted with derision.

"Don't make no mistake!" shouted Haney; "he's the meanest critter on the upper fork."

A young lad named Jimmy Kincaid first tackled the job, and as he ran alongside and tried the cinch, the roan dropped an ear back— the ear toward Jimmy, and the knowing ones giggled with glee. "He's wakin' up! Look out, Jim!"

The lad gathered the reins in his left hand, seized the pommel with his right, and then the roan disclosed his true nature. He was an old rebel. He did not waste his energies on common means. He plunged at once into the most complicated, furious, and effective bucking he could devise, almost without moving out of his tracks—and when the boy, stunned and bleeding at the nose, sprawled in the dust, the roan moved away a few steps and dozed, panting and tense, apparently neither angry nor frightened.

One of the Reynolds gang tried him next and "stayed with him" till he threw himself. When he arose the rider failed to secure his stirrups and was thrown after having sat the beast superbly. The miners were warming to the old roan. Many of them had never seen a pitching broncho before, and their delight led to loud whoops and jovial outcries.

"Bully boy, roan! Shake 'em off!"

Denver Dan tried him next and sat him, haughtily contemptuous, till he stopped, quivering with fatigue and reeking with sweat.

"Oh, well!" yelled a big miner, "that ain't a fair shake for the pony; you should have took him when he was fresh." And the crowd sustained him in it.

"Here comes one that is fresh," called the marshal, and into the arena came a wicked-eyed, superbly-fashioned black roan horse, plainly wild and unbroken, led by two cowboys, one on either side.

Joe Grassi shook a handfull of bills down at the crowd. "Here's a hundred dollars to the man who'll set that pony three minutes by the watch."

"This is no place to tackle such a brute as that," said Reynolds.

Mose was looking straight ahead with a musing look in his eyes.

Denver Dan walked out. "I need that hundred dollars; nail it to a post for a few minutes, will ye?"

This was no tricky old cow pony, but a natively vicious, powerful, and cunning young horse. While the cowboys held him Dan threw off his coat and hat and bound a bandanna over the bronchos's head and pulled it down over his eyes. Laying the saddle on swiftly, but gently, he cinched it strongly. With determined and vigorous movement, he thrust the bit into his mouth.

"Slack away!" he called to the ropers. The horse, nearly dead for lack of breath, drew a deep sigh.

Haney called out: "Stand clear, everybody, clear the road!"

And casting one rope to the ground, Dan swung into the saddle.

For just an instant the horse crouched low and waited—then shot into the air with a tigerish bound and fell stiff-legged. Again and again he flung his head down, humped his back, and sprang into the air grunting and squealing with rage and fear. Dan sat him, but the punishment made him swear. Suddenly the horse dropped and rolled, hoping to catch his rider unawares. Dan escaped by stepping to the ground, but he was white, and the blood was oozing slowly from his nose. As the brute arose, Dan was in the saddle. With two or three tremendous bounds, the horse flung himself into the air like a high-vaulting acrobat, landing so near the fence that Dan, swerving far to the left, was unseated, and sprawled low in the dust while the squealing broncho went down the track bucking and lashing out with undiminished vigor.

Dan staggered to his feet, stunned and bleeding. He swore most terrible oaths that he would ride that wall-eyed brute if it took a year.

"You've had your turn. It was a fair fight," called Kelly.

"Who's the next ambitious man?" shouted Haney.

"I don't want no truck with that," said the cowboys among themselves.

"Not in a place like this," said Jimmy. "A feller's liable to get mashed agin a fence."

Mose stood with hands gripping a post, his eyes thoughtful. Suddenly he threw off his coat.

"I'll try him," he said.

"Oh, I don't think you'd better; it'll bung you all up," cautioned Reynolds.

Mose said in a low voice: "I'm good for him, and I need that money."

"Let him breathe awhile," called the crowd as the broncho was brought back, lariated as before. "Give him a show for his life."

Mose muttered to Reynolds: "He's due to bolt, and I'm going to quirt him a-plenty."

The spectators, tense with joy, filled the air with advice and warning. "Don't let him get started. Keep him away from the fence."

Mose wore a set and serious look as he approached the frenzied beast. There was danger in this trick—a broken leg or collar bone might make his foolhardiness costly. In his mind's eye he could foresee the broncho's action. He had escaped down the track once, and would do the same again after a few desperate bounds—nevertheless Mose dreaded the terrible concussion of those stiff-legged leapings.

Standing beside the animal's shoulder he slipped off the ropes and swung to the saddle. The beast went off as before, with three or four terrible buck jumps, but Mose plied the quirt with wild shouting, and suddenly, abandoning his pitching, the horse set off at a tearing pace around the track. For nearly half way he ran steadily—then began once more to hump his back and leap into the air.

"He's down!" yelled some one.

"No, he's up again—and Mose is there," said Haney.

The crowd, not to be cheated of their fun, raced across the oval where the battle was still going on.

The princess was white with anxiety and ordered her coachman to "Get there quick as God'll let ye." When she came in sight the horse was tearing at Mose's foot with his teeth.

"Time's up!" called Haney.

"Make it ten," said Mose, whose blood was hot.

The beast dropped and rolled, but arose again under the sting of the quirt and renewed his frenzied attack. As Mose roweled him he kicked with both hind feet as if to tear the cinch from his belly. He reared on his toes and fell backward. He rushed with ferocious cunning against the corral, forcing his rider to stand in the opposite stirrup, then bucked, keeping so close to the fence that Mose was forced to hang to his mane and fight him from tearing his flesh with his savage teeth. Twice he went down and rolled over, but when he arose Mose was on his back. Twice he flung himself to the earth, and the second time he broke the bridle rein, but Mose, catching one piece, kept his head up while he roweled him till the blood dripped in the dust.

At last, after fifteen minutes of struggle, the broncho again made off around the track at a rapid run. As he came opposite the judge's stand Mose swung him around in a circle and leaped to the ground, leaving the horse to gallop down the track. Dusty, and quivering with fatigue, Mose walked across the track and took up his coat.

"You earned your money, Mose," said Grassi, as he handed out the roll of bills.

"I'll think so to-morrow morning, I reckon," replied Mose, and his walk showed dizziness and weakness.

"You've had the easy end of it," said Dan. "You should have took him when I did, when he was fresh."

"You didn't stay on him long enough to weaken him any," said Mose in offensive reply, and Dan did not care to push the controversy any further.

"That spoils my shooting now," Mose said to Haney. "I couldn't hit the side of a mule."

"Oh, you'll stiddy up after dinner."

"Good boy!" called the crisp voice of Mrs. Raimon. "Come here, I want to talk with you."

He could not decently refuse to go to the side of her carriage. She had with her a plain woman, slightly younger than herself, who passed for her niece. The two men who came with them were in the judge's stand.

Leaning over, she spoke with sudden intensity. "My God! you mustn't take such risks—I'm all of a quiver. You're too good a man to be killed by a miserable bucking broncho. Don't do it again, for my sake—if that don't count, for *her* sake." And he in sudden joy and confidence replied: "That's just why I did it; for her sake."

Her eyes set in sudden alarm. "What do you mean?"

"You'll know in a day or two. I'm going to quit my job."

"I know," she said with a quick indrawn breath, "you're going away. Who's that girl I saw you talking with to-day? Is that the one?"

He laughed at her for the first time. "Not by a thousand miles."

"What do you mean by that? Does she live in Chicago?"

He ceased to laugh and grew a little darker of brow, and she quietly added: "That's none o' my business, you'd like to say. All right—say it isn't. But won't you get in and go down to dinner with me? I want to honor the champion—the Ivanhoe of the tournament."

He shook his head. "No, I've promised to picnic with some old friends of mine."

"That girl over there?"

"Yes."

"Well, just as you say, but you must eat with me to-night, will you? Come now, what do you say?"

With a half promise Mose walked away toward the Reynolds' carriage—not without regret, for there was charm in the princess, both in her own handsome person and because she suggested a singular world of which he knew nothing. She allured and repelled at the same time.

Beside the buggy Cora and Mrs. Reynolds had spread a substantial lunch, and in such humble company the victor of the tournament ate his dinner, while Dan and the rest galloped off to a saloon.

"I don't know what I can do with the gun," he said in reply to a question from Cora. "My nerves are still on the jump; I guess I'll keep out of the contest—it would hurt my reputation to miss." He turned to Reynolds: "Capt'n, I want you to get me a chance to punch cattle on a car down to Chicago."

Reynolds looked surprised. "What fur do you want to go to Chicago, Mose? I never have knew you to mention hit befo'."

Mose felt his skin growing red. "Well, I just thought I'd like to take a turn in the States and see the elephant."

"You'll see the hull circus if you go to Chicago," said Mrs. Reynolds. "They say it's a terrible wicked place."

"I don't suppose it's any worse than Wagon Wheel, ma," said Cora.

"Yes, but it's so much bigger."

"Well, mother," said Reynolds, "a bear is bigger than a ho'net, but the ho'net can give him points and beat him, suah thing."

Mose was rather glad of this diversion, for when Reynolds spoke again it was to say: "I reckon I can fix it for you. When do you want it?"

"Right off, this week."

"Be gone long?"

Cora waited anxiously for his answer, and his hesitation and uncertainty of tone made her heart grow heavy.

"Oh, no—only a short trip, I reckon. Got to get back before my money gives out."

He did not intend to enter the revolver contest, but it offered so easy to his hand that he went in and won hands down. His arm was lame, but his nerves, not fevered by whisky, swiftly recovered tone. He was careful, however, not to go beyond the limits of the contest as he should have done had his arm possessed all of its proper cunning. He had no real competitor but Dan, who had been drinking steadily all day and was unfitted for his work. Mose lost nothing in the trial.

That night he put into his pocket one hundred and twenty dollars as the result of his day's work, and immediately asked to be released of his duties as guard.

The manager of the Express Company said: "I'm sorry you're leaving us, and I hope you'll return to us soon. I'll hold the place open for you, if you say so."

This Mose refused. "I don't like it," he said. "I don't think I earn the money. Hire a good driver and he'll have no trouble. You don't need me."

Mindful of his promise to eat dinner with the princess, he said to Reynolds: "Don't wait for me. Go on—I'll overtake you at Twelve Mile Creek."

The princess had not lost sight of him for a single moment, and the instant he departed from his friends she drove up. "You are to come to my house to-night, remember."

"I must overtake my folks; I can't stay long," he said lamely.

Her power was augmented by her home. He had expected pictures and fine carpets and a piano and they were there, but there was a great deal more. He perceived a richness of effect which he could not have formulated better than to say, "It was all *fine*." He had expected things to be costly and gay of color, but this mysterious fitness of everything was a marvel to one like himself, used only to the meager ornaments of the homes in Rock River, or the threadbare poverty of the ranches and the squalid hotels of the cow country. The house was a large new frame building, not so much different from other houses with respect to exterior, but as he entered the door he took off his hat to it as he used to do as a lad in the home of Banker Brooks, deacon in his father's church.

His was a sensitive soul, eye and ear were both acute. He perceived, without accounting for it, that the walls and hangings were complementary in color, that the furniture matched the carpet, and that the pictures on the wall were unusually good. They were not all highly-colored, naked subjects, as he had been led to expect. His respect for Mrs. Raimon rose, for he remembered that Mary's home, while just as different from this as Mary was different from Mrs. Raimon, had, after all, something in common—both were beautiful to him, though Mary's home was sweeter, daintier, and homelier. He was in the midst of an analysis of these subtleties when Mrs. Raimon (as he now determined to call her) returned from changing her dress.

He was amazed at the change in her. She wore a dark gray gown with almost no ornament, and looked smaller, older, and paler, but incomparably more winning and womanly than she had ever seemed before. She appeared to be serious and her voice was gentle and winning.

"Well, boy, here you are—under my roof. Not such an awful den after all, is it?" she said with a smile.

"Beats a holler log in a snowstorm," he replied, looking about the room. "Must have shipped all this truck from the States, it never was built out here—it would take me a couple of months to earn a whole outfit like this, wouldn't it?"

She remained serious. "Mose, I want to tell you——"

"Wait a minute," he interrupted; "let's start fair. My name is Harold Excell, and I'm going to call you Mrs. Raimon."

She thrust out her hand. "Good boy!" He could see she was profoundly pleased. Indeed she could not at once resume. At last she said: "I was going to say, Harold, that you can't earn a home trailin' around over these mountains year after year with a band of Indians."

He became thoughtful. "I reckon you're right about that. I'm wasting time; I've got to picket old Kintuck somewhere and go to work if I——"

He stopped abruptly and she smiled mournfully. "You needn't hesitate; tell me all about it."

He sat in silence—a silence that at last became a rebuke. She arose. "Well, suppose we go out to supper; we can talk all the better there."

He felt out of place and self-conscious, but he gave little outward sign of it as he took his seat at the table opposite her. For reasons of her own she emphasized the domestic side of her life and fairly awed the stern youth by her womanly dignity and grace. The little table was set for two, with pretty dishes. Liquor had no place on the cover, but a shining tea-pot, brought in by a smiling negress, was placed at her right hand. Her talk for a time was of the tea, the food, his taste as to sugar and other things pertaining to her duties as hostess. All his lurid imaginings of her faded into the wind, and a thousand new and old conceptions of wife and home and peaceful middle age came thronging like sober-colored birds. If she were playing a game it was well done and successful. Mose fell often into silence and deep thought.

She respected his introspection, and busying herself with the service and with low-voiced orders to the waitress, left him free for a time.

Suddenly she turned. "You mustn't judge me by what people say outside. Judge me by what I am to you. I don't claim to be a Sunday-school teacher, but I average up pretty well, after all. I appear to a disadvantage. When Raimon died I took hold of his business out here and I've made it pay. I have a talent for business, and I like it. I've got enough to be silly with if I want to, but I intend to take care of myself—and I may even marry again. I can see you're deeply involved in a love affair, Mose, and I honestly want to help you—but I shan't say another word about it—only remember, when you need help you come to Martha Jane Williams Raimon. How is that for a name? It's mine; my father was Lawrence Todd Williams, Professor of Paleontology at Blank College. Raimon was an actor of the tenth rate—the kind that play leading business in the candlestick circuit. Naturally Doctor Todd objected to an actor as a son-in-law. I eloped. Launt was a good fellow, and we had a happy honeymoon, but he lost his health and came out here and invested in a mine. That brought me. I was always lucky, and we struck it—but the poor fellow didn't live long enough to enjoy it. You know all," she ended with a curious forced lightness of utterance.

After another characteristic silence, Mose said slowly: "Anyhow, I want you to understand that I'm much obliged for your good will; I'm not worth a cuss at putting things in a smooth way; I think I'm getting worse every day, but you've been my friend, and—and there's no discount on my words when I tell you you've made me feel ashamed of myself to-day. From this time on, I take no other man's judgment of a woman. You know my life—all there is that would interest you. I don't know how to talk to a woman—any kind of a woman—but no matter what I say, I don't mean to do anybody any harm. I'm getting a good deal like an Indian—I talk to make known what's on my mind. Since I was seventeen years of age I've let girls pretty well alone. The kind I meet alongside the trail don't interest me. When I was a boy I was glib enough, but I know a whole lot less now than I did then—that is about some things. What I started to say is this: I'm mighty much obliged for what you've done for me here—but I'm going to pull out to-night———"

"Not for good?" she said.

"Well—that's beyond me. All I know is I hit the longest and wildest trail I ever entered. Where it comes out at I don't know. But I shan't forget you; you've been a good friend to me."

Her voice faltered a little as she said: "I wish you'd write to me and let me know how you are?"

"Oh, don't expect that of me. I chew my tongue like a ten-year-old kid when I write. I never was any good at it, and I'm clear out of it now. The chances are I'll round up in the mountains again; I can't see how I'd make a living anywhere else. If I come back this way I'll let you know."

Neither of them was eating now, and the tension was great. She knew that no artifice could keep him, and he was aware of her emotion and was eager to escape.

He pushed back his chair at last, and she arose and came toward him and took his hand, standing so close to him that her bosom almost touched his shoulder.

"I hate to see you go!" she said, and the passionate tremor in her voice moved him very deeply. "You've brought back my interest in simple things—and life seems worth while when I'm with you."

He shook her hand and then dropped it. "Well, so long."

"So long!" she said, and added, with another attempt at brightness, "and don't stay away too long, and don't fail to let me know when you make the circuit."

As he mounted his horse he remembered that there was another good-by to speak, and that was to Cora.

"I wish these women would let a man go without saying good-by at all," he thought in irritation, but the patter of Kintuck's feet set his thought in other directions. As he topped the divide, he drew rein and looked at the great range to the southeast, lit by the dull red light of the sun, which had long since set to the settlers in the valley. His heart was for a moment divided. The joys of the trail— the care-free life—perhaps after all the family life was not for him. Perhaps he was chasing a mirage. He was on the divide of his life. On one side were the mountains, the camps, the cattle, the wild animals—on the other the plains, the cities, and Mary.

The thought of Mary went deep. It took hold of the foundations of his thinking and decided him. Shuddering with the pain and despair of his love he lifted rein and rode down into the deep shadow of the long cañon through which roared the swift waters of the North Fork on their long journey to the east and south. Thereafter he had no uncertainties. Like the water of the cañon he had but to go downward to the plain.

CHAPTER XIX

THE EAGLE ADVENTURES INTO STRANGE LANDS

It can not be said that the Black Eagle of the Rocky Mountains approached civilization in any heroic disguise. At its best, accompanying a cattle train is not epic in its largeness. To prod cattle by means of a long pole, to pull out smothered sheep, are not in themselves degrading deeds, but they are not picturesque in quality. They smell of the shambles, not of the hills.

Day by day the train slid down the shining threads of track like a long string of rectangular green and brown and yellow beads. The caboose was filled with cattlemen and their assistants, who smoked, talked politics, told stories, and slept at all hours of the day, whenever a spare segment of bench offered. Those who were awake saw everything and commented on everything in sight. To some the main questions were when and where they were to get dinner or secure a drink. The train, being a "through freight," ran almost as steadily as a passenger train, and the thirsty souls became quite depressed or savage at times by lack of opportunities to "wet their whistles."

Mose was singularly silent, for he was reliving his boyish life on the plains and noting the changes which had taken place. The towns had grown gray with the bleach of the weather. Farms had multiplied and fences cut the range into pasture lands. As the mountains sank beneath the level horizon line his heart sank with them. Every hour of travel to the East was to him dangerous, disheartening. On the second day he was ready to leap from the caboose and wave it good-by; but he did not—he merely sat on the back platform and watched the track. He felt as if he were in one of those aerial buckets which descend like eagles from the mines in the Marshall Basin; the engine appeared to proceed eastward of its own weight, impossible to check or turn back.

The uncertainty of finding Mary in the millions of the city weakened his resolution, but as he was aboard, and as the train slid while he pondered, descending, remorselessly, he determined to "stay with it" as he would with a bucking broncho.

Kansas City with its big depot sheds filled with clangor and swarming with emigrants gave him a foretaste of Chicago. Two of his companions proceeded to get drunk and became so offensive that he was forced to cuff them into quiet. This depressed him also—he had no other defense but his hands. His revolvers were put away in his valise where they could not be reached in a hurry. Reynolds had said to him, "Now, Mose, you're going into a country where they settle things with fists, so leave your guns at home. Keep cool and don't mix in where there's no call to mix in. If a man gives you lip—walk off and leave him—don't hunt your guns."

Mose had also purchased a "hard" hat and shaved off his mustache in Cañon City, and Reynolds himself would not have known him as he sauntered about the station room. Every time he lifted his fingers to his mustache he experienced a shock, and coming before a big mirror over the fireplace he stared with amazement—so boyish and so sorrowful did he appear to himself. It seemed as though he were playing a part.

As the train drew out of the town, night was falling and the East grew mysterious as the thitherward side of the river of death. Familiar things were being left behind. Uncertainties thickened like the darkness. All night long the engine hooted and howled and jarred along through the deep darkness, and every time the train stopped the cattle and sheep were inspected. Lanterns held aloft disclosed cattle being trampled to death and sheep smothering. Wild shouting, oaths, broke forth accompanied by thumpings, and the rumbling and creaking of cars as the cattle surged to and fro, and at the end, circles of fire—lanterns signaling "Go ahead"—caused a wild rush for the caboose.

Morning brought to light a land of small farms, with cattle in minute pastures, surrounded by stacks of hay and grain, plowed fields, threshing crews, and teams plodding to and fro on dusty roads. The plainsman was gone, the prairie farmer filled the landscape. Towns thickened and grew larger. At noon the freight lay at a siding to let the express trains come in at a populous city, and in the wait Mose found time to pace the platform. The people were better dressed, the cowboy hat was absent, and nearly everybody wore not merely a coat but a vest and linen collar. Some lovely girls looking crisp as columbines or plains' poppies looked at him from the doors of the parlor cars. They suggested Mary to him, of course, and made him realize how far he was getting from the range.

These dainty girls looked and acted like some of those he had seen in Cañon City and the Springs. They walked with the same step and held their dresses the same way. That must be the fashion, he thought. The men of the town were less solemn than plainsmen, they smiled oftener and they joked more easily. Mose wondered how so many of them made a living in one place. He heard one girl say to another, "Yes—but he's awful sad looking, don't you think so?" and it was some minutes before he began to understand that they were talking about him. Then he wished he knew what else they had said.

There was little chance to see the towns for the train whirled through them with furious jangle of bell and whiz of steam—or else drew up in the freight yard a long way out from the station. When night fell on this, the third day, they were nearing the Great River and all the cattlemen were lamenting the fact. Those who had been over the line before said:

"Too bad, fellers! You'd ought to see the Mississippi, she's a loo-loo. The bridge, too, is worth seein'."

During the evening there was a serious talk about hotels and the amusements to be had. One faction, led by McCleary, of Currant Creek, stood for the "Drovers' Home." "It's right out near the stockyards an' it's a good place. Dollar a day covers everything, unless you want a big room, which is a quarter extra. Grub is all right—and some darn nice girls waitin' on the table, too."

But Thompson who owned the sheep was contemptuous. "I want to be in town; I don't go to Chicago to live out in the stockyards; I want to be where things go by. I ante my valise at the Grand Palace or the New Merchants'; the best is good enough for me."

McCleary looked a little put down. "Well, that's all right for a man who can afford it. I've got a big family and I wouldn't feel right to be blowing in two or three dollars a day just for style."

"Wherever the girls are thickest, there's where you'll find me," said one of the young fellows.

"That's me," said another.

Thompson smiled with a superior air. "You fellers'll bring up down on South Clark Street before you end. Some choice dive on the levee is gappin' for you. Now, mind you, I won't bail you out.

- 188 -

You go into the game with your eyes open," he said, and his banter was highly pleasing to the accused ones.

McCleary turned to Harold, whom he knew only as "Hank," and said:

"Hank, you ain't sayin' a word; what're your plans?"

"I'll stay with you as long as you need me."

"All right; I'll take care o' you then."

Night fell before they came in sight of the city. They were woefully behindhand and everything delayed them. After a hundred hesitations succeeded by fierce forward dashes, after switching this way and that, they came to a final halt in a jungle of freight cars, a chaos of mysterious activities, and a dense, hot, steaming atmosphere that oppressed and sickened the men from the mountains. Lanterns sparkled and looped and circled, and fierce cries arose. Engines snorted in sullen labor, charging to and fro, aimlessly it appeared. And all around cattle were bawling, sheep were pleading for release, and swine lifted their piercing protests against imprisonment.

"Here we are, in Chicago!" said McCleary, who always entered the city on that side. "Now, fellers, watch out for yourselves. Keep your hands on your wallets and don't blow out the electric light."

"Oh, you go to hell," was their jocular reply.

"We're no spring chickens."

"You go up against this town, my boys, and you'll think you're just out o' the shell."

Mose said nothing. He had the indifferent air of a man who had been often to the great metropolis and knew exactly what he wished to do.

It was after twelve o'clock when the crowd of noisy cattlemen tramped into the Drovers' Home, glad of a safe ending of their trip. They were all boisterous and all of them were liquorous except Harold, who drank little and remained silent and uncommunicative. He had been most efficient in all ways and McCleary was grateful and filled with admiration of him. He had taken him without knowing who he was, merely because Reynolds requested it, but he now said:

"Hank, you're a jim-dandy; I want you. When you've had your spree here, you come back with me and I'll do the right thing by ye."

Harold thanked him in offhand phrase and went early to bed.

He had not slept in a hotel bed since the night in Marmion when Jack was with him, and the wonderful charm and mystery and passion of those two days, so intimately wrought in with passionate memories of Mary, came back upon him now, keeping him awake till nearly dawn. He arose late and yet found only McCleary at breakfast; the other men had remained so long in the barroom that sleep and drunkenness came together.

After breakfast Harold wandered out into the street. To his left a hundred towers of dull gray smoke rose, and prodigious buildings set in empty spaces were like the cliffs of red stone in the Quirino. Beyond, great roofs thickened in the haze, farther on in that way lay Chicago, and somewhere in that welter, that tumult, that terror of the unknown, lived Mary.

With McCleary he took a car that galloped like a broncho, and started for the very heart of the mystery. As the crowds thickened, as the cars they met grew more heavily laden, McCleary said:

"My God! Where are they all goin'? How do they all make a livin'?"

"That beats me," said Harold. "Seems as if they eat up all the grub in the world."

The older man sighed. "Well, I reckon they know what they're doin', but I'd hate to take my chances among 'em."

If any man had told Harold before he started that he would grow irresolute and weak in the presence of the city he would have bitterly resented it, but now the mass and weight of things hitherto unimagined appalled and bewildered him.

A profound melancholy settled over his heart as the smoke and gray light of the metropolis closed in over his head. For half a day he did little more than wander up and down Clark Street. His ears, acute as a hound's, took hold of every sound and attempted to identify it, just as his eyes seized and tried to understand the forms and faces of the swarming pavements. He felt his weakness as never before and it made him sullen and irritable. He acknowledged also the folly of thrusting himself into such a world, and had it not been for a certain tenacity of purpose which was beyond his will, he would have returned with his companions at the end of their riotous week.

Up till the day of their going he had made no effort to find Mary but had merely loitered in the streets in the daytime, and at night had visited the cheap theaters, not knowing the good from the bad. The city grew each day more vast and more hateful to him. The mere thought of being forced to earn a living in such a mad tumult made him shudder. The day that McCleary started West Harold went to see him off, and after they had shaken hands for the last time, Harold went to the ticket window and handed in his return coupon to the agent, saying, "I'd like to have you put that aside for me; I don't want to run any chances of losing it."

The agent smiled knowingly. "All right, what name?"

"Excell, 'XL,' that's my brand."

"All right, she's right here any time you want her—inside of the thirty days—time runs out on the fifteenth."

"I savvy," said Harold as he turned away.

He disposed his money about his person in four or five small wads, and so fortified, faced the city. To lose his little fund would be like having his pack mule give out in the desert, and he took every precaution against such a calamity.

Nothing of this uncertainty and inner weakness appeared in his outward actions, however. No one accused him of looking like an "easy mark" or "a soft thing." The line of his lips and the lower of his strongly marked eyebrows made strangers slow of approach. He was never awkward, he could not be so any more than could a fox or a puma, but he was restless, irresolute, brooding, and gloomy.

He moved down to the Occidental Grand, where he was able to secure a room on the top floor for fifty cents per day. His meals he picked up wherever he chanced to be when feeling hungry. When weary with his wanderings he often returned to his seat on the sidewalk before the hotel and watched the people pass, finding in this a melancholy pleasure.

One evening the night clerk, a brisk young fellow, took a seat beside him. "This is a great corner for the girls all right. A feller can just about take his pick here along about eight. They're after a ticket to the theater and a supper. If a feller only has a few seemolleons to spare he can have a life worth livin'."

Mose turned a curious glance upon him. "If you wanted to find a party in this town how would you go at it?"

"Well, I'd try the directory first go-off. If I didn't find him there I'd write to some of his folks, if I knew any of 'em, and get a clew. If I didn't succeed then I'd try the police. What's his name?"

Harold ignored this query.

"Where could I try this directory?"

"There's one right in there on the desk."

"That big book?"

"Yes."

"I didn't know what that was. I thought it was a dictionary."

The clerk shrieked with merriment. "The dictionary! Well, say, where have you been raised?"

"On the range."

"You mean cowboy?"

"Yes; we don't need directories out there. Does that book tell where everybody lives?"

"Well no, but most everybody shows up in it somewhere," replied the clerk quite soberly. It had not occurred to him that anybody could live outside a directory.

Harold got up and went to the book which he turned over slowly, looking at the names. "I don't see that this helps a man much," he said to the clerk who came in to help him. "Here is Henry Coleman lives at 2201 Exeter Street. Now how is a man going to find that street?"

"Ask a policeman," replied the clerk, much interested. "You're not used to towns?"

"Not much. I can cross a mountain range easier than I can find one of these streets."

Under the clerk's supervision Harold found the Yardwells, Thomas and James, but Mary's name did not appear. He turned to conservatories and located three or four, and having made out a slip of information set forth. The first one he found to be situated up several flights of stairs and was closed; so was the second. The third was in a brilliantly lighted building which towered high above the street. On the eighth floor in a small office a young girl with severe cast of countenance (and hair parted on one side) looked up from her writing and coldly inquired:

"Is there anything I can do for you?"

"Is there a girl named Mary Yardwell in your school?" he asked with some effort, feeling a hot flush in his cheek—a sensation new to him.

"I don't think so, I'll look," replied the girl with business civility. She thumbed a book to see and at length replied, "No, sir, there is not."

"Much obliged."

"Not at all," replied the girl calmly, resuming her work.

Harold went down the steps to avoid the elevator. The next place was oppressive with its grandeur. A tremendous wall, cold and dark (except for a single row of lighted windows), loomed high overhead. In the center of an arched opening in this wall a white hot globe flamed, lighting into still more dazzling cleanliness a broad flight of marble steps which led by a half turn to unknown regions above. Young people were crowding into the elevator, girls in dainty costumes predominating. They seemed wondrously flowerlike and birdlike to the plainsman, and brought back his school days at the seminary, and the time when he was at ease with young people like this. He had gone far from them now— their happy faces made him sad.

He walked up the stairway, four flights, and came to a long hall, which rustled and rippled and sparkled with flights of young girls—eager, vivid, excited, and care-free. A few men moved about like dull-coated robins surrounded by orioles and canary birds.

A bland old man with clean-shaven mouth seemed to be the proper source of information, and to him Harold stepped with his question.

The old man smiled. "Miss Yardwell? Yes—she is one of our most valued pupils. Certainly—Willy!" he called to a small boy who carried a livery of startling newness, "go tell Miss Yardwell a gentleman would like to see her."

"I suppose you are from her country home?" said the old gentleman, who imagined a romance in this relation of a powerful and handsome young man to Miss Yardwell.

"I am," Harold replied briefly.

"Take a seat—she will be here presently."

Harold took the offered seat with a sick, faint feeling at the pit of his stomach. The long-hoped-for event was at hand. It seemed impossible that Mary could be there—that she was about to stand before him. His mind was filled with the things he had arranged to say to her, but they were now in confused mass, circling and circling like the wrack of a boat in a river's whirlpool.

He knew her far down the hall—he recognized the poise of her head and her walk, which had always been very fine and dignified. As she approached, the radiance of her dress, her beauty, scared him. She looked at him once and then at the clerk as if to say, "Is this the man?"

Then Harold arose and said, "Well, Mary, here I am."

For an instant she looked at him, and then a light leaped into her eyes.

"Why, Harold Excell!—" she stopped abruptly as he caught her outstretched hands, and she remembered the sinister association of the name. "Why, why, I didn't know you. Where do you come from?" Her face was flushed, her eyes eager, searching, restless. "Come in here," she said abruptly, and before he had time to reply, she led him to a little anteroom with a cushioned wall seat, and they took seats side by side.

"It is impossible!" she said, still staring at him, her bosom pulsating with her quickened breath. "It is not you—it can't be you," she whispered, "Black Mose sitting here—with me—in Chicago. You're in danger."

"I don't feel that way."

He smiled for the first time, and his fine teeth shining from his handsome mouth led her to say:

"Your big mustaches are gone—that's the reason I didn't know you at once—I don't believe I like you so well——"

"They'll grow again," he said; "I'm in disguise." He smiled again as if in a joke.

Again the thought of who he really was flamed through her mind. "What a life you lead! How do you happen to be here? I never expected to see you in a city—you don't fit into a city."

"I'm here because you are," he replied, and the simplicity of his reply moved her deeply. "I came as soon as I got your letter," he went on.

"My letter! I've written only one letter, that was soon after your visit to Marmion."

"That's the one I mean. I got it nearly four years after you wrote it. I hope you haven't changed since that letter."

"I'm older," she said evasively. "My father died a little over a year ago."

"I know, Jack wrote me."

"Why didn't you get my letter sooner?"

"I was on the trail."

"On the trail! You are always on the trail. Oh, the wild life you lead! I saw notices of you once or twice—always in some trouble." She looked at him smilingly but there was sadness in her smile.

"It's no fault of mine," he exclaimed. "I can't stand by and see some poor Indian or Chinaman bullied—and besides the papers always exaggerate everything I do. You mustn't condemn me till you hear my side of these scrapes."

"I don't condemn you at all but it makes me sad," she slowly replied. "You are wasting your life out there in the wild country— oh, isn't it strange that we should sit here? My mind is so busy with the wonder of it I can't talk straight. I had given up ever seeing you again——"

"You're not married?" he asked with startling bluntness.

She colored hotly. "No."

"Are you engaged?"

"No," she replied faintly.

"Then you're mine!" he said with a clutch upon her wrist, a masterful intensity of passion in his eyes.

"Don't—please don't!" she said, "they will see you."

"I don't care if they do!" he exultingly said; then his face darkened. "But perhaps you are ashamed of me?"

"Oh, no, no—only——"

"I couldn't blame you if you were," he said bitterly. "I'm only a poor devil of a mountaineer, not fit to sit here beside you."

"Tell me about yourself," she hastened to say. "What have you been doing all these years?" She was determined to turn him from his savage arraignment of himself.

"It won't amount to much in your eyes. It isn't worth as much to me as I thought it was going to be. When I found King had your promise—I hit the trail and I didn't care where it led, so it didn't double on itself. I didn't want to see or hear anything of you again. What became of King? Why did you turn him loose?"

Her eyelids fell to shut out his gaze. "Well—after your visit I couldn't find courage to fulfill my promise—and so I asked him to release me—and he did—he was very kind."

"He couldn't do anything else."

"Go on with your story," she said hurriedly.

As they sat thus in the corner of the little sitting room, the pupils and guests of the institution came and went from the cloak rooms, eyeing the intent couple with smiling and curious glances. Who could that dark, handsome young man be who held Miss Yardwell with his glittering eyes? The girls found something very interesting in his bronzed skin and in the big black hat which he held in his hands.

On his part Harold did not care—he scarcely noticed these figures. Their whispers were as unimportant as the sound of aspen leaves, their footfalls as little to be heeded as those of rabbits on the pine needles of his camp. Before him sat the one human being in the world who could command him and she was absorbed in interest of his story. He grew to a tense, swift, eager narration as he went on. It pleased him to see her glow with interest and enthusiasm over the sights and sounds of the wild country. At last he ended.

"And so—I feel as though I could settle down—if I only had you. The trail got lonesome that last year—I didn't suppose it would—but it did. After three years of it I was glad to get back to my old friends, the Reynolds. I thought of you every day—but I didn't listen to hear you sing, because I thought you were King's wife—I didn't want to hear about you ever—but that's all past now—I am here and you are here. Will you go back to the mountains with me this time?"

She looked away. "Come and see me to-morrow, I must think of this. It is so hard to decide—our lives are so different——" She arose abruptly. "I must go now. Come into the concert, I'm going to sing." She glanced at him in a sad, half-smiling way. "I can't sing If I Were a Voice for you, but perhaps you'll like my aria better."

As they walked along the corridor together they formed a singularly handsome couple. He was clad in a well-worn but neat black suit, which he wore with grace. His big-rimmed black hat was crushed in his left hand. Mary was in pale blue which became her well, and on her softly rounded face a thoughtful smile rested. She always walked with uncommon dignity, and the eyes of many young men followed her. There was something about her companion not quite analyzable to her city friends—something alien and savage and admirable.

Entering the hall they found it well filled, but Mary secured a seat near the side door for Harold, and with a smile said, "I may not see you till to-morrow. Here is my address. Come up early. At three. I want a long talk with you."

Left to himself the plainsman looked around the hall which seemed a splendid and spacious one to him. It was filled with ladies in beautiful costumes, and with men in clawhammer coats. He had seen pictures of evening suits in the newspapers but never before had he been privileged to behold live men in them. The men seemed pale and puny for the most part. He had never before seen ladies in low-necked dresses and one just before him seemed shamelessly naked, and he gazed at her in astonishment. He was glad Mary had more modesty.

The concert interested him but did not move him. The songs were brilliant but without meaning. He waited with fierce impatience for Mary to come on, and during this wait he did an inordinate amount of thinking. A hundred new conceptions came into his besieged brain—engaging but by no means confusing him. He perceived that Mary was already as much a part of this high-colored life as she had been of the life of Marmion, quite at ease, certain of herself, and the cañon between them widened swiftly. She was infinitely further away from him than before. His cause now entirely hopeless, he had no right to ask any such sacrifice of her—even if she were ready to make it.

As she stepped out upon the stage in the glare of the light, she seemed as far from him as the roseate crown of snow on Sierra Blanca, and he shivered with a sort of awe. Her singing moved him less than her delicate beauty—but her voice and the pretty way she had of lifting her chin thrilled him just as when he sat in the little church at Marmion. The flowerlike texture of her skin and the exquisite grace of her hands plunged him into gloom.

He did not join in the generous applause which followed—he wondered if she would sing If I Were a Voice for him. He felt a numbness creeping over his limbs and he drew his breath like one in pain. Mary looked pale as a lily as she returned and stood waiting for the applause to die away. Then out over the tense audience, straight toward him, soared her voice quivering with emotion—she dared to sing the old song for him.

Suddenly all sense of material things passed from the wild heart of the plainsman. He saw only the singer who stood in the center of a white flame. A soft humming roar was in his ears like the falling of rain drops on the leaves of maple trees. He remembered the pale little girl in the prison—this was not Mary—but she had the voice and the spirit of Mary——

Then the song stopped! The singer went away—the white light went with her and the yellow glare of lamps came back. He heard the passionate applause—he saw Mary reappear and bow, a sad smile on her face—a smile which he alone could understand—her heart was full of pity for him. Then once more she withdrew, and staggering like one suffering from vertigo—the eagle-hearted youth went out of the hall and down the polished stairway like an outcast soul, descending from paradise into hell.

That radiant singer was not for such as Black Mose.

CHAPTER XX

A DARK DAY WITH A GLOWING SUNSET

The clerk at the station window was not the kindly young man who had received Harold's ticket for safe keeping. He knew nothing of it and poked around for several minutes before finding it. After glancing keenly at its date he threw it down and brusquely said:

"Time's out on this, my friend."

Harold looked at him sharply. "Oh, no, that can't be; it's a thirty-day trip."

The agent grew irritable. "I know it is; it was good to the fifteenth; this is the seventeenth; the ticket is worthless."

Harold took up the slip of paper and stared at it in bewilderment. The agent was right; he had overstayed the limit and was without five dollars in his pocket. He turned weak with a sudden sense of his helplessness and the desolation of his surroundings. He was like a man whose horse fails him on a desert. Taking a seat on a bench in a dark corner of the waiting room he gave himself up to a study of the situation. To be alone in the Needle Range was nothing to worry about, but to be alone and without money in a city scared him.

For two hours he sat there, his thoughts milling like a herd of restless cattle, turning aimlessly around and around in their tracks. He had foolishly neglected his opportunity to escape, and the mountains became each moment more beautiful as they swiftly receded into unattainable distance. He had expected to be riding back into the safe and splendid plains country, back to friends and familiar things, and had trusted to the joy of his return to soften the despair of his second failure to take Mary back with him.

It was a sorrowful thing to see the young eagle in somber dream, the man of unhesitating action becoming introspective. Floods of intent business men, gay young girls, and grizzled old farmers in groups of twos and threes, streamed by, dimly shadowed in his reflective eyes. All these people had purpose and reward in their lives; he alone was a stray, a tramp, with no one but old Kintuck to draw him to any particular spot or keep him there.

"I am outside of everything," he bitterly thought. "There is nothing for me."

Yes, there was Cora and there was little Pink—and then he thought of Mrs. Raimon, whose wealth and serenity of temper had a greater appeal than ever before. He knew perfectly well that a single word from him would bring her and her money to his rescue at once. But something arose in him which made the utterance of such a word impossible. As for Cora and the little one, they brought up a different emotion, and the thought of them at last aroused him to action.

"I'll get something to do and earn money enough to go back on," he finally said to himself; "that's all I'm fit for, just to work by the day for some other man; that's my size. I've failed in everything else I've ever undertaken. I've no business to interfere with a girl like Mary. She's too high class for a hobo like me; even if I had a ranch it would be playing it low down on a singer like her to ask her to go out there. It's no use; I'm worse than a failure—I'm in a hole, and the first thing I've got to do is to earn money enough to get out of it."

He was ashamed to go back to the little hotel to which he had said good-by with so much relief. It was too expensive for him, anyhow, and so he set to work to find one near by which came within his changed condition. He secured lodging at last in an old wooden shack on a side street not far from the station, where rooms could be had for twenty cents a night—in advance. It was a wretched place, filled with cockroaches and other insects, but it was at least a hole in which he could den up for a few nights when sleep overcame him. Thus fortified, he wandered forth into the city, which was becoming each moment more remorseless and more menacing in his eyes.

Almost without knowing it, he found himself walking the broad pavement before the musical college wherein he found Mary. He had no definite hope of seeing her again, but that doorway was the one spot of light in all the weltering black chaos of the city, which now threatened him with hunger and cold. The awe and terror he felt were such as a city dweller would feel if left alone in a wild swamp filled with strange beasts and reptiles.

After an hour's aimless walking to and fro, he returned to his bed each night, still revolving every conceivable plan for earning money. His thought turned naturally to the handling of cattle at the stockyards, and one morning he set forth on his quest, only to meet with a great surprise. He found all the world changed to him when it became known that he was looking for a job. When he said to the office boys, "I want to see the man who has charge of hiring the hands," they told him to wait a while in a tone of voice which he had never before encountered. His blood flamed hot in an instant over their calm insolence. Eventually he found his way into a room where a surly fat man sat writing. He looked up over his shoulder and snarled out:

"Well, what is it? What do you want?"

Harold controlled himself and replied: "I want to get a job; I'm a cattleman from Colorado, and I'd like——"

"I don't care where you're from; we've got all the men we want. See Mr. White, don't come bothering me."

Harold put his hand on the man's shoulder with the gesture of an angry leopard, and a yellow glare filled his eyes, from which the brutal boss shrank as if from a flame.

With a powerful effort he pulled himself up short and said: "Treat the next cattleman that comes your way a little more decent or you'll get a part of your lung carried away. Good day."

He walked out with the old familiar numbness in his body and the red flashes wavering before his eyes. His brain was in tumult. The free man of the mountain had come in contact with "the tyrant of labor," and it was well for the big beast that Harold was for the moment without his gun.

Going back to his room he took out his revolver and loaded every chamber. In the set of his lips was menace to the next employer who dared to insult and degrade him.

In the days that followed he wandered over the city, with eyes that took note of every group of workmen. He could not bring himself to go back to the stockyards, there was danger of his becoming a murderer if he did; and as he approached the various bosses of the gangs of men in the street, he found himself again and again without the resolution to touch his hat and ask for a job. Once or twice he saw others quite as brutally rebuffed as he had been, and it was only by turning away that he kept himself from taking a hand in an encounter. Once or twice, when the overseer happened to be a decent and sociable fellow, Harold, edging near, caught his eye and was able to address him on terms of equality; but in each case the talk which followed brought out the fact that men were swarming for every place; indeed Harold could see this for himself. Ultimately he fell into the ranks of poor, shivering, hollow-cheeked fellows who stood around wistfully watching the excavation of cellars or hanging with pathetic intentness above the handling of great iron beams or pile drivers.

Work came to be a wonderful thing to possess. To put hand to a beam or a shovel seemed now a most desirable favor, for it meant not only warm food and security and shelter, but in his case it promised a return to the mountains which came each hour to seem the one desirable and splendid country in the world—so secure, so joyous, so shining, his heart ached with wistful love of it.

Each night he walked over to the Lake shore, past the college and up the viaduct, till he could look out over the mysterious, dim expanse of water. It reminded him of the plains, and helped him with its lonely sweep and its serene majesty of reflected stars. At night he dreamed of the cattle and of his old companions on the trail; once he was riding with Talfeather and his band in the West Elk Mountains; once he was riding up the looping, splendid incline of the Trout Lake Trail, seeing the clouds gather around old Lizard Head. At other times he was back at the Reynolds ranch taking supper while the cattle bawled, and through the open door the light of the setting sun fell.

He had written to Reynolds, asking him to buy his saddle and bridle (he couldn't bring himself to sell Kintuck) and each day he hoped for a reply. He had not stated his urgent need of money, but Reynolds would know. One by one every little trinket which he possessed went to pay his landlord for his room. He had a small nugget, which he had carried as a good-luck pocket-piece for many months; this he sold, and at last his revolvers went, and then he seemed helpless.

No word from Reynolds came, and the worst of it was, if the money did come it would not now be enough to carry him back. If he had been able to put it with the money from his nugget and revolvers it would at least have taken him to Denver. But now it was too late.

At last there came a day when he was at his last resource. He could find no work to do in the streets, and so, setting his teeth on his pride, he once more sought the stockyards and "Mr. White." It was a cold, rainy day, and he walked the entire distance. Weak as he was from insufficient food, bad air, and his depression, he could not afford to spend one cent for car fare.

White turned out to be a very decent fellow, who knew nothing whatever of Harold's encounter with the other man. He had no work for him, however. He seemed genuinely regretful, and said:

"As a matter of fact, I'm laying off men just now; you see the rush is pretty well over with."

Harold went over to the Great Western Hotel and hung about the barroom, hoping to meet some one he knew, even though there was a certain risk of being recognized as Black Mose. Swarms of cattlemen filled the hotel, but they were mainly from Texas and Oklahoma, and no familiar face met his searching eyes. He was now so desperately homesick that he meditated striking one of these prosperous-looking fellows for a pass back to the cattle country. But each time his pride stood in the way. It would be necessary to tell his story and yet conceal his name—which was a very difficult thing to do even if he had had nothing to cover up.

Late in the evening, faint with hunger, he started for his wretched bunk as a starving wolf returns, after an unsuccessful hunt, to his cold and cheerless den. His money was again reduced to a few coppers, and for a week he had allowed himself only a small roll three times a day. "My God! if I was only among the In-jins," he said savagely; "*they* wouldn't see a man starve, not while they had a sliver of meat to share with him; but these Easterners don't care; I'm no more to them than a snake or a horned toad."

The knowledge that Mary's heart would bleed with sorrow if she knew of his condition nerved him to make another desperate trial. "I'll try again to-morrow," he said through his set teeth.

On the way home his curious fatalism took a sudden turn, and a feeling that Reynolds' letter surely awaited him made his heart glow. It was impossible that he should actually be without a cent of money, and the thought filled his brain with an irrational exaltation which made him forget the slime in which his feet slipped. He planned to start on the limited train. "I'll go as far from this cursed hole of a city as I can," he said; "I'll get out where men don't eat each other to keep alive. He'll certainly send me twenty dollars. The silver on the bridle is worth that alone. Mebbe he'll understand I'm broke, and send me fifty."

He became so sure of this at last that he stepped into a saloon and bought a big glass of brandy to ward off a chill which he felt coming upon him, and helped himself to a lunch at the counter. When he arose his limbs felt weak and a singular numbness had spread over his whole body. He had never been drunk in his life—but he knew the brandy had produced this effect.

"I shouldn't have taken it on an empty stomach," he muttered to himself as he dragged his heavy limbs out of the door.

When he came fairly to his senses again he was lying in his little room and the slatternly chambermaid was looking in at him.

"You aind seek alretty?" she asked.

"Go away," he said with a scowl; "you've bothered me too much."

"You peen trinken—aind it. Chim help you up de stairs last nide."

"What time is it?" he asked, with an effort to recall where he had been.

"Tweluf o'clock," she replied, still looking at him keenly, genuinely concerned about him.

"Go away. I must get up." As she went toward the door he sat up for a moment, but a terrible throbbing pain just back of his eyes threw him back upon his pillow as if he had met the blow of a fist. "Oh, I'm used up—I can't do it," he groaned, pressing his palms to his temples. "I'm burning up with fever."

The girl came back. "Dat's vat I tought. You dond look ride. Your mudder vouldn't known you since you gome here. Pedder you send for your folks alretty."

"Oh, go out—let me alone. Yes, I'll do it. I'll get up soon."

When the girl returned with the proprietor of the hotel Harold was far past rational speech. He was pounding furiously on the door, shouting, "Let me out!" When they tried to open the door they found it locked. The proprietor, a burly German, set his weight against it and tore the lock off.

Harold was dangerously quiet as he said: "You'd better let me out o' here. Them greasers are stampeding the cattle. It's a little trick of theirs."

"Dot's all right; you go back to bed; I'll look out for dot greaser pisness," said the landlord, who thought him drunk.

"You let me out or I'll break you in two," the determined man replied, and a tremendous struggle took place.

Ultimately Harold was vanquished, and Schmidt, piling his huge bulk on the worn-out body of the young man, held him until his notion changed.

"Did you ever have a tree burn up in your head?" he asked.

"Pring a policeman," whispered Schmidt to the girl, "and a doctor. De man is grazy mit fevers; he aindt trunk."

When the officer came in Harold looked at him with sternly steady eyes. "See here, cap, don't you try any funny business with me. I won't stand it; I'll shoot with you for dollars or doughnuts."

"What's the matter—jim-jams?" asked the officer indifferently.

"No," replied Schmidt, "I tondt pelief it—he's got some fever onto him."

The policeman felt his pulse. "He's certainly hot enough. Who is he?"

"Hank Jones."

"That's a lie—I'm 'Black Mose,'" said Harold.

The policeman smiled. "'Black Mose' was killed in San Juan last summer."

Harold received this news gravely. "Sorry for him, but I'm the man. You'll find my name on my revolver, the big one—not the little one. I'm all the 'Black Mose' there is. If you'll give me a chance I'll rope a steer with you for blood or whisky; I'm thirsty."

"Well now," said the policeman, "you be quiet till the doctor comes, and I'll go through your valise." After a hasty examination he said: "Damned little here, and no revolvers of any kind. Does he eat here?"

"No, he only hires this room."

"Mebbe he don't eat anywhere; he looks to me like a hungry man."

"Dot's what I think," said the maid. "I'll go pring him some soup."

The prisoner calmly said: "Too late now; my stomach is all dried up."

"Haven't you any folks?" the policeman asked.

Harold seemed to pause for thought. "I believe I have, but I can't think. Mary could tell you."

"Who's Mary?"

"What's that to you. Bring me some water—I'm burning dry."

"Now keep quiet," said the policeman; "you're sick as a horse."

When the doctor came the policeman turned Harold over to him. "This is a case for St. Luke's Hospital, I guess," he said as he went out.

The doctor briskly administered a narcotic as being the easiest and simplest way to handle a patient who seemed friendless and penniless. "The man is simply delirious with fever. He looks like a man emaciated from lack of food. What do you know about him?"

The landlord confessed he knew but little.

The doctor resumed: "Of course you can't attend to him here. I'll inform the hospital authorities at once. Meanwhile, communicate with his friends if you can. He'll be all right for the present."

This valuable man was hardly gone before a lively young fellow with a smoothly shaven, smiling face slipped in. He went through every pocket of Harold's clothing, and found a torn envelope with the name "Excell" written on it, and a small photo of a little girl with the words, "To Mose from Cora." The young man's smile became a chuckle as he saw these things, and he said to himself: "Nothing here to identify him, eh?" Then to the landlord he said; "I'm from The Star office. If anything new turns up I wish you'd call up Harriman, that's me, and let me in on it."

The hospital authorities were not informed, or paid no attention to the summons, and Harold was left to the care of the chambermaid, who did her poor best to serve him.

The Star next morning contained two columns of closely printed matter under the caption, "Black Mose, the Famous Dead Shot, Dying in a West Side Hotel. After Years of Adventure on the Trail, the Famous Desperado Succumbs to Old John Barley Corn." The article recounted all the deeds which had been ascribed to Harold and added a few entirely new ones. His marvelous skill with the revolver was referred to, and his defense of the red men and others in distress was touched upon so eloquently that the dying man was lifted to a romantic height of hardihood and gallantry. A fancy picture of him took nearly a quarter of a page and was surrounded by a corona of revolvers each spouting flame.

Mrs. Raimon seated at breakfast in the lofty dining room of her hotel, languidly unfolded The Star, gave one glance, and opened the paper so quickly and nervously her cup and saucer fell to the floor.

"My God! Can that be true? I must see him." As she read the article she carried on a rapid thinking. "How can I find him? I must see that reporter; he will know." She was a woman of decision. She arose quickly and returned to her room. "Call a carriage for me, quick!" she said to the bell boy who answered to her call. "No name is given to the hotel, but The Star will know. Good Heavens! if he should die!" Her florid face was set and white as she took her seat in the cab. "To The Star office—quick!" she said to the driver, and there was command in the slam of the door.

To the city editor she abruptly said: "I want to find the man who wrote this article on 'Black Mose.' I want to find the hotel where he is."

The editor was enormously interested at once. "Harriman is on the night force and at home how, but I'll see what I can do." By punching various bells and speaking into mysteriously ramifying tubes he was finally able to say: "The man is at a little hotel just across the river. I think it is called the St. Nicholas. It isn't a nice place; you'd better take some one with you. Mind you, I don't vouch for the truth of that article; the boy may be mistaken about it."

Mrs. Raimon turned on her heel and vanished. She had her information and acted upon it. She was never finer than when she knelt at Harold's bedside and laid her hand gently on his forehead. She could not speak for a moment, and when her eyes cleared of their tears and she felt the wide, dry eyes of the man searching her, a spasm of pain contracted her heart.

"He don't know me!" she cried to the slatternly maid, who stood watching the scene with deep sympathy.

Harold spoke petulantly: "Go away and tell Mary I want her. It costs too much for her to sing, or else she'd come. These people won't let me get up, but Reynolds will be here soon and then something will rip wide open. They took my guns and my saddle. If I had old Kintuck here I could ride to Mary. She said she'd sing for me every Sunday. Look here, I want ice on my head. This pillow has been heated. I don't want a hot pillow—and I don't want my arms covered. Say, I wish you'd send word to old Jack. I don't know where he is, but he'd come—so will Reynolds. These policemen will have a hot time keeping me here after they come. It's too low here, I must take Mary away—it's healthier in the mountains. It ain't so hot——"

Out of this stream of loosely uttered words the princess caught and held little more than the names "Jack" and "Mary."

"Who is Jack?" she softly asked.

Harold laughed. "Don't you know old freckle-faced Jack? Why, I'd know Jack in the dark of a cave. He's my friend—my old chum. He didn't forget me when they sent me to jail. Neither did Mary. She sung for me."

"Can't you tell me Mary's name?"

"Why, it's just Mary, Mary Yardwell."

"Where does she live?"

"Oh, don't bother me," he replied irritably. "What do you want to know for?"

The princess softly persisted, and he said: "She lives in the East. In Chicago. It's too far off to find her. It takes five days to get down there on a cattle train, and then you have to look her up in a directory, and then trail her down. I couldn't find her."

The princess took down Mary's name and sent a messenger to try to find the address of this woman who was more to the delirious man than all the rest of the world.

As he tossed and muttered she took possession of the house. "Is this the worst room you have? Get the best bed in the house ready. I want this man to have the cleanest room you have. Hurry! Telephone to the Western Palace and ask Doctor Sanborn to come at once—tell him Mrs. Raimon wants him."

Under her vigorous action one of the larger rooms was cleared out and made ready, and when the doctor came Harold was moved, under his personal supervision. "I shall stay here till he is out of danger," she said to the doctor as he was leaving, "and please ask my maid to go out and get some clean bed linen and bring it down here at once—and tell her to send Mr. Doris here, won't you?"

The doctor promised to attend to these matters at once.

She sat by the bedside of the sufferer bathing his hands and face as if he were a child, talking to him gently with a mother's grave cadences. He was now too weak to resist any command, and took his medicine at a gulp like a young robin.

Late in the afternoon as Mrs. Raimon returned from an errand to the street she was amazed to find a tall and handsome girl sitting beside the sick man's bed holding his two cold white hands in both of hers. There was a singular and thrilling serenity in the stranger's face—a composure that was exaltation, while Harold, with half-closed eyelids, lay as if in awe, gazing up into the woman's face.

Mrs. Raimon waited until Harold's eyes closed like a sleepy child's and the watcher arose—then she drew near and timidly asked:

"Are you Mary?"

"Yes," was the simple reply.

The elder woman's voice trembled. "I am glad you've come. He has called for you incessantly. You must let me help you—I am Mrs. Raimon, of Wagon Wheel—I knew him there."

Mary understood the woman's humble attitude, but she did not encourage a caress. She coldly replied: "I shall be very grateful. He is very ill, and I shall not leave him till his friends come."

She thought immediately of Jack, and sent a telegram saying: "Harold is here ill—come at once." She did not know where to reach Mr. Excell, so could only wait to consult Jack.

Mrs. Raimon remained with her and was so unobtrusively ready to do good that Mary's heart softened toward her—though she did not like her florid beauty and her display of jewels.

A telegram from Jack came during the evening: "Do all you can for Harold. Will reach him to-night."

He came in at eleven o'clock, his face knotted into anxious lines. They smoothed out as his eyes fell upon Mary, who met him in the hall.

"Oh, I'm glad to see you here," he said brokenly. "How is he—is there any hope?"

In his presence Mary's composure gave way. "O Jack! If he should die now——" She laid her head against his sturdy shoulder and for a moment shook with nervous weakness. Almost before he could speak she recovered herself. "He only knew me for a few moments. He's delirious again. The doctor is with him—oh, I can't bear to hear him rave! It is awful! He calls for me, and yet does not know me. O Jack, it makes my heart ache so, he is so weak! He came to see me—and then went away—I didn't know where he had gone. And all the time he was starving here. O God! It would be too dreadful—if he should die!"

"We won't let him die!" he stoutly replied. "I'm going in to see him."

Together they went in. The doctor, intently studying his patient, sat motionless and silent. He was a young man with a serious face, but his movements were quick, silent, and full of decision. He looked up and made a motion, stopping them where they were.

Out of a low mutter at last Harold's words grew distinct: "I don't care—but the water is cold as ice—I wouldn't put a cayuse into it—let alone Kintuck. Should be a bridge here somewhere."

"Oh, he's on the trail again!" said Mary. "Harold, don't you know me?" She bent over to him again and put forth the utmost intensity of her will to recall him. "I am here, Harold, don't you see me?"

His head ceased to roll and he looked at her with eyes that made her heart grow sick—then a slow, faint smile came to his lips. "Yes—I know you, Mary—but the river is between us, and it's swift and cold, and Kintuck is thin and hungry—I can't cross now!"

"Doctor," said Jack, as the physician was leaving, "what are the chances?"

The doctor's voice carried conviction: "Oh, he'll pull through—he has one of the finest bodies I ever saw." He smiled. "He'll cross the river all right—and land on our side."

Two days later Mr. Excell, big and brown, his brow also knotted with anxiety, entered the room, and fell on his knees and threw his long arm over the helpless figure beneath the coverlet. "Harry! My boy, do you know me?"

Harold looked up at him with big staring eyes and slowly put out his hand. "Sure thing! And I'm not dead yet, father. I'll soon be all right. I've got Mary with me. She can cure me—if the doctor can't."

He spoke slowly, but there was will behind the voice. His wasted face had a gentleness that was most moving to the father. He could not look at the pitiful wreck of his once proud and fearless boy without weeping, and being mindful of Harold's prejudice against sentiment, he left the room to regain his composure. To Mary Mr. Excell said: "I don't know you—but you are a noble woman. I give you a father's gratitude. Won't you tell me who you are?"

"I am Mary Yardwell," she replied in her peculiarly succinct speech. "My home was in Marmion, but I attended school in your village. I sang in your church for a little while."

His face lighted up. "I remember you—a pale, serious little girl. Did you know my son there?"

She looked away for a moment. "I sang for him—when he was in jail," she replied. "I belonged to the Rescue Band."

A shadow fell again upon the father's face.

"I did not know it," he said, feeling something mysterious here—something which lay outside his grasp. "Have you seen him meanwhile? I suppose you must have done so."

"Once, in Marmion, some four years ago."

"Ah! Now I understand his visit to Marmion," said Mr. Excell, with a sudden smile. "I thought he came to see Jack and me. He really came to see you. Am I right?"

"Yes," she replied. "He wanted me to go back with him, but I—I—couldn't do so."

"I know—I know," he replied hastily. "He had no right to ask it of you—poor boy."

"It seems now as though I had no right to refuse. I might have helped him. If he should die now there would be an incurable ache here"—she lifted her hand to her throat; "so long as I lived I should not forgive myself."

CHAPTER XXI

CONCLUSION

As he crawled slowly back to life and clear thinking, Harold's wild heart was filled with a peace and serenity of emotion such as it had not known since childhood. He was like a boy in a careless dream, forecasting nothing, remembering nothing, content to see Mary come and go about the room, glad of the sound of her skirts, thrilling under the gentle pressure of her hand.

She, on her part, could not realize any part of his dark fame as she smiled down into his big yellow-brown eyes which were as pathetic and wistful as those of a gentle animal.

Mrs. Raimon spoke of this. "I saw 'Black Mose' as he stood in the streets of Wagon Wheel, the most famous dead-shot in the State. I can't realize that this is the same man. He's gentle as a babe now; he was as terrible and as beautiful as a tiger then."

Reynolds sent fifty dollars with an apology for the delay and Mr. Excell offered his slender purse, but Mrs. Raimon said: "I'll attend to this matter of expense. Let me do that little for him—please!" And he gave way, knowing her great wealth.

But all these things began at last to trouble the proud heart of the sick man, and as he grew stronger his hours of quiet joy began to be broken by disquieting calculations of his indebtedness to Mrs. Raimon as well as to Mary and Jack. He wished to be free of all obligations, even gratitude. He insisted on his father's return to his pastorate—which he did at the end of the week.

Meanwhile Mary and Jack conspired for the Eagle's good. Together they planned to remove him to some fairer quarter of the city. Together they read and discussed the letters which poured in upon them from theatrical managers, Wild West shows, music halls, and other similar enterprises, and from romantic girls and shrewd photographers, and every other conceivable kind of crank. The offers of the music halls Jack was inclined to consider worth while. "He'd be a great success there, or as a dead-shot in a Wild West show. They pay pretty well, too."

"I don't believe he'd care to do anything like that," Mary quietly replied.

They both found that he cared to do nothing which involved his remaining in the East. As his eyes grew brighter, his longing for the West came back. He lifted his arms above his quilts with the action of the eaglet who meditates leaping from the home ledge. It was a sorrowful thing to see this powerful young animal made thin and white and weak by fever, but his spirit was indomitable.

"He must be moved to the West before he will fully recover," said the doctor, and to this Mrs. Raimon replied:

"Very well, doctor. You name the day when it is safe and we'll go. I'll have a special car, if necessary, but first of all he must go to a good hotel. Can't he be moved now?"

Outwardly Mary acknowledged all the kindness of this rich and powerful woman, but inwardly she resented her intimacy. Drawing all her little store of ready money she quietly began paying off the bills. When all was settled she took a seat beside Harold one day when they were alone and laying one strong, warm hand on his thin, white arm, she said:

"Harold, the doctor says you can be moved from here, and so— you must give me the right to take you home with me."

There was a piercing pathos in his wan smile as he replied, "All right, you're the boss. It's a pretty hard come down, though. I thought once I'd come back after you in a private car. If you stand by me I may be a cattle king yet. There's a whole lot of fight in me still—you watch me and see."

The next day he was moved to a private hotel on the north side, and Mary breathed a sigh of deep relief as she saw him sink back into his soft bed in a clean and sunny room. He, with a touch of his old fire, said: "This sure beats a holler log, but all the same I'll be glad to see the time when I can camp on my saddle again."

Mary only smiled and patted him like a mother caressing a babe. "I'll hate to have you go and leave me—now."

"No danger of that, Mary. We camp down on the same blanket from this on."

Mr. Excell came on to marry them, but Jack sent his best wishes by mail; he could not quite bring himself to see Mary give herself away—even to his hero.

Mrs. Raimon took her defeat with most touching grace. "You're right," she said. "He's yours—I know that perfectly well, but you must let me help him to make a start. It won't hurt him, and it'll please me. I have a ranch, I have mines, I could give him something to do till he got on his feet again, if you'd let me, and I hope you won't deny me a pleasure that will carry no obligation with it."

She was powerfully moved as she went in to say good-by to him. He was sitting in a chair, but looked very pale and weak. She said: "Mose, you're in luck; you've got a woman who'll do you good. She's loyal and she's strong, and there's nothing further for me to do—unless you let me help you. See here, why not let me help you get a start; what do you say?"

Harold felt the deep sincerity of the woman's regard and he said simply:

"All right; let me know what you find, and I'll talk it over with Mary."

She seized his thin hand in both hers and pressed it hard, the tears creeping down her cheeks. "You're a good boy, Mose; you're the kind that are good to women in ways they don't like, sometimes. I hope you'll forget the worst of me and remember only the best. I don't think she knows anything about me; if she hears anything, tell her the truth, but say I was better than women think."

One day about ten days later a bulky letter came, addressed to "Mose Excell." It was from Mrs. Raimon, but contained a letter from Reynolds, who wrote:

"Yesterday a young Cheyenne came ridin' in here inquirin' for you. I told him you was in Chicago, sick. He brought a message from old Talfeather who is gettin' scared about the cattlemen. He says they're crowdin' onto his reservation, and he wants you to come and help him. He wants you to talk with them and to go to Washington and see the Great Father. He sent this medicine and said it was to draw you to him. He said he was blind and his heart was heavy because he feared trouble. I went up to Wagon Wheel and saw the princess, who has a big pull. She said she'd write you. Kintuck is well but getting lazy."

Mrs. Raimon wrote excitedly:

"DEAR FRIEND: Here is work for you to do. The agent at Sand Lake has asked to be relieved and I have written Senator Miller to have you appointed. He thought the idea excellent. We both believe your presence will quiet the cattlemen as well as Talfeather and his band. Will you accept?"

As Harold read, his body uplifted and his eyes grew stern. "See here, Mary, what do you think of this?" and he read the letter and explained the situation. She, too, became tense with interest, but, being a woman who thought before she spoke, she remained silent.

Harold, after a moment, arose from his chair, gaunt and unsteady as he was. "That's what I'm fitted for, Mary. That solves my problem. I know these cattlemen, they know me. I am the white chief of Talfeather's people. If you can stand it to live there with me, Mary, I will go. We can do good; the women need some one like you to teach 'em to do things."

Mary's altruistic nature began to glow. "Do you think so, Harold? Could I be of use?"
"Of use? Why, Mary, those poor squaws and their children need you worse than they need a God. I know, for I've lived among 'em."
"Then I will go," she said, and out of the gray cloud the sun broke and shone from the west across the great lonely plains.
Again "Black Mose" rode up the almost invisible ascent toward the Rocky Mountains. Again he saw the mighty snow peaks loom over the faintly green swells of the plain, but this time he left nothing behind. The aching hunger was gone out of his heart for beside him Mary sat, eager as he to see the wondrous mountain land whose trails to her were script of epic tales, and whose peaks were monuments to great dead beasts and mysterious peoples long since swept away by the ruthless march of the white men.
If she had doubts or hesitations she concealed them, for hers was a nature fitted for such sacrifice as this—and besides, each day increased her love for the singular and daring soul of Harold Excell.

CPSIA information can be obtained
at www.ICGtesting.com
Printed in the USA
BVHW031533070521
606757BV00003B/419

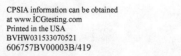